# MARGARET MANCHESTER

# Briar Place

*First published by Amazon 2022*

*Copyright © 2022 by Margaret Manchester*

*All rights reserved. No part of this publication may be reproduced, stored or transmitted in any form or by any means, electronic, mechanical, photocopying, recording, scanning, or otherwise without written permission from the publisher. It is illegal to copy this book, post it to a website, or distribute it by any other means without permission.*

*Margaret Manchester asserts the moral right to be identified as the author of this work.*

*This novel is a work of fiction based on a historical event. Some characters and incidents portrayed in it are real, others are the work of the author's imagination. For further clarification, please see the Author's Historical Note at the end of the book.*

*First edition*

*ISBN: 9798837088766*

*This book was professionally typeset on Reedsy.
Find out more at reedsy.com*

*This book is dedicated to
my sisters, Linda and Dawn,
and my brother, Carl,
with love.
Siblings so often drift apart.
I'm thankful that we've remained close.*

# Acknowledgement

I want to thank my husband, Alec, for his patience, understanding and support while I was writing this book, and for providing feedback throughout the process. I could not have completed it without him.

I am very grateful to my sister, Linda Brown, my father-in-law, Leslie Manchester and friend, Judit Porszasz, for reading and commenting on my final draft before publication.

# Prologue

Eighteen forty-nine: that was the year that my whole life changed.

I had an idyllic childhood growing up in the village of Allenheads, running wild on the fells, wandering through the woods, and splashing in the river with my sisters. Don't get me wrong; it wasn't all rosy. There were times when money was short, and we felt hunger in our bellies, but there was love and laughter in abundance.

We enjoyed playing games with our brother, Jack, whom we all adored. He was a fine young man, and he had all the time in the world for us back then. I remember he would stand his dominoes in a line, and we'd watch in wonder as he knocked over the first, and then the others tumbled, one by one.

To my mind, that's what happened in 1849. One fateful decision triggered a series of events, and once the sequence had begun, it seemed that there was no way to stop it.

I, Lizzie Lowery, was simply an observer. I had no say in what happened. On reflection, perhaps there were times that year when things could have been done differently, the escalation of events stopped, and our lives might have taken a different path. That hindsight is an affliction to me now, knowing that what passed might have been prevented.

But at the time, the lead miners of Allenheads could not have known the heartbreak that would follow their paltry demands. Neither could have Mr Sopwith, for if anyone had known, surely they would have yielded and halted the progression of unfortunate events, saving us all from the suffering that was 1849.

# Chapter 1

**Allenheads Hall, Northumberland
October 1848**

A military officer stood on the doorstep. Heavy raindrops pounded the ground around him. He removed his hat and held it in both hands against his chest, but he didn't smile.

'Good afternoon,' he said, 'Is Mr Sopwith at home?'

'Yes, sir. Please, come in.'

As Bella Dixon showed the man into the hallway, water dripped off his clothes onto the chequered floor. 'May I take your coat?' she asked.

The man peeled off his topcoat, and Bella hung it on the wooden coat stand.

'Who shall I say is here, sir?'

'Captain Wilson,' he replied curtly.

Bella showed the Captain into the drawing-room and watched him traverse the room to stand by the window that looked out over the manicured gardens, and then went to her master's study and tapped lightly at the door.

'Come in!' a man's voice bellowed.

Thomas Sopwith was seated at his desk, writing neatly in a leather-bound book. Bella knew better than to disturb him when he was working, so she waited silently. A few seconds later, he put down his pen and lifted his head.

'Captain Wilson is here to see you, sir.'

'Oh! I wasn't expecting him. Where is he?'

'In the drawing-room, sir.'

Mr Sopwith closed his diary and rose from his leather-studded chair. 'Please, bring us some tea,' he said as he passed Bella in the doorway.

Bella heard the men greet each other warmly while she walked to the kitchen, and as she made their tea, she imagined them shaking hands and sitting on the armchairs facing each other in front of the white marble fireplace, cordially sharing their news. When she returned to the drawing-room with the tea tray, she was surprised to see the two men standing in the middle of the room. Captain Wilson held her master's shaking shoulders firmly in his large hands and spoke to him in a soothing voice.

'Excuse me!'

Embarrassed at having intruded on a private moment and not knowing quite what to do, Bella began to withdraw from the room.

Mr Sopwith looked towards her, his eyes full of tears. Grabbing a handkerchief from his trouser pocket, he rapidly wiped his eyes, blew his nose, and pointed at a small table. Bella put down the tray where he indicated.

The Captain patted Mr Sopwith on the arm and followed her out of the room. In the hallway, he said, 'Excuse me - I'm sorry, I don't know your name.'

'Bella. Bella Dixon.'

'Miss Dixon, I've just brought Mr Sopwith some news and he's taken it rather badly. I'm afraid Jacob is dead. He died of

# CHAPTER 1

fever out in India.'

'Jacob?'

'His son.' The officer sighed.

Bella was shocked by his reply; she had worked for the Sopwiths for several years, yet was unaware that they had a son named Jacob.

'The mistress is resting upstairs. The doctor advised it because of her condition. Should I go and fetch her?' Bella asked, her voice full of concern.

'No, please don't disturb her. Give Thomas some time to come to terms with the news first.' Seeing the puzzled expression on Bella's face, he said sadly, 'Jacob was the son of his first wife. She died just days after giving birth to the boy. It was an absolute tragedy.'

'Oh! I had no idea,' she said, and then added hastily, 'not that it's any of my business.'

Realising that he'd spoken out of turn about his friend's private affairs, Captain Wilson cleared his throat and said, 'Quite right! You know what? I think that something stronger than tea might be in order today.'

Bella smiled kindly at him and said, 'I'll see to it.'

'Thank you,' said the Captain, smiling for the first time since his arrival at the Hall. He returned to the drawing-room to comfort his friend.

When Bella delivered a tray containing a decanter of scotch and two crystal glasses, Mr Sopwith was sitting on the sofa staring out the window, seemingly oblivious to her presence. The officer lifted the tea tray from the table so she could set down the one that she carried.

'Thank you,' she said as she took the tea tray from him. 'Should I ask Cook to set another place for dinner tonight?'

'No, thank you. That's very kind of you, but I shall be leaving soon.'

Bella nodded and left the room. She wandered to the kitchen, where a middle-aged woman kneaded a large lump of dough on the kitchen table. Mrs Vickers looked up and asked, 'Are you alright, lass?'

'Aye, I am,' she said, despite feeling unsettled by the turn of events, 'but the master's not.' Bella informed the cook about Jacob's death.

Mrs Vickers stopped what she was doing and sighed. 'That poor lad. And hardly a man yet.'

'Did you know him?' asked Bella.

'Aye, since the day he was born.' The cook expertly cut the dough and placed it in bread trays. 'I've been with Mr Sopwith since the day he wed his first wife. I moved with him from Alston to Newcastle and then down to London and back. This Mrs Sopwith didn't like London. I can't say I cared for it much meself. Filthy place, it was.'

'I don't remember anyone mentioning Jacob before,' said Bella, hovering in the doorway.

'No, I don't suppose you would. He disgraced the family by runnin' off to sea when he was just a lad of sixteen.' Ignoring Bella's shocked expression, she continued, 'The master never had any time for him. As daft as it sounds, I think he blamed the poor boy for his wife's death.' Mrs Vickers set the bread trays on the hearth and wiped her floury hands on her pinny. 'Anyway, after he lost his wife,' she continued, 'the master threw himself into his work. He travelled a lot in them days - sometimes overseas. And Jacob wasn't an easy child when he was growin' up. I could tell you some tales, I could.' The cook smiled to herself as she placed the bread trays on top

## CHAPTER 1

of the stove. Turning back to Bella, she said, 'The governess couldn't do a thing with him, so Mr Sopwith sent him off to school. I know I shouldn't say it, but the master has a good right to be feelin' bad. The situation's all of his own makin'. He never gave the lad as much as a kind word, never mind showed him any love. He chased him away, he did.'

Bella, touched by the story of Jacob's short and tragic life, wiped away a tear and wondered how Mr Sopwith could treat Jacob in that manner yet be so distressed by his passing.

'Howay hinny, there's no need for you to get yersel' all upset. You didn't even know the lad. Come on, sit down for a bit, and I'll make us a pot of tea.'

# Chapter 2

**Allenheads Lead Mine, Northumberland
October 1848**

Jack Lowery and Frank Dixon finished drilling the last hole in the rock face. Jack stood back and put down the heavy hammer that he'd been wielding. Wiping beads of sweat from his brow, he said, 'That's it. We're done.'

His father, Johnny Lowery, moved to stand in front of the rock face and cleared the holes of dust. Then, gingerly, he placed a small amount of black powder at the back of each hole and packed the holes with clay.

Frank's father, Bill Dixon, took an iron pricker, and with a steady hand, he punctured a hole through the clay until it reached the void at the back where the explosive powder lay, being careful not to let it touch the rock and create a spark. He withdrew it cautiously and then pushed a fuse through the clay to reach the powder.

'Get back!' Bill shouted to his workmates, 'I'm goin' to light the fuse.'

Jack, Johnny and Frank walked away briskly, stopping at a safe distance to wait for Bill. They heard him strike a match against a stone and then the sound of his footsteps as he ran

## CHAPTER 2

towards them.

The miners walked through the tunnel in single file. They hadn't gone far before they heard an almighty explosion and the rumbling of rocks falling in the near distance, and moments later, the air around them filled with fine particles of dust.

'That was another good day, lads,' said Bill, chuckling. 'I can't wait to come back in tomorrow and see how much ore there is in that lot. Who'd like to make a bet?'

'What's in it for the winner?' asked Johnny.

'I reckon we'll be celebratin' in the pub tomorrow night,' replied Bill, 'so how about the winner doesn't pay for a round all night.'

'Alright, you're on!' said Johnny enthusiastically. 'I bet there's half a ton.'

'Half a ton? There won't be that much, will there?' asked Frank.

'I think me father could be right, you know,' said Jack. 'Lead ore's heavy stuff.'

'I know it's heavy stuff,' said Frank, huffily, 'I've been shovellin' it on the washin' floor for years.'

'I'll go higher than half a ton,' said Bill. 'In all the years I've worked here, I've never seen a better bit of vein than that. I reckon it could be nearer a ton that we'll be shiftin' tomorrow mornin'. What do you say, Jack?'

'I'll go down the middle. Three-quarters of a ton.'

'What about me?' asked Frank expectantly. 'Can I place a bet?'

Bill laughed because Frank had never been in the pub before, never mind bought a round of drinks. He said, 'Sixteen years old, two weeks' work in the mine, and you think you know it all. Go on, have a guess if you want, but if you win, we'll buy you a bag of bullets from the sweetie shop.'

Frank looked down, looking agitated, but he held his tongue.

Jack didn't like how Bill had belittled Frank in their company, but he didn't say anything. He didn't think it was right to interfere between a father and his son.

After twelve hours underground, the men reached the bottom of the Gin Hill shaft, and they began the long climb up the wooden ladders to the surface. The light at the mine entrance was visible above them. Jack squinted and pulled down his hat to shield his eyes from the sunlight.

Shovelling rocks and drilling holes in sandstone was hard work, and they'd been working at least twelve hours a day, six days a week, for about a month now. Despite the men taking turns to do the heavy work, Jack's muscles ached from the long hours they'd put in lately, and he walked wearily across the yard for a man of twenty years.

He noticed Mr Sopwith talking to a well-dressed gentleman beside the yard gate. From the conversation he heard as they passed, Jack presumed the man was Mr Armstrong, who had designed the hydraulic engines for the mine.

'Good evening,' said Mr Sopwith, and the men tilted their caps at their boss.

'Good evening,' said the other gentleman, inclining his head to the miners. Bill replied respectfully, 'And to you too, Mr Armstrong.'

Jack smiled to himself for identifying the man correctly. He didn't consider himself a nosy person, but he liked to know who was who and what was what when it came to the mine.

Although the men were physically exhausted, they made

## CHAPTER 2

their way home in good spirits. Jack knew that the bargain they'd made with the mining company this quarter might be the best of his life, and he would work until he dropped to make as much money from it as possible. The others, he knew, felt the same way. Jack thought ahead to the pays that they would receive in January, and his eyes lit up, and his step lightened.

'Fancy a pint after dinner?' Bill asked Johnny when they reached Briar Place, where they lived in neighbouring cottages.

'Aye, why not?' Johnny grinned at his friend.

Jack shook his head. He didn't know why Bill bothered to ask that question every night because his father's answer was always the same. Bill and Johnny went to the village inn after their evening meal without fail.

# Chapter 3

### Allenheads, Northumberland
### October 1848

When Bella left the Hall late that afternoon, gold and copper leaves swirled to the ground around her as she walked down the driveway, out through the large wrought iron gates and down the bank into the small village of Allenheads, situated at the head of the Allen valley, high in the North Pennine hills. As she did every evening, Bella admired the newly built row of honey-coloured sandstone cottages as she strolled through the peaceful village. She saw nobody as she passed the shop, the inn and the mine yard on her way home to Briar Place.

The two stone-built cottages nestled against the hillside on the outskirts of the village and were mirror images of one another. Bella lived with her family at *Number One*, and, for as long as she could remember, the Lowerys had resided at *Number Two*. She let herself in and went straight to her room to change out of her work clothes, after which she returned downstairs to help her mother prepare dinner.

About an hour later, Bella sat down at the table in the front room. At the head of the table sat her father, Bill, a tall, muscular man with sandy hair and a ruddy complexion. Next

## CHAPTER 3

to him sat her younger brother, Frank, who looked exactly like their father had in his younger days. The pair of them ate their meals heartily, laughing loudly together. She guessed that they'd had a good day at the mine from what they said. Her mother, Martha, sat at the opposite end of the table to her husband. She was slim and wore her dark hair, which was streaked with grey, tied back in a bun. An empty chair stood at the table where her sister Lucy used to sit.

After he'd finished eating, Bill wiped his mouth with the back of his hand and said, 'That pie was good, an' I know what would finish it off nicely – a cold pint of beer.' He got up and grabbed his jacket from a hook on the back of the door. 'Me and Johnny are goin' out tonight.'

'That'll make a change,' said Martha sarcastically.

Bill pretended that he hadn't heard her comment and opened the door.

'Can I come with you?' asked Frank.

'I'm sure you can find somethin' better to do,' said his mother sharply.

'Howay, lad,' said Bill, smiling at his son. 'You work with the men now so, aye, why not? Come and have a drink with us.'

Frank grabbed his jacket and cap and followed his father outside. When the door closed behind them, Bella looked at her mother sympathetically. Her father went out with Johnny Lowery every night, leaving her mother at home. It was a standing joke in the village that Bill and Johnny spent more time with each other than they did with their wives and children; working together all day and drinking together at night, they were inseparable. Now, thought Bella, it looked as though Frank would follow in his father's footsteps.

As soon as Bella and her mother were alone, Martha asked,

'So, what's with the long face?'

'Nothing.'

'There's somethin' botherin' you. I can read you like a book. You've not been yourself since you came home.'

'Aye, you're right,' agreed Bella reluctantly. 'Something happened up at the Hall today, and it got me all upset, but you know I'm not supposed to talk about what goes on up there.'

'I know, love. But bottlin' things up isn't good for you either. Anythin' you say to me won't go any further. You have my word.' Her mother smiled at her reassuringly.

Unsure whether or not to confide in her mother, Bella gathered up the dishes and carried them through to the kitchen, remembering how Mr Sopwith had warned the staff that gossiping would not be tolerated under any circumstances. Bella didn't want to get into trouble or lose her job; she liked working at the Hall.

Martha followed her daughter into the kitchen, carrying the rest of the dirty dishes. 'Well?' she prompted, keeping a steady gaze on her daughter until Bella finally relented.

'Mr Sopwith's son died.'

'Oh, no! Not Arthur?' exclaimed her mother. 'He was such a sweet boy. And it's not long since they lost their little Edmund, and they're still in mourning dress for him. Me heart goes out to them, it does.'

'It wasn't Arthur. He's fit and well. Mr Sopwith had another son. An older one. I never knew him.'

'Well, it doesn't matter how old they are,' said Martha sadly, 'they're still your bairns, and losin' your child is one of the worst things that can happen to anyone. I should know.' Bowing her head, she whispered, 'Our Lucy would have been thirteen next week.'

## CHAPTER 3

'Oh, I'm sorry, Mother. I shouldn't have said anything.' Bella hugged her mother. 'I borrowed a new book from the library yesterday. Would you like me to read it to you tonight? Or we could do some matting if you want?'

Bella would willingly do anything to divert her mother's attention from Lucy.

'Never mind me,' said Martha, wiping a tear from her eye. 'I'll be alright. It's a nice night out there tonight. I thought you might like to go for a walk. With Jack, maybe?' Her mother raised her eyebrows.

'Why would you think that?' Bella turned away and began to wash the dishes.

'I might be gettin' on a bit, but I'm not blind.' Martha laughed and smiled knowingly at her daughter. 'Jack's a good lad, and it would make us all happy if the two of you got together.'

Martha picked up a tea towel and dried the dinner plates.

'I don't know,' said Bella. 'I think I should stay in tonight and keep you company.'

'If you do that every night that your father goes to the pub, you'll end up a lonely old woman like me. Anyway, I think you could do with cheering up. Go and see the lad!'

That wasn't a request; it was an order. So, as soon as the dishes were washed and dried and the kitchen was clean and tidy, Bella picked up her shawl, wrapped it around her shoulders, and went next door.

Without knocking, she opened the Lowerys' front door and saw Jack sitting at the table with his mother and six younger sisters.

'Come on in, love.' Eliza Lowery pointed at the teapot and said, 'If you're stayin', help yourself to a cup. It's fresh.'

'Thank you, Mrs Lowery, but I just popped round to see if

Jack wants to come out.'

Eliza raised her eyebrows and smiled at her son.

'Aye, alright,' said Jack, blushing slightly. He stood up, took his jacket off the back of his chair and slipped it on, and then ushered Bella outside, closing the door behind them. They stood on the roadside and looked at each other shyly.

'That's what you used to say when you came callin' for me when we were bairns.' He chuckled and nudged her with his elbow. 'By, we used to get up to some mischief back then, didn't we?'

'Aye, we did.' Bella laughed too.

'So, what do you want to do?'

Repeating her mother's words, she said, 'It's a nice night. I thought we could go for a walk.'

'Aye, alright. Which way do you want to go?' he asked, looking up and down the road.

'I don't know. We could go down the road towards Sparty Lea or up the carrier's way onto the fell?'

'Sparty Lea way, it is,' said Jack decisively.

As they set off down the road, he said, 'They mightn't work you very hard up at the Hall, but I've done a long shift at the mine today. I was up at dawn and just made it back in time for me tea.'

'Why have you all been starting so early?' she asked.

Jack looked at her in surprise. 'What! You don't know?'

Bella shook her head.

'I'm surprised your father hasn't said anythin'. The vein that we're workin' on is good - very good, in fact. So we're working longer hours to get as much ore out as we can before the end of the year.'

'It must be nice to come and go whenever you want,' said

## CHAPTER 3

Bella. 'Mr Sopwith's a stickler for time-keeping. He docks me pay if I'm not at the Hall and ready to start work at seven on the dot. You'll never believe this, but he has a clock in every room!'

'He hasn't! You're pullin' me leg.'

'Aye, he has,' she said, nodding her head for emphasis.

Jack laughed, and then his expression turned serious.

'It might seem like we work whatever hours we want, but that's not how it is. There's always a reason for the hours we do. Some days we can't work because the air is bad. It's frustratin' for us, and it's frustratin' for the bosses, but we cannot work if we cannot breathe.'

As they walked, Bella studied Jack, her childhood friend. As bairns, they'd been inseparable. They'd wandered over the moors looking for adders and birds' nests, made camps in the woods, and plodged and fished in the river together, but their fun and adventures had ended abruptly on Jack's tenth birthday when he left school and began work on the washing floor at the mine. Since then, despite being neighbours, she hadn't taken much notice of him. That was until a few weeks ago when she'd visited the Lowerys. She had gone into the house and seen Jack sitting at the table, reading a story from a well-read book with his youngest sister on his knee. Their eyes had met, and at that moment, Bella realised the scruffy lad she'd once been best friends with had become an attractive man.

Jack wasn't handsome in the traditional sense, but Bella was drawn to him like a moth to a flame. He was familiar, yet she hardly knew him; it was so long since they had spoken more than a greeting. Jack was slightly taller than Bella and stockily built, with broad shoulders and strong limbs. His shoulder-length hair was as black as a crow, and it shone in the early evening light.

'Do you want to go down to the river?' he asked, stopping next to a wooden gate. 'This is where we used to paddle. Do you remember?'

'Aye, I do. The times we went home looking like a pair of drowned rats.' She grinned as she shook her head.

'It was always you that splashed me first,' said Jack, with a cheeky smile.

'A little bit of water never hurt anybody!' Bella said in mock seriousness, and they laughed as they walked side by side down the path.

'Do you remember that time you fell face down in the clarts in the Pearson's farmyard?' she asked.

'How could I forget it? Me clothes were in such a state that day, caked in muck, that me mother made me sit under the outside tap and swill it off.'

Bella laughed loudly.

'Don't laugh! It was bloody freezing!'

As he smiled at their memories, Bella noticed tiny creases form at the corners of his dark eyes, making them look even more striking.

Jack picked up a pebble on the river bank and threw it into the slow-flowing water, where it broke the surface with a splash.

'We'll not see any fish now,' said Bella, looking into the shallows. 'You doing that will have scared them all away.'

'There was nothin' bigger than tiddlers here, anyway.'

They stood in silence for a while, looking into the water and listening to it trickle over the rocky riverbed until the silence became awkward.

## CHAPTER 3

'Can I ask you somethin', Bella?' asked Jack. 'Why did you come over to ours tonight? Was it just because you fancied a walk, or did you want to see me?' Jack cleared his throat. 'You know what I'm tryin' to say.'

Shifting uncomfortably, Bella looked up at Jack shyly through her eyelashes and said, 'It was you I wanted to see, Jack.'

He let out the breath he had been holding and smiled at her. Then, looking down into the river, he said, 'I've been meanin' to ask you out for a while.'

'Why didn't you?'

Turning back to face her, he said, 'It's a long time since we were best mates. And with you workin' up at the big house now and mixin' with the well-to-do, I didn't know if … I thought you might look down on me, you know, that I mightn't be good enough for you. What I'm tryin' to say is that I thought you might have set your sights higher than someone like me.'

'Aww, Jack. How could you think that? I've always….' She stopped, her eyes wide, surprised by what she'd been about to say.

'So, you feel the same way?' Jack's eyes brightened as he watched her face for confirmation.

'Aye, Jack Lowery. I like you, an' all.' Bella's cheeks felt so hot that she thought she must be blushing as red as a beetroot.

Jack stepped tentatively towards her and raised his hand to cup her cheek. He leaned forward and gently kissed her lips, and then taking her hand, he stepped back to admire her.

'Did you know that Bella means beautiful?' he whispered.

'Aye, so I've heard,' she said bashfully, looking down at the ground.

'The name suits you. You are very beautiful, Bella.' He ran his fingers through her long, golden hair and then traced a line down the side of her face and touched her lips with his fingertips. She looked up at him, and when their eyes met, he kissed her again, pulling her towards him and holding her firmly in his strong arms.

Then stepping back, he sighed and held out his hand. 'Come on. I'd better get you back. I'm sure your mother would appreciate some company tonight.'

Bella took his hand, and as they set off for home, she wondered how Jack knew that her mother was alone. As if reading her mind, he said, 'I saw your Frank go out with them earlier. He's so much like his father; it's uncanny.'

They strolled back to Briar Place, chatting contentedly, and when they reached the cottages, they turned to face one another.

'Can we go out again tomorrow night?' asked Jack. 'After tea?'

'Aye, I'd like that.'

Jack looked like he wanted to kiss her again, but his sisters piled out of the house and teased them for holding hands.

'Goodnight,' Bella said softly, 'I'll see you tomorrow.'

He nodded at her warmly and then accompanied his sisters inside, closing the door behind them.

Bella went into her house smiling broadly, relieved that her affection for Jack was reciprocated.

# Chapter 4

### Allenheads Village, Northumberland
### October 1848

When Bella left Allenheads Hall the following night, Mr Sopwith was in the garden, peering through his telescope that was pointed towards the village. Looking past him, she saw a group of miners milling around outside the mine yard, gesticulating wildly and looking far from happy. Even from that distance, she could hear their raised voices.

As she drew nearer, Bella saw that Jack was amongst them. She considered going to meet him so they could walk home together but decided against it because the men looked preoccupied and more than a little agitated. She walked through the village with hardly a glance in their direction, but Jack saw her and ran over.

'Bella! Hold on,' he shouted.

'Hello, Jack. Is there something wrong? I could hear me father shouting all the way from the Hall.'

'Aye, you could say that,' he said as they walked down the road together. 'Sopwith's taken on some men to keep track of the hours we work at the mine. We don't need bloody watcher men.' He almost spat out the last few words. 'They were at the mine this mornin' when we went down, lookin' at their fob watches and scribblin' the time in their notebooks, and they were back again tonight, an' all, checkin' on what time we came out. The lads are all up in arms about it.'

'I'm sorry, Jack,' said Bella, shrugging her shoulders. 'But I don't understand what the problem is.'

'The problem is that Sopwith wants us to work eight hours a day, startin' and finishin' at the same time every day, like the fellas in his factory in Newcastle do. But lead miners cannot do that. We never have and we never will.' Counting on his fingers, Jack said, 'There's the bad air for one thing. Floodin' for another. In the winter, not all of us can get to the mine 'cos of the snow. And then there's hay time. A lot of the lads have a bit of land and have to cut the grass when the weather's right. You see, we work hard when we can, and we take time off when we need to. That's the way it's always been and there's no need for anythin' to change.' Gesturing towards Allenheads Hall, he asked, 'Who does he think he is, anyway, sittin' up there lordin' it over us all?'

'I don't think it's just me father that's upset,' said Bella, rolling her eyes but silently admiring the fire in Jack's dark eyes and the passion in his voice.

'No, it's not just your father. We're all stottin' about it, and we're goin' to do somethin' about it. We cannot let him get away with it.' He said, 'Watchin' over us like that, he's treatin' us like bairns!'

They walked in silence for a few minutes, and when she thought Jack had calmed down, she asked, 'Do you still want to go for a walk later?'

'Aww, I'm sorry, Bella. We're havin' a meetin' tonight. It's important. It's to discuss what's goin' on and what we should do about it. I'm sorry but I have to go. We're meetin' at the pub at seven.'

Bella had been looking forward to spending the evening with Jack, and she was upset that he'd changed his plans and not thought to tell her, but she tried not to show it.

'Never mind,' she said, 'we can go out tomorrow night. I might take me mother over to your place instead. It's a while since we've had a sing-song with the girls.'

'They'd love that.' Jack smiled warmly at the mention of his sisters.

As there was nobody around when they got back to the cottages, Jack kissed Bella softly on her lips and said, 'You could meet me in the village later and walk me home, if you want?'

'I might just do that, Jack Lowery.' And with that, she turned and disappeared into her house.

Inside, her mother was in the kitchen preparing the evening meal. She popped her head around the door and asked, 'Was that Jack's voice I heard outside?'

When Bella didn't reply, Martha raised her eyebrows and said, 'Last night must have gone well if he's walkin' you home from work!'

'There's nowt wrong with your hearing, Mother.'

Bella heard her mother chuckle as she climbed the stairs, smiling to herself. Last night had gone well, she thought, but it was a shame that she wouldn't be able to spend as much time with Jack that evening as she'd hoped. As Bella changed out of her work clothes, she heard the front door close and raised voices coming from downstairs. Her father and brother were home, and they weren't happy. Not only that, she could hear Mr Lowery shouting next door too. She'd never known the men at Briar Place to be so upset.

While the Dixons ate rabbit stew, potatoes, and cabbage for their teas, Bella listened to the same story about the watcher men from her father.

'Miners are proud men,' said Bill, sitting straight on his chair. 'They're capable of workin' on their own account. They don't need to be managed, and they certainly don't need anyone to record what time they start and finish work. Why change a system that's worked for centuries?' He shrugged his shoulders.

'It doesn't need to be changed,' said Frank firmly.

'Damn right, it doesn't.'

As Bella sat and listened, she could feel trouble brewing. She thought about Mr Sopwith, her employer and Chief Agent for the lead mines, for it was he who was demanding that the miners work an eight-hour day, and was determined that they would do so. As far as Bella was concerned, hiring men to supervise the miners' hours showed a lack of respect for the men and she wondered if he might come to regret that action. She knew Mr Sopwith wasn't a man to be crossed. He was well-connected and well-respected throughout the country. Perhaps it would be the miners who would regret standing up to him. Then, the image of her master grieving for his son came to mind, and she couldn't help but feel a little sympathy for the man.

When the men at Briar Place left for the meeting in the village, Bella and Martha went next door.

Lizzie Lowery answered the door to her neighbours and invited them inside. Her younger sisters had been so excited when Jack told them Bella and Mrs Dixon were coming over

## CHAPTER 4

for a sing-song that they had spent over an hour cleaning and tidying in preparation for their visit. The girls sat expectantly on chairs lining the edge of the room, and they all had smiles on their faces. Lizzie looked at them proudly.

At seventeen, Lizzie felt older than her years. Since she'd left school at ten, she'd spent her time caring for her sisters, whom she loved dearly. She wondered cynically if God had given her lots of siblings so she could experience what motherhood would be like because, with her wayward red hair and thin frame, she thought it unlikely that a man would find her attractive and want to marry her, although she hoped that one day when her sisters were grown up and no longer needed her, she might find someone who would take her on. But for now, she was content with her life.

Her sister, Hannah, was just a couple of years younger than her. She was a pretty girl with dark brown hair, and the men and the boys in the village were already paying her attention. Unlike herself, Hannah would have no trouble finding a husband, thought Lizzie.

Jane, Catherine, and Deborah were lively girls who were always laughing, teasing and joking amongst themselves, and then the youngest sister was Mary, a sweet child who refused to be separated from her rag doll, which she clutched in her tiny hands.

As Lizzie pointed at the empty chairs by the window and said, 'Please, sit down,' she noticed that Bella looked ill at ease, as though she had something on her mind. Lizzie sat back and listened while Bella and Martha chatted to her mother, Eliza Lowery, for a short while and then she suggested that they should start the evening by singing a few hymns. With going to church every Sunday, even the youngest children knew the more common hymns, and they adored the new one that they had just learned, *All Things Bright And Beautiful*. Afterwards, they sang some popular ballads and folk songs, finishing with *Bobby Shafto*. After an hour or so of singing, Lizzie saw that Bella was smiling brightly and looked much more relaxed. Singing could certainly lift a person's spirits, she thought.

While Hannah took the younger girls to bed, Lizzie made a pot of tea. The women shared more news and gossip over a cup of tea and a slice of fruit cake, and when Bella and her mother rose to leave, Eliza said, 'Don't forget about Saturday night.'

'What's on Saturday night?' asked Bella, looking from her mother to Eliza.

'It's our Jack's birthday,' replied Eliza. 'It's his twenty-first. We're havin' a bit of a do for him.'

'We'll all be here,' said Martha. 'I'll come over in the afternoon and give you a hand puttin' the spread together.'

'Thanks, Martha. That's very kind of you.'

Lizzie was surprised that her brother hadn't told Bella about his birthday, but that was men for you, she thought. They didn't pay as much attention to family events and special occasions as women did. She was so glad that Jack and Bella were walking out together at last. She had always hoped that they would get together, and now that they were a couple, she was pleased for them.

Bella and her mother stepped out of the Lowerys' cottage and through their front door.

'I don't know about you, lass, but I'm ready for me bed,' said Martha as she tended to the fire. 'I wonder what time your

## CHAPTER 4

father and Frank will be back tonight?'

'I don't know,' said Bella, still standing by the door. She took her shawl off the hook and said, 'I'm just going out for some fresh air.' She left before her mother had time to reply.

It was dark as Bella walked up the road towards the village of Allenheads, but the sky was clear, and the moon was almost full, lighting her way. She hoped that the meeting had gone well and that Jack would be in a better mood than earlier in the day. She stood by the gate to the mine yard, from where she had a good view of the pub doorway, and it wasn't long before Jack stepped outside and looked around. When his eyes found hers, he waved and ran across the road to where she stood.

'Thanks for comin',' he said, kissing her cheek. 'I wasn't sure if you would.'

'Where are the others?' Bella asked, wondering if her father, Frank, and Johnny might be joining them.

'They're stoppin' for another pint.'

'Don't you want to stay with them?'

'I'd rather be here with you,' he said, grinning at her. 'I don't mind a pint or two, but that's enough for me. I've seen me father, and yours for that matter, rollin' in drunk every night since I was a bairn.'

'They always seem happy when they come home.'

'It makes them senseless, is what it does,' replied Jack.

As they set off to walk home, Jack took Bella's hand and said, 'I don't want to talk about them. What they do is their own business. What have you been up to today?'

Bella told him about her day, which had been spent working at the Hall and singing with his sisters, and he listened as she spoke. Then, she asked, 'What did they decide to do about the watcher men?'

'Don't worry about that. The men have got something planned. Something that should get them off our backs.'

She was a little disappointed that Jack hadn't shared their plans with her but thought he must have his reasons. 'I'm glad it will be sorted out soon.'

Before they reached the cottages, Jack stopped by a large tree, pulled Bella behind it and said, 'Nobody can see us here.'

She had been about to say that there was nobody on the road to see them anyway, but before she could open her mouth, Jack's lips descended onto hers, and he pulled her into his embrace.

'I've wanted to do that all day,' he said.

'Me too,' said Bella, nestling against his firm chest.

They stood and held each other for quite some time before Jack broke away. He took her hand and said, 'I'm pleased you came to meet me tonight, Bella. I really wanted to see you.'

She smiled up at him. 'I'm glad I did. It's not often that I get to see you when there's nobody else about.' Bella reached up to kiss him again, and Jack took her in his arms and kissed her lovingly.

When they parted, he said, 'It must be late. I should take you home.'

They walked back to Briar Place holding hands, their fingers entwined.

Lying in her bed that night, familiar voices outside the house disturbed Bella's sleep. It was her father, Frank, and Johnny returning from the pub, clearly very drunk by the way they were shouting and carrying on. As they approached the cottages, one of them shushed the others loudly, and she heard

## CHAPTER 4

Johnny say, 'Be quiet, lads. We don't want to wake the lasses. Our lives wouldn't be worth living!' Bill and Frank laughed in response. Bella doubted that anyone at Briar Place could have slept through the racket.

The noise eventually subsided when her father and brother retired for the night. As Bella drifted back to sleep, thinking about her parent's relationship, she felt sorry for her mother, who only saw her husband at mealtimes and at church. Over the years, she'd given him three children, spent her life cooking and cleaning for him, done his laundry and mended his clothes, and she had asked for little in return. Couldn't her father see how lonely her mother was?

# Chapter 5

### Allenheads Hall, Northumberland
### October 1848

Bella prepared the dining room for the guests from London who were expected for dinner that evening. She polished the silver cutlery until she could see her reflection in it and then set the places at the table with precision. There was a large empty space at the centre of the table. Mrs Sopwith's favourite centrepiece was a beautiful silver epergne, which she liked filled with flowers.

Bella went to the window to look for any flowers that might be left in the garden and sighed. There were so few plants that flowered at this time of year in Allenheads. Still, she spotted a bush in the far corner of the garden, sparsely covered with miniature white roses. With some evergreen foliage, of which there was an abundance, she thought she could make an attractive display.

She went to the kitchen, donned her shawl and boots, picked up a basket and a pair of scissors, and went outside to the garden. The grass was damp. She crossed the lawn leaving a trail of footprints behind her. When she reached the rosebush, she snipped off a flower with the scissors and sniffed the

## CHAPTER 5

pleasant scent. She cut the remaining blooms, placed them delicately into the basket and then turned her attention to the greenery. As she clipped small twigs from the shrubbery, she heard voices and looked towards the drive, where she saw five men walking towards the front door. Then, to her surprise, an enormous group of miners marched through the gateway and stood inside the grounds. Her father and Frank were at the edge of the crowd, and Johnny and Jack stood beside them.

Glued to the spot, she watched one of the five men, Mr Heslop from the village, step forward and knock at the door. He stood back and waited. If she'd been in the house, she would have been the one to open the door, but instead, she caught a fleeting glimpse of Mrs Vickers in the doorway before it closed again. It was several minutes before it reopened and Mr Sopwith stepped outside.

The Chief Agent stood on his gravel drive, facing the miners, and said, 'Good afternoon, gentlemen. What is the meaning of this intrusion?'

'I speak on behalf of us all,' replied Mr Heslop, projecting his voice to be heard by everyone in the vicinity. 'There's nearly three hundred of us in number here today, and we're all agreed that the watcher men you've employed at the mine should be dismissed. There's no need for them to be there. Our fathers and grandfathers had nobody watching over them when they worked at this mine, and it was the best lead mine in the country in their time! So why should we endure it? Standing there with their notebooks and pencils, recording our every move, there's no need for it. Let them go now, and you'll hear no more about the matter.'

In the background, the miners murmured and nodded in agreement.

Bella realised why Jack had been vague about the miners' plan. It was because she worked for Mr Sopwith. Had she known what they intended to do, she could have forewarned him, taking away their element of surprise and giving Mr Sopwith time to prepare a response.

She wondered where Jack thought her loyalties lay - with her family and friends or her employer. Did Jack trust her? He mustn't, she thought, or he would have confided in her.

Bella glanced up at the front of the building. Mrs Sopwith was watching the proceedings from an upstairs window, her hand resting on her pregnant belly.

'I hear what you say,' said Mr Sopwith, 'but I must disagree that my agents are unnecessary. When the bargains were let, you all agreed to work a forty-hour week, yet I have seen for myself that some of you work nowhere near that number. The gentlemen are employed to monitor your time-keeping so that we all know where we stand.'

'We don't get an hourly rate of pay like your factory men. We're paid on the weight of ore we fetch out of the mine, or the depth of rock that we dig. Time-keeping isn't relevant in our case.'

'That's true,' said Mr Sopwith, 'but for this mine to be profitable in the future, I need men to work regular hours. Forty hours a week is fewer than most men work. It's not a lot to ask.'

One of the miners by the gate, Nelson Kidd, shouted, 'I'd like to see you drilling holes and shovelling rock for forty bloody hours a week!' His comment was followed by jeering from the crowd.

'Gentlemen, I must stop you there,' said Mr Sopwith angrily. Dramatically pointing at the crowd of miners, he said, 'I will

## CHAPTER 5

not stand here and listen to your grievances against my under-agents in this unruly manner, with this mob of ignorant, Irish ruffians watching on.'

'Then, what are we supposed to do to show you that we all stand together in our complaint?' asked Mr Heslop, taken aback by Mr Sopwith's reaction.

'Do as any civilised group of men would do. Present your sentiments in writing.'

'Aye, alright. We'll do that. But believe me, Mr Sopwith, you haven't heard the last of this.'

'I bid you farewell.' Mr Sopwith turned his back on them and returned to his house, further infuriating the miners.

Bella returned to the kitchen, removed her shawl and wet boots, and then went to the dining room to collect the epergne. As she passed Mr Sopwith's office, she heard him cursing to himself and then a loud thud, which sounded like his fist hitting the desk.

She popped her head around the door and asked, 'Are you alright, sir?'

He looked at her strangely. 'Am I alright? No! I am not alright. I am shocked by their impertinence! How dare they come to my home and speak to me in that manner in front of my family?'

'I'm sorry, sir. They don't mean any harm. They're just upset about the watcher men, that's all.'

Mr Sopwith shook his head slowly, 'Bella, I'm so sorry I took out my indignation on you. I can't believe that I have just behaved as badly as they did. My sincerest apologies. Please bring me a cup of tea, would you? And then continue with the preparations for tonight. Our guests will be arriving soon. Thank God they didn't witness that demonstration out there!'

'Yes, sir.'

Bella collected the epergne and then went to the kitchen, where Mrs Vickers was calmly preparing a four-course meal for six people. While Bella waited for the kettle to boil, she decorated the centrepiece with the roses and foliage from the garden, and the cook smiled approvingly at her efforts.

The dinner guests were late to arrive. Mrs Vickers had expected to serve the meal at seven o'clock, and she fussed around the kitchen, checking on the pots and pans, trying to keep the food hot.

The kitchen was so warm that Bella went to stand outside for a while to cool down. It was a pleasant evening for the time of year, and she looked up to the skies and admired the full moon and the twinkling stars in the heavens. Bats flew around the garden, and she watched them dart around, quickly changing direction, and she wondered why they never collided with the buildings or the trees.

'They're here!' shouted Mrs Vickers.

Bella went inside, refreshed after a short break.

'With it bein' only gentlemen tonight,' said Mrs Vickers, 'it'll only take about ten minutes for the master to make his guests comfortable and get them seated at the table. Are you ready for this?'

'Aye, I'm ready.'

Mrs Vickers ladled the soup into bowls, and Bella carried them into the dining room, two at a time, and set them in front of the guests. A white-haired man who Bella didn't recognise smiled up at her and thanked her for the food.

'You're very welcome, sir,' she replied automatically because the man's words had taken her by surprise; Mr Sopwith's guests usually ignored her when she served at the table. Mr

## CHAPTER 5

Sopwith glared at her for speaking to a guest.

When she returned to the kitchen, she told Mrs Vickers about the man's kind gesture and asked if she knew who the master's guests were that evening.

'I know who that one will be. Mr Faraday. He's a lovely man. He doesn't have any airs and graces like most of them do.' With a towel wrapped around her hands, Mrs Vickers carried the heated dinner plates to the table and spread them out so she could serve the main course. 'He's a scientist from London and a good friend of Mr Sopwith. He was a regular visitor at the London house.'

'That must be him. He seemed very nice.'

'Mr Armstrong, you'll know. He comes here regularly.'

'Yes, I recognised him.'

'The others must be scientists or engineers. They're the sort of men that he mixes with.'

Mrs Vickers placed a roasted breast of duck on each plate, quickly served the potatoes and vegetables, and then carefully spooned the gravy so as not to spill it on the edges of the plates. Bella thought the meal looked delicious, and her mouth watered. She hadn't eaten since midday, and her stomach rumbled.

'I've put a bit to the side for us,' the cook confided with a wink. 'We'll have it when they're eatin' their desserts. Go and clear the table, and then I'll help you carry these through.'

After serving at Mr Sopwith's dinner party, Bella returned home late that evening. She found her mother at home alone, sitting in front of the fire with her knitting.

'They've gone to another meetin',' said Martha. 'Your father and Frank said somethin' about them havin' to put everythin' down in writin' for the bosses.'

Bella took off her shawl and boots and then sat next to her mother.

Martha put her knitting in a basket by her chair and looked up at her daughter. 'You look tired, love. Have you had somethin' to eat?'

'Aye, Mrs Vickers made a bit extra.' In a posh voice, she added, 'We had duck with vegetables, roast potatoes and gravy for our teas this evening.'

'Very grand, I'm sure. I kept you a bit of mutton stew, but it'll keep for tomorrow.'

'Thanks, Mother. You know you do a great job of looking after us all.'

Martha smiled at the compliment, and Bella thought her mother looked years younger when she smiled and that it was a shame she didn't smile more often.

The front door opened, and Bill and Frank barged into the living room, grinning broadly and reeking of beer. The meeting must have gone well, Bella thought.

'Jack's waitin' outside for you,' said her brother, with a wink.

Bella hadn't expected to see Jack that night. She quickly put on her boots, wrapped her shawl around her body, and went outside. Despite the full moon glowing overhead, her eyes took a second to adjust to the darkness before she saw Jack standing on the other side of the road.

'Bella,' he said, taking her into his arms and hugging her. 'I missed you. Last night seems such a long time ago.'

'I know, it does. I saw you at the Hall this afternoon. I was in the garden.'

Jack released Bella and stepped back, his face hard and eyes wide. 'Did you hear what that stuck-up bastard called us? An ignorant mob of Irish ruffians. Hmph! There's none of us Irish, and none of us is ignorant either. We've all been schooled!'

'Don't let it upset you, Jack. I'm sure he didn't mean what he said.'

'Oh! He meant it alright. Did you see the look on his face? I don't know why he thinks he has the right to look down on us the way he does. Chief Minin' Agent! What does he know about minin'? He's never done a day's minin' in his life.'

'Jack!'

Jack stopped his rant and looked down at Bella. She leaned forward and kissed him gently on the lips. Pulling her to him, he returned her kiss with the passion that still ran through his veins until they were both breathless. They stood together in silence, holding each other until their heartbeats slowed. Jack leaned back and looked deeply into Bella's eyes. He was about to speak when they heard a door open, and Frank called out, 'Mother said you have to come in now.'

'I'll be there in a minute,' she replied and turned her attention to Jack. 'What were you goin' to say?'

'It doesn't matter. Goodnight, love.' He kissed her gently before releasing her from his arms.

'Goodnight, Jack.'

# Chapter 6

**Allenheads Hall, Northumberland
October 1848**

On Saturday morning, Bella sang to herself as she dusted the vases on the sideboard in the hallway.

'Someone sounds happy!'

Bella turned towards the staircase and was surprised to see Mrs Sopwith.

'Are you alright, ma'am? Can I get you anything?'

'I'm fine, Bella. I'm a bit restless, that's all. It's so tedious staying in my bedroom all day every day.'

'But the doctor said you should rest.'

Ignoring Bella's words, Mrs Sopwith said, 'You've been singing all morning. It's rather cheered me up. Tell me, what's made you so happy?'

'No reason, in particular.'

'I know!' Mrs Sopwith beamed. 'You're courting, aren't you?'

Bella's blush gave her away.

'How sweet! Does the young man live near here?'

'Yes, he lives next door to us.'

'The boy next door. How wonderful! Have you plans to see

## CHAPTER 6

him this weekend?'

'Yes, it's his birthday today and his family are having a party for him later. It's his twenty-first.'

Looking at Bella's tiny waist, Mrs Sopwith said, 'As I've had so much time on my hands, I've been sorting through my wardrobe. There are a couple of dresses that will never fit me again, not after six pregnancies, but they may fit you. If you'd like them, you're welcome to them.'

'That's very generous of you, ma'am,' said Bella in disbelief. 'Thank you. Thank you very much.'

'I'm tired now. I'll leave the dresses outside my bedroom door.' Mrs Sopwith began to climb the stairs, but, after a few steps, she turned back to Bella and said, 'It must be months since you've had a day off. You're like a permanent fixture in this house. Take the rest of the afternoon off to prepare for your party and we'll see you on Monday.'

'Thank you, ma'am.'

Bella watched Mrs Sopwith ascend the wide staircase and listened to her footsteps cross the landing. A bedroom door closed and then opened again. At that point, Bella ran upstairs to retrieve the dresses from the landing. Without looking too closely at them, she quickly wrapped them in brown paper and left the Hall, unable to believe her luck.

When she entered the cottage, her mother instantly saw the package that she carried and asked, 'What's that you've got there?'

'Mrs Sopwith gave me some dresses.'

'By! They must like you up there if they're givin' you their cast-offs.' Getting up from her chair, she said, 'Come on, then. Let's have a look.'

They went upstairs to Bella's bedroom and unwrapped the

dresses. The first was an emerald green dress with a wide neckline and flowing skirt. Bella tried it on, and it fitted well. Feeling the material, her mother said, 'That's quality, that is, and what a lovely colour! You should wear it tonight at the party. Jack won't be able to keep his eyes off you.'

'Oh, Mother!' said Bella, but as she looked at her reflection in the old, chipped mirror on her bedroom wall, she hardly recognised herself. The dress was so elegant and she had to admit that it looked good on her.

The other was a pale blue silk dress, which fitted her perfectly. When her mother saw her wearing it, she gasped, and her voice broke as she said, 'This one should be your wedding dress, Bella. You look absolutely beautiful in it. You couldn't wish for better.'

After packing the blue dress carefully, Bella left the green one on her bed and went downstairs. She carried in the tin bath from the backyard and placed it in front of the living room fire. Martha heated the water to fill it, and each family member had a bath. When it was Bella's turn, her mother helped wash her hair.

'We should curl your hair for the party,' said Martha as she rinsed out the soap. 'It's how all the ladies wear their hair now.'

'How do you know that?' asked Bella.

'I used to be a lady's maid before I married your father, and I take notice of such things.'

'You've never told me that before. Where did you work?'

'At a large house near Hexham. Mrs Hedley was an elderly lady but very graceful. She had a room full of clothes and shoes - and powdered wigs!'

'Wigs?' laughed Bella.

## CHAPTER 6

'Aye, they weren't in fashion even then, but she'd kept them. She sometimes asked me to help her put them on. I think they reminded her of her youth. I remember there was a painting of her hanging in the hall, and if that was anythin' to go by, she'd been a real beauty. Age is cruel to a woman.'

Her mother disappeared upstairs and came back with a comb and some long strips of cloth. 'Get some clothes on, and then come and sit on the cracket in front of me chair. I'm goin' to do your hair.'

'I thought you were going to help Mrs Lowery with the food today.'

'That's all taken care of. We were up at the crack of dawn and got finished by noon.'

Bella sat in front of the fire, reading the book she'd borrowed from the library until her hair dried. Then, her mother removed the rags from her hair and teased the ringlets into beautiful golden curls.

They went to Bella's room, and her mother helped Bella into the green dress.

'For a neckline that wide, you need a necklace,' said Martha. 'I don't have much in the way of jewellery, but Mrs Hedley did give me a locket when I left her service.' Her mother went to her room and came back holding a small locket, which she fastened around Bella's neck.

'Is it gold?' asked Bella, touching the oval locket with her fingers.

'Aye, it is.' Martha smiled proudly. 'I wore it on me weddin' day, and I've never had an occasion to wear it since. Stand back and let me have a look at you.' After inspecting her daughter, she said, 'You're ready. Come on, let's go!'

Downstairs, Bill and Frank both turned to look at Bella in

her fancy frock.

'You'll be the belle of the ball, our Bella,' said Frank.

'Thank you,' she smiled at her brother's compliment.

When Bella stepped outside, she heard her father say, 'How do you expect Jack to keep his hands off our daughter when she's dressed like that?'

Bella felt wonderful in her new dress. Her mother had dressed her to look like a lady for Jack's party, and she wasn't going to let her father's words stop her from enjoying the night.

When the Dixons went next door, Johnny Lowery was already playing his fiddle. The Lowery girls wore ribbons in their hair and danced a jig in the centre of the room. Several tables, covered with mismatched tablecloths and laden with food, lined one wall. The house was full of family and friends from the village. Some guests stood around the edges of the living room, while others were outside the front door, but all were chatting and drinking either ale or tea. When Jack saw the Dixons arrive, he went to greet them. He held out his hand to Bill and Frank, who congratulated him on his coming of age, then he kissed Martha on her cheek, and she wished him many happy returns. They mingled with the crowd, leaving Bella and Jack alone.

'Happy Birthday!' said Bella.

'I hardly recognised you standin' there,' Jack said in his rich, deep voice. 'You look good. Really good.' He whispered into her ear, 'I've never seen you lookin' so beautiful, ever.'

His dark eyes were focused intensely on her when he kissed her on the cheek, lingering longer than necessary, and then he took her hand and led her into the room.

'Hello, Bella! Do you want to dance with us?' asked Hannah

## CHAPTER 6

excitedly.

'Of course, I do!' Bella moved to the centre of the room and danced with Jack's sisters, aware that he was watching her. It wasn't long before she heard him say, 'Can I join you?'

Bella held out her hand, and they danced together to the cheers of family and friends, which made them blush. Bella loved dancing with Jack, especially when he lifted her up and swung her around. She didn't think that she had ever been so happy in her life, and if Jack's grin was anything to go by, she thought he must be feeling the same way.

When they stopped for refreshments, Bella stood with Lizzie and Hannah and watched the guests dance on the makeshift dance floor until Lizzie decided that it was time to take the younger girls upstairs to bed. Bella doubted that they would be able to sleep with the noise from the party, but they did look tired, so perhaps they would.

Voices and laughter carried over the sound of the violin music. Everyone was having a wonderful time. Jack chatted with his guests, but Bella was aware that his eyes were on her for most of the night. The men got louder as the drink flowed, and Bella heard much good-humoured cursing.

Martha came to Bella's side and took her arm. 'I think it's time we went home and left the men to it.'

Jack saw that Bella and Martha were leaving and rushed to the door. 'Thank you for coming tonight,' he said. 'I hope you enjoyed the party?' He addressed them both, but his eyes were fixed firmly on Bella.

'It was a lovely evening,' said Martha. 'We've had a lovely time.'

'Goodnight, Mrs Dixon,' said Jack, and he kissed her cheek before she stepped outside.

'Have you enjoyed your birthday?' asked Bella.

'It was the best!' Jack kissed her lightly on the lips, which surprised her when they were in company. 'Goodnight, Bella.'

'Goodnight, Jack,' whispered Bella, and then she followed her mother next door.

# Chapter 7

### Allenheads Hall, Northumberland
### October 1848

Bella added the finishing touches to a display of dried flowers and grasses on the stand in the hallway. She heard Mr Sopwith sigh loudly, and when she glanced in his direction, she saw that he was checking his pocket watch. He was standing by the door, waiting to say farewell to his wife and children who were travelling to Newhouse, the mine agent's house at Ireshopeburn in Weardale. He had hired a coach to take them, and it had been standing on the drive for fifteen minutes already.

'Ah! There you are,' said Mr Sopwith when his wife appeared at the top of the staircase. 'Are you ready, my dear?'

'Yes, we are. Would you help the nanny with the bags please?'

Mr Sopwith called for the coach driver to come inside and asked him to take the bags from the landing out to the coach. The young man willingly obliged.

The children went to their father one by one. He wished them a speedy journey and a good vacation in Weardale. Finally, his wife faced him, and he kissed her on the cheek as he said goodbye.

'I feel as though we're being cast out of our home at a most inopportune time,' said Mrs Sopwith, resting her hand on her large belly.

'It's just for a week, my dear,' he replied. 'The baby isn't due for a month yet.'

Bella felt uncomfortable listening to their conversation and considered leaving the hallway, but thought that moving would draw attention to her presence.

'Mr Beaumont wants his son to come here and learn about the lead industry from me,' continued the master, 'and to do a little shooting. I've already explained that Wentworth is bringing some friends with him. We need the children's rooms to accommodate them, and that it's hardly appropriate for you or the children to be here when the house is full of young men. It wouldn't be right.'

'Our daughters need to meet eligible young men. Any friend of Wentworth Beaumont would be a suitable husband for our girls.'

'This is neither the time nor the place for that, my dear. I will see you at Newhouse when we visit on Tuesday morning.' He took her gloved hand and kissed it.

Mrs Sopwith walked out to the coach, and Mr Sopwith returned to his office.

As soon as the way was clear, Bella escaped to the kitchen, where Mrs Vickers was taking delivery of supplies for the young Mr Beaumonts' imminent stay. Bella helped her store the food items and beverages in the appropriate places, and then they shared a pot of tea and discussed the plan for the visit.

Around mid-afternoon, the party arrived at Allenheads Hall. Mr Sopwith warmly greeted the four young men as they

## CHAPTER 7

climbed down from their carriage and invited them inside. In the absence of a manservant, the carriage driver carried the men's bags upstairs, and Bella deposited them into their rooms.

Mrs Vickers had prepared a feast for their first evening. The soup was onion with stilton, the fish course was rainbow trout with minted peas, followed by the main course of roast venison and vegetables, the dessert was apple and cream made in a pineapple-shaped mould, and then there was a selection of cheeses and biscuits with the coffee. Bella served a different wine or port with each course, and by the end of the meal, there was much raucous laughter in the dining room.

After the men retired to the drawing-room with a decanter of brandy, Bella cleared the table and helped Mrs Vickers to wash the dishes. She had enjoyed the night serving the visitors. They were different from Mr Sopwith's usual guests; they were younger, around her age, and much more fun.

In the next few days, Mr Sopwith and his visitors rode to Newhouse, Coalcleugh, and the smelt mill at Rookhope. They went shooting on the moors and spent their evenings eating, drinking, telling stories, and playing games.

As she left work on Friday night, Bella was delighted to see Jack waiting by the gates and she walked quickly down the drive to meet him.

'This is a nice surprise. I didn't expect to see you tonight.'

She took his hand, and they wandered home together.

'You've been working late all week,' said Jack. 'I've hardly seen you. Is there somethin' goin' on up there?'

'He's got some people staying. That's all.' Smiling up at him, she said, 'Because I've put in a lot of extra hours this week, he's given me the day off tomorrow.'

'A full Saturday off. That's great! I could finish early if you want to spend the afternoon together?'

'Aye, that would be lovely,' she said. 'If it's a nice day, we could go up onto the fells and take a picnic.'

'We could.' Jack pulled Bella to a stop, kissed her gently, and whispered, 'And if I take you up onto the moors, I'll have you all to myself.'

Bella felt excited by his words and blushed furiously.

Bella rose early the next day and spent the morning baking scones, cakes and bread. She packed two scones, two slices of cake, some cheese, ham, and bread in a basket and then changed into a pretty lilac dress.

Her father and Frank came home around noon, so she guessed that Jack must have finished work too. She sat in the living room and waited for him. He arrived at the door about half an hour later, his hair brushed back, still damp from being washed, and he was wearing his Sunday clothes.

'You look very handsome,' she said with a smile and grabbed the basket and her shawl.

'And you look beautiful as always.'

'We're off now, Mother,' she called through to the kitchen.

'Make sure you're back before dark,' shouted Martha.

'We will,' said Bella, rolling her eyes.

Jack took the basket from her and hooked it over his arm. They held hands as they strolled to the bottom of the carrier's track and then they began to climb the hill towards the fell. Bella was pleased that the stony path was dry underfoot. The moor was autumnal now that the heather had turned brown and the bracken russet.

The couple continued the long trek to the top of the hill

and stood on Killhope Law, admiring the beautiful views in all directions. Hills and secluded valleys stretched for miles, and there was not another person in sight. The only sounds they heard were the bleating of a sheep and the call of a red grouse in the distance. Jack put down the picnic basket. He stood behind Bella, wrapped his arms around her, his chin resting on her shoulder, and held her close.

'It's much nicer up here than I remember,' said Bella. They had walked to Killhope Law many times as children but never before had she appreciated the magnificent landscape.

'It's beautiful, just like you.' Jack turned her around and kissed her forehead.

Retrieving the basket, he said, 'I saw a nice spot further down where we could have our picnic. The ground looked nice and dry.'

Bella felt reluctant to leave the peaceful seclusion of the hilltop, but she took his proffered hand and walked down the bank with him. They found the place that Jack had seen earlier, a circular patch of grazed grass surrounded by tall bracken and old woody heather. It was sheltered and private. Bella bent down and touched the grass to check that it was dry and then sat down.

Jack sat by her side and lifted the tea towel that covered the basket. 'I've been wondering what's in here,' he said, taking out a square of cheese and holding it to Bella's lips. To his delight, she ate the cheese from his fingers.

They ate heartily after the long walk, and when they had finished, Bella packed up the basket and was about to get to her feet when Jack took her hand.

'What's the rush?' he asked. 'We have the whole afternoon together, and this is as good a place as any to spend it. It's quiet.

It's peaceful. And we're alone.' He put his arm around her shoulder, and she turned to face him. Their lips touched and before long they were kissing heatedly, their hands exploring each other's bodies over their clothes.

They heard the sound of horses' hooves, which gradually became louder as the horses drew near.

'The carrier ponies won't be up here on a Saturday,' said Jack. 'Anyone on horseback won't see us here until they're on top of us. Maybe we should stand up so we don't get trampled.'

Horrified by his words, Bella jumped up and waved her arms in the air and called out to the riders to let them know they were there.

Startled, one of the horses reared and the rider swore loudly as he tumbled to the ground. The horse bolted in the opposite direction, and another man turned his horse around and galloped after it.

'Wentworth, are you alright?' asked Mr Sopwith, getting down from his horse to check on his guest.

The young gentleman rubbed the debris off his clothes and said, 'I'm fine, thank you. Absolutely fine.'

'Bella, is that you?' asked Mr Sopwith, peering at her and closing the distance between them. 'What are you doing up here, scaring the horses like that? Mr Beaumont could have been killed!'

Jack stood up and put a hand protectively on Bella's shoulder.

'I'm sorry, Mr Sopwith. I didn't mean to frighten the horses. We were having a picnic at the side of the track here and we heard the horses coming. We didn't want to get trampled.'

'I see,' he looked at the young couple suspiciously and remounted his horse. 'It's just as well Mr Armstrong is only carrying out a reconnaissance of the moor today, and not testing his new armaments as he will be soon. Had you been picnicking then, you could have been blown to smithereens, never mind trampled.'

Bella shivered at his words.

'Tommy, you're frightening the girl,' Mr Armstrong said to his friend.

Mr Sopwith looked away uncomfortably before saying, 'I know you meant Mr Beaumont no harm, but still, I think you owe him an apology. After all, you were responsible for his fall.'

Bella walked over to the young man and said sincerely, 'I'm very sorry for what happened, Mr Beaumont. I hope you're not hurt.'

'Thank you, Bella. There's no harm done.' Looking in the direction that his horse bolted, he said, 'Here comes Hartley with my horse now.'

Mr Beaumont mounted the chestnut mare, and the men set off and continued along the track, nodding to Bella and Jack as they passed.

As they rode away, Bella began to cry. Jack held her and said, 'It's alright, Bella. The fella wasn't hurt. He said there was no harm done. So what's the matter? Why are you crying?'

When Bella didn't answer, he asked, 'Are those lads the ones that are staying at the Hall?'

Bella nodded.

'Have they done something to upset you?'

Bella shook her head, and when she could speak, she asked, 'Did you see the way he looked at us?'

'Who?'

'Mr Sopwith. He thinks we were-'

'Is that what you're upset about?' Jack chuckled. 'We were doin' what he thought. So what?'

'I don't want him to think that I'm not a good sort. That I'm a loose woman.'

'Bella, there's nothin' wrong in what we were doin'. It's what all courtin' couples do when they get the chance to be alone. Anyway, I don't know why you're so bothered about what he thinks. He's a pompous old fool.'

Bella hung her head, and said, 'He's not like you think he is.'

'Tell me, then. What is he like?'

'I cannot talk about him and his family. It's not allowed. I'd lose me job if he found out I'd been gossiping about him.'

'So, he must have something to hide,' reasoned Jack.

'No, he hasn't. He just doesn't want everybody to know his business, that's all.'

'You know somethin', Bella. I think you care more about him that you do me sometimes.' Jack picked up the basket and began to stride down the hill.

Bella followed behind him but didn't try to catch up. She didn't want to talk to him and didn't think he'd want to talk to her either. She was still upset about the incident with the horses and the encounter with Mr Sopwith. She and Jack had been having a wonderful afternoon until the riders had turned up, and they would have stayed in their secluded hideaway, kissing, cuddling and caressing all afternoon if they hadn't been interrupted. But instead, they had argued, which they seemed fated to do when either of them mentioned Mr Sopwith's name.

# Chapter 8

### Allenheads, Northumberland
### November 1848

It was a foggy afternoon and almost dusk when the disgruntled miners and their families gathered outside the inn at Allenheads to hear the latest news from their representative in the dispute. Mr Heslop stood on the steps of the public house, waiting to deliver his speech.

The Dixons and the Lowerys stood together at the back of the assembly. Bella was there, not so much to hear what Mr Heslop had to say, but because she'd wanted to see Jack. He stood by her side and slipped his arm around her waist, an action that did not go unnoticed by the villagers, and she wondered if he'd done it purposely to declare to the world that she was his girl.

Mr Heslop addressed the group. 'My fellow men, it has been a whole week since we presented Mr Sopwith with our grievances in writing, as he, himself, requested that we should do, and yet we have heard nothing from him in return. There has been no letter of reply, no request for a meeting, nor notice of an enquiry.

'But without reason, the five of us who represented you

have been dismissed from our employment and evicted from our homes - and without notice! What does that say about the man?

'We have all been unjustly deprived of our privileges. As workers, we have every right to rise up against oppression and tyranny in our workplace, as many of our comrades across Europe have done of late. They have won their fights, and we can win ours too!

'Mr Sopwith has resigned from the Loyal Miners' Association. He said he does not want to be affiliated with such a 'mobbish body' as ours. He is our Chief Agent, yet he has turned his back on us. What does that say about the man?

'But all is not lost. I have requested an interview with Mr Atkinson, who many of you will know. He worked with our former and beloved Chief Agent, Mr Crawhall, God rest his soul. And some of you may have met him in his other role - that of a magistrate!'

The miners laughed and called out names in jest, although few of them had been in enough trouble to warrant standing in front of the magistrate.

'Mr Atkinson has agreed to an interview,' continued Mr Heslop, 'and we'll speak next Friday. Please be assured that this matter will be dealt with in one way or another. By Christmas, I promise you, this disagreement will be resolved.'

The miners shouted words of encouragement and thanks. One of the miners, Tom Carr, took off his cap and shouted, 'We should have a collection for the men who lost their work and homes in our cause.' He walked amongst the crowd, and people eagerly donated what they could afford to the families who had been evicted on Mr Sopwith's orders.

Some men followed Mr Heslop into the pub, while others

## CHAPTER 8

stood outside chatting in groups. Bella heard Mrs Carr ask, 'How could he chuck them out without givin' them any notice? That's not right. Where will they go?' and the reply from Mrs Heslop, 'He doesn't care what happens to them or their bairns. The Lord will judge him for his actions when his time comes.'

Eventually, the crowd dispersed, and Bella walked back to Briar Place with Jack. The speech had unsettled her. Why had the miners started a dispute with Mr Sopwith? Or was it Mr Sopwith who had started it? She wasn't sure. It was difficult for her to believe that the amiable man she worked for at the Hall was the same man the miners' representative had portrayed as a tyrant and whom Mrs Heslop thought might go to Hell for his actions.

She realised that Jack had been right. Her loyalties were divided. She loved her job at Allenheads Hall and cared for the Sopwith family. They had been good to her. But her closest family and friends were miners, and she wanted nothing more than for them to be happy again.

As though reading her mind, Jack said, 'You never say a word against him.'

'Who?'

'Sopwith. You see him day in and day out. What's he like, really?'

When Bella didn't reply, Jack took her arm and stopped her, and she turned towards him.

'Come on, Jack. I've already said I can't talk about him. He's a good employer, though, and they're decent people.'

'S'pose you have to say that. He pays your wages.'

'He pays your wages an' all. Don't you get that? You rely on him for your job just as much as I do for mine.'

'Hmph. There are other mines,' said Jack, huffily, setting off again at a slower pace.

They walked the rest of the way in silence, and when they reached Briar Place, Jack stood in front of his house and turned to face Bella.

'We're not going to agree about him,' said Jack, 'so let's not talk about him anymore.'

'That's fine by me,' she said. 'Look, Jack, I don't want to leave things like this. Why don't you come over to ours later? We could play cards or something.'

'Aye, I'll pop round after I've had me tea.' Jack kissed her on the cheek before going inside.

As good as his word, Jack came round later that evening and played a few hands of whist with Bella and her mother, and Bella was relieved that he was back to his usual charming self. She hoped that their disagreement about Mr Sopwith had been forgotten.

On Friday morning, Bella arrived at the Hall early and was greeted by Mr Sopwith himself. 'Bella, there you are. Would you come with me today, please?'

'Where to, sir?

'There is to be a meeting at the mine office and I want to ensure that the - the guests are catered for.'

'Yes, sir. Of course. How many guests are you expecting?'

'Plan for ten. The meeting will start at nine o'clock sharp.' Mr Sopwith returned to his study.

Bella had never been asked to serve refreshments at the mine office before. She took what she thought she would need from the kitchen and walked down the drive to the office building, which stood beside the gates to the Hall.

She had the kettle boiling on the fire before anyone arrived

## CHAPTER 8

and set the tea to stew as soon as she heard voices in the meeting room. Mr Sopwith's voice rang out louder than the others as he greeted each guest amiably. She carried in the large teapot, filled ten cups with tea, and handed out the cups and saucers to the men.

She recognised the five men who had represented the miners and the two watcher men. The other well-dressed man, she presumed, must be Mr Atkinson, the justice of the peace.

After she had finished serving them, one cup of tea remained. Bella took it to the small room and sat in front of the fire to drink it herself. As she took a sip, Mr Sopwith popped his head around the door, and Bella almost spat out the tea in surprise.

'We'll take tea at eleven. Perhaps you could clear up in here and come back at ten thirty?'

'Yes, sir.'

Bella collected the empty cups and saucers and took them back to the Hall kitchen to wash and dry. After completing a few tasks, she returned at the allotted time, and as she approached the door, she heard the voices of the aggrieved miners complaining about their plight. The conversation appeared heated as Bella set the kettle over the fire, but they all chatted amicably during the break. While she cleared up afterwards, the talks resumed in a similar fashion to earlier in the debate. From the snippets of the meeting that she witnessed, she thought the miners put across a convincing argument.

Just minutes after one o'clock, Mr Sopwith, Mr Atkinson and the two watcher men returned to the Hall for lunch. Bella served them salmon sandwiches and sponge cake with Earl

Grey tea.

'We need to reach a resolution,' said Mr Atkinson. 'We've heard what they have to say. Clearly, they are disgruntled by the recent changes that have been imposed. We need to give them something to appease them.'

'I agree,' replied Mr Sopwith. 'But the eight hour day is not negotiable.'

'So, what is negotiable?'

Bella left the room and smiled. She was pleased that Mr Atkinson had listened to the miners and was treating their request seriously. She imagined the miners sitting in the village inn, eating meat pies and washing them down with a pint of ale, discussing the progress they'd made and their tactics for the afternoon talks, and she thought that the people up at the Hall weren't all that different from the miners in reality.

Later that afternoon, Bella heard Mr Sopwith return to the Hall. She glanced at the clock in the drawing-room and was surprised that the meeting had lasted a full eight hours. She passed his study on her way to the kitchen and heard him rehearsing a speech. She stopped outside the door for a minute and chided herself for eavesdropping, but she couldn't stop grinning at what she heard. She wished she could tell Jack and her father what he planned to say to them, but she couldn't. No doubt they would hear it for themselves soon enough.

The next day, as Bella returned home from work, she met her father, Frank, Johnny and Jack coming out of the mine yard, and they were all smiling.

'We've bloody done it!' said Bill, taking his daughter into his

## CHAPTER 8

arms and swinging her around. 'Sopwith said the spy system's gonna be stopped and the watcher men are goin' to be called off. Thank God for that!'

'And Mr Atkinson said he'll pass our case about the eight hour day on to Mr Rodham and Mr Nevin to consider,' said Johnny. 'They're not involved, so I reckon they should come to a fair decision.'

'He said our liberties and privileges won't be increased, Bella,' said Frank, 'but they won't be reduced either. That's good, isn't it? That means things will stay the same as they were before. That's what we wanted.'

'Aye, it is good news,' said Bella, grinning, pretending that she was hearing it for the first time. 'Hopefully, things will get back to normal now.'

'I'm sure they will,' said her father. 'But just in case, we're sending a man down to see Mr Beaumont who owns the mine. If Sopwith doesn't keep to his word this time, I'm sure Mr Beaumont will put him in his place!'

Jack took Bella's hand, and they dawdled behind the others on their way back to Briar Place.

'I'm pleased it's all over,' said Bella. 'It's lovely to see everyone smiling again.'

'Aye, it is. And I'm sorry I gave you such a hard time about workin' for Sopwith.'

'I told you he was a decent bloke, didn't I?'

'Yes, you did.' Jack leaned towards Bella and kissed her cheek. 'I should never have doubted you.'

# Chapter 9

**Allenheads, Northumberland
November 1848**

When Bella arrived at Allenheads Hall the following day, she felt an air of nervous anticipation as soon as she entered the house. Mrs Vickers was flustered, which was very unlike her.

'Are you alright?' Bella asked the cook.

'It's Mrs Sopwith. The baby's on its way.'

'Has the doctor been to see her?'

'He's up there now, and the midwife. They're both attending her. I'd better get them some breakfast. They've been up there since the early hours, so they're bound to be hungry.'

Mrs Vickers went into the pantry and brought out some eggs and bacon. 'I'll not make any for Mr Sopwith,' she said, as she placed some fat in a skillet and put it on the stove. 'He'll not want anything. He's all churned up.'

'What should I do?' asked Bella.

'The nursery will need to be prepared. Could you do that?'

'Shouldn't the nanny do that?'

'She's not here,' said Mrs Vickers, as she placed the bacon into the pan, and it began to sizzle. 'She's taken the bairns to Newcastle. They left in a hurry yesterday when Mrs Sopwith

## CHAPTER 9

thought she was startin'. She didn't want them in the house when the baby was born.'

'Alright, I'll get the nursery ready.'

Bella ran up the stairs and took the newly-laundered cot sheets and blankets from the linen press on the landing and carried them into the nursery, the room adjacent to Mrs Sopwith's bedroom. She wasn't familiar with the children's rooms because the nanny usually cleaned and tidied them. The fire had already been set in the grate. Bella lit a match and held the flame below the crumpled newspaper, which caught fire immediately, and soon, the sticks above it were alight. She used the fire tongs to place small pieces of coal on top of the sticks, and very quickly, she had a good fire burning.

She opened the sash window to let in some air and looked outside. It was a blustery day, and she could feel the fine raindrops on her face. She closed the window immediately. She thought a damp room would be worse for the baby than an unaired room. Through the thick stone walls, Bella could hear Mrs Sopwith in the next room and expected the baby would be born soon. After making up the crib, she returned downstairs.

As she passed his office, Mr Sopwith appeared to be engrossed in drawing a plan, but the tapping of his foot under the desk betrayed his anxiety.

In the kitchen, Mrs Vickers had finished cooking breakfast.

'I'll take the Doctor's plate into the dining room,' she said to Bella. 'You go and knock quietly on Mrs Sopwith's door and ask him to come down. The midwife can have hers after. One of them will have to stay with her.' Turning to the boiler, she said, 'And then I'd better get some water on to boil.'

Bella did as she had been asked. The doctor followed her

downstairs, and on their way to the dining room, he stopped to give Mr Sopwith an update on his wife's progress, and from what he said, Bella learned that her mistress's labour was going well.

When all was done that could be done to prepare for the imminent arrival, everyone in the house listened to the clocks ticking and the guttural sounds coming from the mistress's bedroom. By this time, Mr Sopwith was pacing up and down the hallway, muttering to himself, and Bella suspected that he was saying a prayer. She recalled the story Captain Wilson had told her about Mr Sopwith losing his first wife shortly after she had given birth, and she thought it was no wonder that he was so anxious while he waited for news.

Eventually, they heard the shrill cry of a baby.

Mrs Vickers was so relieved that she hugged Bella, and said, 'Thank the Lord!'

A few minutes later, the doctor came downstairs and said to Mr Sopwith, 'I'm delighted to say that your wife has a healthy daughter and that they are both very well.'

Mr Sopwith let out a large breath and then smiled broadly. He shook the doctor's hand firmly. 'Thank you! Thank you so much. Would you care to join me for a drink?'

The doctor nodded and followed Mr Sopwith into the drawing-room. Bella quickly prepared a tray with a decanter of scotch and a couple of crystal glasses and took it in for them.

'Congratulations, sir,' she said as she placed the tray on the side table.

'Thank you, Bella.'

Mr Sopwith poured the drinks and then proposed a toast to the new baby, and he and the doctor raised their glasses.

## CHAPTER 9

The doctor was a frequent visitor at the Hall that week. The baby was unsettled, and the whole household was tired of the constant noise. Bella had never known a newborn to cry so much. The piercing sound was impossible to ignore.

'What's the matter with her?' Bella asked Mrs Vickers one afternoon when the infant had cried non-stop for hours.

'I wish I knew so I could put a stop to it. I cannot concentrate with all this racket goin' on. I forgot to put the sultanas in the scones this morning. The master doesn't like them plain, without any fruit in them, so I've had to make another batch. He's vexed enough already.'

'Because of the bairn crying?'

'No, he's on the warpath about somethin' else this mornin'.'

'What's happened now?'

'Apparently, one of the miners went to visit Mr Beaumont down at Bretton Hall in Yorkshire. He's the father of the young Mr Beaumont who stayed here and he owns the mine. Anyway, I heard the fella didn't get the time of day down there, but all the same, the master got to hear about it and he's furious. I don't know this for sure, but I think he's been told to get the Allenheads' miners under control.'

Bella knew that her father had been involved in the plan to send Mr Shield to Bretton Hall to inform Mr Beaumont about what was happening at the mine, hoping that he would end Mr Sopwith's time-keeping arrangement and the proposed eight-hour day. It looked like the mission had failed. She couldn't understand why Mr Shield had been sent all that way after Mr Sopwith had removed the watcher men from the mine. That was what the miners had wanted and they'd achieved it already.

Bella couldn't tell Mrs Vickers that she knew anything

about the situation, so she feigned disinterest and changed the subject. 'About the scones,' she said, 'The children can have them when they get home.'

'Oh! I forgot to tell you. They're stayin' in Newcastle for a bit longer. Mr Sopwith doesn't want them comin' home until the baby's settled. The nanny couldn't teach them here with all this noise goin' on, could she?'

'That's true enough.'

'Take the scones home with you, hinny.' The cook put them in a tin. 'And I don't want any argument.'

'Thank you, Mrs Vickers. My lot won't mind that they're plain!' Bella laughed as she took the tin from the cook.

# Chapter 10

**Allenheads, Northumberland
November 1848**

Jack and his partners waded through a blanket of thick fog to the mine at Allenheads, and when they reached the yard, they peered through the low-lying cloud, unable to believe what they saw.

'Is that what I think it is?' asked Johnny.

'Aye, I reckon so,' replied Bill. 'The nerve of that bloody man.'

'Who?' asked Frank.

'Who do you think?' replied his father, pointing up the hill towards the Hall. 'Him up there. Sopwith!'

As they approached the mine shaft, they could see two men standing by the entrance. One of them was a large man, tall and broad, and he looked to be in his thirties. The other was a middle-aged man of average height and build. He held a notebook and pencil in his hands. 'Mornin' gents,' he called out, his pencil poised to write. 'Can I take your names?'

'I've worked in this mine for twenty-five years,' replied Bill. 'If you don't know who I am, that's your problem, not mine.'

He pushed past the time-keeper and entered the shaft.

'Hoy!' the older man shouted. 'Ower here, quick!'

The large man stood by the shaft, blocking it so that Bill's partners couldn't follow him underground.

Bill climbed back up and stood on the top rung of the ladder. 'Shift out of the way,' he shouted as he pushed the man hard on the back with both hands, forcing him to fall forward. Looking at the prone figure lying in the mud, Bill barked, 'You've no right to stop these men from doin' a day's work

Before he'd finished speaking, they heard the sound of footsteps running towards them, and three more men appeared from the mist and stood in a circle around them.

'What's this got to do with you lot?' asked Bill menacingly, stepping out of the shaft.

A parish constable stepped forward, bearing a truncheon in his hand, and he stood right in front of Bill, nose to nose, and they glared at each other.

'Is there a problem here, gents?' asked the constable. He looked from the watcher men to the miners and back to Bill.

The large man who had fallen stood up, his clothes covered in mud.

No matter how hard he tried, Frank could not smother his laughter. He turned away and creased up laughing.

'Settle yourself, Frank,' warned Jack.

Frank stood tall and turned to face the men, a smirk still showing on his lips.

The constable took his handcuffs out of his jacket pocket and looked slowly and deliberately at Frank. 'You would do well to listen to him,' he said, nodding towards Jack. 'Or else I'll have to find a way to wipe that smile off your face.'

Frank stood there, straight-faced, not sure what to say. With the silence making him uncomfortable, he said, 'I'm sorry,'

## CHAPTER 10

which earned him a disapproving look from his father.

The policeman ignored the apology and purposely moved his jacket to show them that he carried a pistol.

Jack didn't like the way things were going. The constable clearly wanted to make trouble. To defuse the situation, he said, 'We're the Dixon partnership. All four of us. Now, can we get on with our work?'

The older man scribbled something in a notebook, looked at his watch, and then nodded, permitting them to enter the mine. The other men moved to the side to let them pass. Jack went in last, keeping an eye on the constable who looked disappointed by their compliance.

When they reached the bottom of the shaft and could no longer be heard by anyone outside, Frank said, 'I thought I was goin' to get arrested for laughin'!' and his hearty laugh bellowed through the hollow tunnels.

Slapping him on the shoulder, Bill said, 'It's not a laughin' matter, son. The watcher men are back in force, and we've got the bloody constables to contend with now an' all. What's brought that on, eh?'

'I dunno,' replied Johnny, shrugging his shoulders. 'We haven't done anythin' wrong.'

Jack shook his head. 'Think about the timin', Bill. When did Mr Shield set off for Bretton Hall? And how long would it have taken for Mr Beaumont to send a letter to Sopwith to say he'd had a miner from Allenheads come to complain about him? I reckon Sopwith's had a tellin' off from his boss, and he blames it on us. I reckon it's retaliation for involvin' Mr Beaumont.'

'Jack, lad, I think you might be right,' said his father, with a proud smile.

'Did our Bella tell you that?' asked Frank, his eyes narrowed.

Everyone looked to Jack for an answer.

'No, she didn't. Bella never talks about what goes on up there.'

Bill didn't look convinced.

'What are we goin' to do about them blokes outside?' asked Johnny. 'We're not goin' to put up with them bein' here, are we?'

'No, we are not goin' to put up with them,' said Bill. 'Don't worry. I'll think of somethin'.'

Her father and Frank were home before Bella that evening, and they stopped talking as soon as she walked through the door.

'What's going on?' she asked.

'You mean you don't know?' asked her father sarcastically. 'Has nothing been said up there?'

'I've no idea what you're talkin' about.'

'The watcher men were back at the mine today, and not just the two of them. Oh, no! There were five of them.' Looking her in the eye, he shouted, 'Five! And a copper, an' all, showin' off his truncheon and his handcuffs and his pistol! That's intimidation, that is. And after Sopwith promised us. You cannot trust a word that bloody man says.'

'Bill!' said Martha. 'Calm down. There's no point gettin' upset about it.'

Bella watched her father's face turn even redder, and then he got to his feet.

'You don't understand. How could you?' said Bill, grabbing his cap. 'I'm goin' out.'

Frank followed his father and slammed the door shut behind

## CHAPTER 10

them.

'They're gettin' themselves all het up about it,' said Martha, sitting down on her chair and picking up her knitting. 'I'm sorry if they've upset you, you know, with you workin' up there.'

'I'm alright,' replied Bella. 'I'm getting used to it.'

'I don't like seein' them upset, and I don't like them havin' a go at you. It's not fair. You've got nothin' to do with it.' Martha's knitting needles began to click rapidly.

'Do you mind if I pop over to see Jack for a few minutes?'

'I'll be fine, love,' she smiled up at Bella. 'You go and see him.'

When Bella opened the Lowerys' door, Jack leapt up from his seat at the table and went outside, closing the door behind them so that they could talk without being overheard.

'It's good to see you,' Jack said, kissing Bella's cheek. He took her hand and led her around the side of the house, where he took her into his arms and kissed her.

'I'm glad you're in a better mood than me father was at tea time.'

'Everyone was upset after what happened this morning,' replied Jack, releasing her from his hold.

'But you're not angry like them,' she said. 'Why's that?'

'I'm seethin' inside, Bella. Don't get me started. It's just that I hardly see anythin' of you, and I don't want to spoil our time together by talkin' about work.'

'I know. I'm sorry.'

Jack put his arm around Bella's shoulders, kissed the top of her head and said, 'I wish it wasn't dark already. I would love to go for a walk with you up onto the fells or down by the river.'

'I wish we could,' she replied longingly. 'I don't like this time of year. It's dark when I walk to work, and it's dark when I come home. I can't wait for the Spring and longer days.'

'It'll be Christmas soon,' said Jack. 'That's somethin' to look forward to, and I love the New Year. The January pays should be good this year, an' all.' He smiled broadly.

Bella shivered with the cold, and Jack wrapped his strong arms around her and pulled her close. 'Do you want to come to Allendale with me? I'd love to see the New Year in with you.'

'Aye, that would be great.'

He kissed her again and said, 'I know I should tell you to go inside where it's warm, but I don't want to let you go.'

'Me too,' she said with a shiver.

'That's it! Go on. Home!' He pushed her gently towards the house.

'Goodnight, Jack.' She grinned cheekily at him.

'Goodnight, love.'

# Chapter 11

### Allenheads Hall, Northumberland
### December 1848

'Bella, there will be men arriving every quarter of the hour today, and for many days to come. When they arrive, please bring them directly to my study.'

'Yes, sir.'

They were interrupted by a knock at the door. Looking at his pocket watch, Mr Sopwith said, 'That will be the first. Very good. Right on time!' He went to his study to await the visitor's arrival.

Bella answered the door to Johnny Lowery, who quickly removed his cap and twisted it in his hands.

'I've never been to the big house afore, Bella, but the boss asked us to come.'

'Come in, Mr Lowery. Mr Sopwith's waiting for you in his study.'

His eyes wide, Johnny looked around the large entrance hall with its beautifully tiled floor, carpeted staircase, ornate lamps, oil paintings, and foreboding large oak doors. Bella stopped outside Mr Sopwith's office. Sensing his discomfort, she put her hand on Johnny's arm and smiled at him reassuringly before knocking at the door. When she heard Mr Sopwith say, 'Come in,' she opened the heavy door.

Johnny entered and sat in a chair at the centre of the oak-panelled room. As she closed the door, Bella heard her master say, 'Mr Lowery, thank you for coming here today. I hope you'll oblige me by helping with my enquiries.'

Johnny was the first visitor of many. Miner after miner came until the end of the day when Bella opened the door and saw Jack standing on the doorstep. He took off his hat and said, 'I've come to see Mr Sopwith.'

'Aye, you and all the rest. He must have talked to over twenty miners today.'

'The lads are sayin' it's like an inquisition in there.'

'He's just asking everybody a few questions. It's nothing to be worried about.'

In the hallway, Jack said, 'You'll be finishin' work soon. Can I walk you home after?'

'Aye, wait for me by the gate. You'd better come in, though. Mr Sopwith doesn't like to be kept waiting.'

Jack looked straight ahead as he walked to the study door, not appearing to be intimidated by the sheer scale of the building or the grandness of the decor as most of the miners had been. When the meeting finished, Bella showed him to the door and then rushed to the kitchen to collect her shawl. She ran down the drive and found Jack leaning nonchalantly against the gatepost. He offered her his arm, and they walked through the village together.

'What was the meeting like?' she asked.

'An inquisition, like they said. He wanted to know everythin' about everybody. Who did this, and who did that? And he wanted to know who the leaders of the conspiracy were.

## CHAPTER 11

That's what he called it - a conspiracy. We're not bein' unreasonable, Bella. All we want is what we always had. You'd think we'd asked him to double our pays the way he's goin' on. Do you know somethin'? That man's a bully.'

'You didn't tell him about me father being involved, did you?'

'Of course not. I didn't tell him anythin'. I wouldn't betray the lads.'

'Thank you,' she said, kissing Jack on the cheek.

'It's got to be awkward for you, though, workin' up there with him and livin' down here with us.'

'Aye, it is.'

'He's gone back on what he said, and not for the first time. He's proven he cannot be trusted. Seriously, Bella, have you thought about leavin' your job?'

'I can't, Jack. It's a good job and the pay's decent. Anyway, I'm sure all of this will blow over soon.'

'I hope you're right.'

When they were standing outside their houses, Bella said, 'Will you come over tonight after you've had your tea?'

'Aye, I'd like that. I'll see you later.'

With a quick kiss on the lips, they went into their houses.

While Bella and her family ate their evening meal, Bill said, 'Promises, promises. They mean nothin' to a man like that. Absolutely nothin'.'

'That's right!' said Frank. 'They don't.'

'I wish you could talk to him, Bella,' said her father. 'He'd listen to you.'

'I'm just a housemaid up there, Father. A man like Mr Sopwith isn't going to listen to a maid. I'd lose me job just for the cheek of bringing it up.'

'Well, if he's that unreasonable, why are you still workin' for him?'

'The same reason you do - for money.'

'Hmph! You won't say a word to Sopwith to help out your family, but you've got the cheek to speak to me like that.'

'I'm sorry, Father. It's just that Jack had a go at me earlier about working up there an' all. I like me job. And as I said to him, this will soon be over and done with.'

'I wouldn't be so sure, lass. We've not had that independent inquiry that he promised us. And now he's embarrassin' us all, questioning us like school bairns, wantin' us to inform on our fellow men. I know he thinks he's got the upper hand here, but he's not finished with us yet. Not by any means.'

The look of determination on her father's face concerned Bella greatly; if anybody was as stubborn as her father, it was Mr Sopwith.

The following evening, Jack sat in the village inn with his friend Robbie Dodd. As they supped their beers, they listened to the miners at the bar discussing the recent events and voicing their grievances. It was clear to Jack that they were all disgruntled that the time-watchers had returned in force and that Sopwith had not kept his promise to hold an independent inquiry, and it occurred to him that after two whole months, the miners were right back to where they'd started. Their efforts to get rid of the watcher men had been in vain.

Bill Dixon rose to his feet and rang the bell on the bar to get everyone's attention.

'Is it last orders already?' shouted Nelson Kidd. 'I've only just got here.' His outburst set off a peal of laughter.

Bill waited for the noise to subside and he stood before the men to propose his idea. After he'd finished speaking, Jack watched the miners' reactions. He saw expressions of surprise, anger, shock, and ultimately agreement on their faces.

'No!' said Robbie. 'It'll never come to that, will it?'

'I hope not, but time will tell,' said Jack.

'Aye, I suppose it will.' Holding up his tankard, Robbie asked, 'Do you want another one?'

Jack nodded, and Robbie went to the bar.

Jack felt numb. He hoped that the dispute wouldn't go that far and that the situation could be resolved without the need for Bill's plan. For if it went ahead, it would affect his future plans; his and Bella's future plans to more be precise. Leaning back in his chair and thinking things through, he decided that Bill's suggestion would be the most likely outcome of the current situation. Sopwith was a stubborn man. He wanted to change and improve the industry just as much as the miners disliked change and would resist it. If neither side backed down soon, the men would have no option but to go along with Bill's plan.

Robbie returned with more ale, and the discussions continued. The more moderate men amongst the miners suggested that they ask Mr Sopwith to arrange a meeting with Mr Nevin and Mr Rodham to resolve the situation in a friendly manner. They agreed that the meeting should take place on the sixteenth of December. That was to be their plan of action - for now, at least.

Jack chatted with Robbie as he drank his pint, and when they were ready to leave, Jack said farewell to his father and friends. That evening, he walked home slowly, his eyes on the glistening road, deep in his thoughts.

# Chapter 12

### Allenheads Hall, Northumberland
### December 1848

When Bella entered the drawing-room to put more coal on the fire, Mrs Sopwith was seated on the sofa. Bella was pleased to see that her mistress was up and about again after her confinement and thought she looked well.

'Morning, ma'am.'

'Good morning, Bella. It looks cold out today.'

'It is. There was a hard frost last night.'

'I hope it warms up before this afternoon. The baby is to be baptised today.'

'You'll need a thick woollen shawl and plenty of blankets. That open carriage you've got won't keep you very warm.'

'Bless you, Bella.'

Mrs Sopwith stood up and walked to the window. Looking out onto the high fells in the distance, she said, 'But really, I don't know what my husband was thinking buying an open-topped phaeton when we live in these hills, where we suffer from the most inclement weather.' Turning back to Bella, she asked. 'Would you come with me this afternoon? In case I'm in need of assistance.'

## CHAPTER 12

'Yes, of course. I'd be glad to.'

When they were ready to leave, Bella helped Mrs Sopwith to the phaeton, which was drawn by two bay horses and driven by Mr Sopwith. Bella fussed around her mistress, ensuring that both she and her baby were warm enough for the short journey to the church. She turned to go back to the house to grab her outdoor clothes, but Mr Sopwith's stern tone halted her, 'Hurry, please. We don't want to keep the vicar waiting. We're already behind schedule.'

Bella climbed into the carriage and sat on the padded leather seat beside Mrs Sopwith, and as they left the yard, she saw the full form of Mrs Vickers chasing after them, waving Bella's thick woollen shawl in the air. She didn't dare ask Mr Sopwith to stop after he had already expressed his concern about arriving at the church on time.

Bella had never been in a carriage before and was surprised by how much smoother and faster it travelled than a cart, but it wasn't long before the icy wind began to rip through her clothes. She longed to ask if she could share the blanket that covered Mrs Sopwith's knees, but it would have been highly improper to do so. By the time they arrived at the church, Bella's hands and feet were numb, and she struggled to stop her teeth from chattering. She climbed down from the carriage. Mrs Sopwith passed her the baby to hold while Mr Sopwith helped his wife down.

Carrying the infant, Bella followed the couple into the church. It was not much warmer inside than outside, but at least she was sheltered from the piercing wind. Bella and Mr Sopwith took a seat on the front pew, and Mrs Sopwith continued to the front of the church, where she knelt before the vicar.

When the vicar began to speak, he addressed Mrs Sopwith, 'For as much as it hath pleased Almighty God of his goodness to give you safe deliverance, and hath preserved you in the great danger of child-birth: You shall therefore give hearty thanks unto God.' Then he finished with, 'O Almighty God, we give thee humble thanks for that thou hast vouchsafed to deliver this woman thy servant from the great pain and peril of childbirth: Grant, we beseech thee, most merciful Father, that she through thy help may both faithfully live and walk according to thy will, in this life present; and also may be partaker of everlasting glory in the life to come; through Jesus Christ our Lord. Amen.'

Psalms and prayers followed his words.

After the vicar had finished the churching ceremony, Mrs Sopwith stood up. Her husband moved swiftly to her side and took her arm to support her. Bella handed the infant to its mother and returned to her seat, from where she watched the parents and godparents move to the font for the baptism of Alice Mary Sopwith. Mr Sopwith looked on proudly as his daughter was named, and Bella had another glimpse of her employer as a family man. It was evident to her how much his wife and children meant to him.

At the end of the service, Mr Sopwith chatted with the godparents. The vicar passed the baby back to her mother, commenting that it was unusual for a child to sleep all the way through the baptism ceremony. Mrs Sopwith appeared preoccupied for a moment before she said urgently, 'Tommy, we need to see the doctor.'

Mr Sopwith looked at his wife and then at the infant, which lay limply in her arms, and announced to the small gathering, 'We need to leave immediately!'

## CHAPTER 12

He ushered his wife out of the church and into the carriage, and Bella ran along behind them. He drove as quickly as he dared to the doctor's house, and then jumped down and banged at the door. The doctor's wife opened the door and listened to what Mr Sopwith had to say, and then pointed down the road, indicating her husband's whereabouts.

Mr Sopwith returned to the carriage, whispered reassurances to his wife, and set off at a canter and within minutes they were leaving the village. Bella sat with Mrs Sopwith and the baby as the carriage tore down the road, and she wondered how far they were going. Eventually, they stopped outside a house in Sparty Lea and Mr Sopwith rushed his wife and child inside.

The wind picked up as Bella waited and she drew the discarded woollen blanket around her shoulders to shield herself from the bitter blast. When the door opened, she was relieved to see the Sopwiths smiling. They thanked the doctor profusely and climbed into the carriage.

'Is she well?' asked Bella.

'She has a slight fever that made her sleepy, but the doctor has assured us that there is nothing to be concerned about and that she will be well again soon.'

'That's great news. I'm so glad,' said Bella, as she wrapped the blanket snuggly around mother and baby.

When they left Sparty Lea, sleet was coming down thick and fast. Large icy water droplets soon drenched Bella's thin bonnet and ran down her neck and inside her clothes. Mr Sopwith drove more slowly on the way back because the road was slippery and the visibility poor. By the time they returned to Allenheads, it was dark, and Bella was chilled to the bone. Mr Sopwith kindly stopped the carriage outside Bella's house and she was grateful for his thoughtfulness. It occurred to her that if he had taken her back to the Hall, she wasn't sure that she would have made it home the way she felt. With a smile to Mrs Sopwith, Bella climbed down and waited until they were out of sight before hobbling to the front door.

Bella lifted the latch, pushed open the door, and almost fell across the threshold. As she dragged herself in, the heat inside the cottage hit her. Her body felt so heavy. She stumbled to the nearest chair and collapsed onto it.

'Are you alright, Bella?' asked Frank. When his sister didn't respond, he shouted, 'Mother! There's somethin' wrong with our Bella.'

Bill got out of his chair and gawped helplessly at his daughter's sodden clothes and colourless face. 'Martha!' he shouted. 'Come, quick!'

Martha ran in from the kitchen, looked at her daughter, and said, 'Frank, get the kettle on and make some tea.'

'How do I...?'

'Just do it!'

Martha sat Bella forward and removed her wet clothes - her dress and petticoats, boots and stockings - until all she had on was her chemise and bloomers. Her parents helped her across the room to the armchair by the fire where her father had been sitting.

Bella slumped into the soft, comfortable chair, and she felt so sleepy that she struggled to keep her eyes open. Her parent's voices sounded like they were coming from a long way away, yet they were standing over her. How could that be?

'Bill, have you got any drink? Whisky or brandy?' asked Martha.

'No. Johnny might have some. I'll pop next door.'

## CHAPTER 12

While her father was out, her mother wrapped a woollen blanket around Bella's shoulders and another around her knees.

Frank brought her a cup of weak tea with lots of sugar in it, and it went through Bella's mind that this was probably the first cup of tea that her brother had made in his sixteen years of life. The thought made her want to laugh aloud, a proper belly laugh like when she'd been a child.

He handed the cup to Bella, but her hands shook too much, and the hot liquid splashed the blankets. Her mother prised the cup from Bella's hands and held it to her lips.

'Frank,' said Martha. 'Don't just stand there. Bring some more peat in, and a few logs, and get this fire built up.'

Suddenly, the room seemed crowded and noisy. Bella was aware that more people were buzzing around her and that Jack was kneeling at her side, holding her hand. She heard him say, 'My God! She's frozen. What happened to her?'

'Get some of this down her,' said Eliza, handing Martha a glass of brandy. 'It'll warm her from the inside out.'

As Martha gently poured the strong liquor into her mouth, Bella coughed and then lay back in the chair, comforted by the warmth in her stomach, the heat from Jack's hand, and the murmuring voices of the people she loved.

After a long while, she was aware of pins and needles stabbing viciously at her hands and feet, and she wanted to cry out from the pain, but she just sat there in silence, trying to understand what everyone was saying in the background. Gradually, the feeling returned to her hands, and she squeezed Jack's hand.

'Bella, are you feelin' better?' he asked, and within an instant, half a dozen faces were looking down on her.

'Aye,' she croaked.

'Leave her be. It'll take time for her to come round,' said Eliza. 'Have you any idea what happened?'

'None,' said Martha. 'She came through the door like that, and she hasn't said a word 'til now. She didn't have her shawl or her hat. Just what she wears indoors up there.'

'Maybe you should go to the big house and find out what happened to her,' suggested Johnny. 'Her stuff must be up there. Why on earth would she have left the Hall without them?'

Everyone had a theory. Bella listened to their concoctions and wanted to protest, but the most she could do was shake her head. As her senses returned, Bella realised that she should have made Mr Sopwith wait for another minute or two while she returned to the kitchen for her shawl. What harm would it have done? As ill as she felt, though, her thoughts were with Mrs Sopwith and her baby, and she hoped that they hadn't suffered from the journey.

Her mother brought another cup of tea, which Eliza laced with brandy. After Bella had finished it, she could finally explain to them what had happened that day, and emotions were running high when she finished her story. Her mother was relieved that Bella was improving after her horrendous ordeal. Her father and brother were angry with Mr Sopwith for putting her life in danger and threatened him with violence. Johnny and Eliza were shocked that she had gone out in that weather without her shawl and that the Sopwiths had allowed it. They wished her a speedy recovery before they left, and as Eliza went out of the door, Bella heard her say to Johnny, 'After a chill like that, she's not in the clear yet.'

## CHAPTER 12

That night, Jack was reluctant to leave Bella. They sat by the fire together, holding hands, staring into the orange glow of the burning peat. Outwardly, Jack remained calm for Bella's sake, but inside, he was livid with Sopwith for allowing Bella to get into such a state. She'd been out with him and his family. Surely he must have noticed that she wasn't dressed well enough for that kind of outing, not in this weather. Bella had been so cold when he'd arrived that he thought she might die, and the thought of losing her tore at his heart. He loved her, and he couldn't bear the thought of losing her, ever. He placed his arm around her shoulders and kissed her tenderly on her brow, and his heart melted when she smiled up at him and leaned into him for comfort.

Early the following day, Jack went to Allenheads Hall and knocked at the kitchen door. It was opened by Mrs Vickers, who had a smudge of flour on her cheek.

'I've come to tell you that Bella won't be coming into work today. She's not well.'

'Oh! She's never had a day off sick before. What's the matter with her?'

'She got chilled to the bone yesterday going to the church with them,' he said, emphasising the last word to show his disdain. 'She'll be lucky if she doesn't come down with the flu or pneumonia.'

'Oh dear! I'm sorry to hear that, but I cannot say I'm surprised. When they left, I went out with her shawl, but they'd already set off. They mustn't have heard me shoutin' because they didn't stop.' Mrs Vickers shook her head. 'Just wait here a minute,' she said as she disappeared inside. Less than a minute later, she returned with a bowl covered with a tea towel. 'Give her this. A bit of beef broth. It'll help her to get her strength back.'

'Thank you,' he said with a smile. 'I can see why Bella talks so highly of you.'

Mrs Vickers' floury cheeks flushed at the compliment, and she said, 'Get away with you,' flapping her hands at him, shooing him away from the door.

Jack laughed, his mood lightened by his encounter with Mrs Vickers and by her generosity. He understood why Bella would enjoy working with such a kind-hearted woman. As he walked home, he whistled to himself.

When he returned to Briar Place, he went straight to the Dixons' house and handed the bowl to Martha.

'What's this?'

'Mrs Vickers sent some beef broth down for Bella. How is she this mornin'?'

'She's still in bed. I didn't see any point in gettin' her up when she's not fit enough to go to work. She might as well get some rest.'

'Is she warm enough up there?'

'Aye, I lit the fire in her room. Do you want to go up and see her?'

'If you don't mind?'

Jack didn't wait for an answer. He quickly climbed the stairs. As a child, he'd played in Bella's room, so he knew that hers was the one at the back of the house. Knocking gently, he asked, 'Bella, can I come in?'

'Jack?'

'Aye, it's me.'

'Where's me mother? Does she know you're up here?'

'Aye, she said I could come up and see you.'

## CHAPTER 12

'You'd better come in then.'

Jack opened the door and went into her bedroom. The curtains were drawn, and the only light was from the glow of the fire in the tiny grate. It gave off just enough heat to warm the air.

'How are you feelin'?' he asked as he moved a chair to her bedside and sat down. He held her hand, noticing that it felt cold in his.

'Much better than last night.' Looking down at their hands, she said, 'I'm sorry I put you all to so much trouble.'

'Bella, it wasn't your fault, and it wasn't any trouble. We just want you to get better. Have you thought about gettin' up and sittin' downstairs? It's much warmer down there.'

'I don't know, Jack. I slept all night, but I still feel tired.'

Jack went to the window and pulled open the curtains; light poured into the room, making Bella squint as she watched Jack move back to her bedside. 'I don't think you've warmed up properly yet. Please, get dressed and come downstairs. I'll be waitin' for you.'

He bent down, stroked her hair, and kissed the corner of her mouth. He left the room and went downstairs, where he chatted to Martha, who was still shaken after her daughter's ordeal, and he was delighted when Bella came downstairs soon afterwards and sat in the chair beside the fireplace. He stoked the fire and then sat on the chair arm. Immediately, Bella wrapped her arms around his waist and rested her head against his side, absorbing the warmth of his body. Within minutes, her breathing slowed, and Jack knew that she had fallen asleep in his arms.

# Chapter 13

**Allenheads, Northumberland
December 1848**

A few days later, Jack and the other miners met outside the mine office. They had been astonished when Mr Sopwith agreed to the meeting that they'd requested with Mr Nevin and Mr Rodham and were excited that an impartial audience would hear their complaint at last. They filed into the meeting room at the arranged time and were shocked to see that only Mr Sopwith was present, seated at a table at the front of the room. There was no sign whatsoever of Mr Nevin or Mr Rodham.

The men grumbled amongst themselves until Mr Sopwith shouted, 'Right! Let's make a start, shall we?' and the room fell silent.

'You called for a meeting, and a meeting you shall have. I will listen to your concerns on one condition, and that is that old charges that have been heard already will not be brought up again. Do you understand?' Without waiting for a response, he asked, 'Are there any new issues you wish to tell me about?'

The men looked from one to another in disbelief. Mr Heslop spoke for them all when he said, 'You agreed for us to meet

## CHAPTER 13

with Mr Nevin and Mr Rodham today. You agreed to an independent hearin'. What's the meanin' of this?'

'It is the meeting that you called for. I am here to listen to any new problems or grievances that the miners at Allenheads may have.'

'What! You mean like you not keeping your promises?' shouted Bill, who turned abruptly and walked out, followed by several more grumbling men.

Mr Sopwith sat quietly with his arms folded across his chest and a smug look on his face.

Jack turned to his father and said, 'Come on, let's go. We're wasting our time here,' and they too left the meeting.

'Nothing's going to come of talks,' said Johnny. 'I hate to say it, but I think Bill has the answer. That's the only thing that goin' to work now.'

Jack had been thinking about Bill's suggestion ever since he'd brought it up that night in the pub, and he still wasn't keen on the idea. A strike was always the last resort, and its success relied on both parties being willing to negotiate and compromise. Sopwith didn't look like he would back down, regardless of their actions. He'd already dismissed five of them and put them out of their homes. If the miners crossed him, what would he be capable of? That question made Jack feel uneasy.

'Are you comin' with us for a pint?' asked his father.

'No, I'm goin' to check on Bella. I want to see how she's gettin' on.'

'Give her our best.'

'Will do. See you later.'

When he arrived at her house, Jack was glad to see that Bella looked brighter. She stood up to greet him, and then they sat together by the fire in the Dixons' front room.

'While you're here to keep an eye on her,' said Martha. 'I'm goin' to the village to pick up a few bits and pieces from the shop.' She wrapped herself in a shawl and braved the cold air outside.

'I think that's an excuse to let us have a bit of time on our own,' said Bella when the door closed. 'There can't be much that she needs.'

'Well, if that's the case, it's very considerate of her.'

'How did the meeting go today?' asked Bella. 'What did Mr Sopwith say?'

'I've got you all to myself for what? Half an hour? You're mad if you think I'm goin' to waste it talkin' about Sopwith.'

He bent down, kissed her lips and then asked, 'How are you feelin'?'

'Much better, thanks.'

'Really? You've got more colour than you had yesterday and you feel like you've warmed up again, thank God.'

'I'm fine, Jack, really.'

'Are you strong enough to get to your feet?' he asked, raising a dark eyebrow. He held out his hand to help Bella up and then enfolded her in his arms.

She held on to him tightly, comforted by the warmth and love she felt in his embrace.

'I'm so pleased you're gettin' better, Bella. I was scared that you might get the flu or somethin'.' Leaving that thought hanging in the air, he whispered, 'If anythin' was to happen to you, I don't know what I'd do.'

A few days later, Bella was well enough to return to work at Allenheads Hall, and she was greeted warmly by Mrs Vickers,

## CHAPTER 13

who seemed to think that she was somehow responsible for what had happened because she had failed to stop the carriage and give Bella her shawl.

After Bella reassured the cook that she was completely well and did not hold her responsible for what had happened, she began her day's work by cleaning and polishing the furniture in the drawing-room. She had only been in the room for a few minutes when she heard a commotion at the front door and the sound of children laughing and squealing. She went into the hallway to see what was causing the fuss and grinned when she saw Mr Sopwith and another man dragging a giant fir tree through the front door.

'Papa! Papa!' shouted Ursula. 'Where will you put it?'

He turned to his daughter and said, 'I think it would look wonderful in the drawing-room, don't you?'

'Yes!' came the reply. 'Can we decorate it?'

'Your mother likes to dress the tree, but I'm sure she'd appreciate your help.'

Bella returned to the drawing-room to clear a space for the Christmas tree, moving the small sofa from the corner so that there was room for the tree between the fireplace and window. The men lifted the tree into a bucket, and they chocked it with logs and sticks to hold it upright. The top of the tree almost touched the ceiling.

'Mrs Sopwith will need the step-ladders to decorate it,' said Bella. 'I'll go and fetch them.'

She remembered that Mrs Sopwith had been weak when she'd helped her at the church and wondered if it was safe for her to be climbing ladders so soon after giving birth.

'Thank you, Bella,' replied Mr Sopwith. 'Perhaps, you could help her place the higher items on the tree.'

'Yes, sir.' Bella was glad that her master was considerate of his wife's delicate condition and she was delighted that she would be helping to decorate the tree. She would never admit it to the Sopwiths, but she has only ever seen pictures of Christmas trees in books. Seeing the awe on the children's faces, she knew exactly how they felt because she felt the same way.

For the next couple of hours, she helped Mrs Sopwith and the children dress the tree with ribbons, pine cones, sweets, glass baubles, and gifts. Bella thoroughly enjoyed the morning and felt like one of the family, working with Mrs Sopwith and her children to complete the task. When they finished, they all stood back to admire their handiwork, and she had to admit that they had done a fantastic job. It looked wonderful.

Bella felt a small hand slipping into hers and looked down to see Arthur standing next to her. 'Thank you,' he said. 'You've made it very pretty.'

'You're welcome,' Bella replied sincerely, smiling down at the boy.

Before Christmas, Mr Sopwith called the miners together in the mine yard. There had been a lot of speculation amongst the men about what he would say, but they held little hope of a resolution. They were sceptical because they had heard his promises before and knew that they were meaningless. But still, Jack went along to listen to what the man had to say.

Thomas Sopwith stood before his workforce and said, 'Gentlemen, I have listened to your grievances, and I have investigated the charges thoroughly. I have heard from each and every one of you who came to see me and, as a result of this comprehensive investigation, I can assure you that the

## CHAPTER 13

charges against my under-agents are unfounded and totally without merit. So let that be the end of it. I want to hear no more. I expect you to work five days a week and eight hours a day as you agreed when you took your bargains. That's forty hours a week. That's all I ask. Forty hours a week from you. Now, this is the end of the matter, and I will hear and say no more about it.

'However, on another matter entirely, I'm afraid I must be the bearer of bad news. Mr Beaumont, the owner of WB Lead and the Allenheads mine, has sadly passed away. His son will take over the ownership of the company when he comes of age, but until then, I expect it will be managed by his guardians. That is all I can tell you for now. I bid you good-day, gentlemen, and a very happy Christmas.'

Mr Sopwith turned away and walked out of the yard, leaving the miners in a state of shock. Jack could not believe what he'd just heard. Not the bit about Mr Beaumont. Yes, it was sad that he'd died and he was sorry for the family's loss, but it was the first announcement that had made his blood boil. Sopwith had dismissed their demands entirely without there being an impartial inquiry. The angry voices of the miners followed the Chief Agent back to the Hall. So, that was that, after all this time.

'How dare he?' Johnny said, turning to Jack. 'He calls that an investigation. Hmph! Of course, people's gonna tell him what he wants to hear. He pays their bloody wages! What choice has a man got? He'd put them out on the street if they told him how it really is. '

'Come on, let's go home,' said Jack. 'There's nothin' we can do here.'

Jack was concerned about his father. He missed the calm,

fun-loving man that he used to be. He seemed to get himself worked up about everything these days. Jack wished that everything could go back to how it had been before the watcher men had turned up at the mine. They had all been content with their lives then.

'You go, Jack,' replied Johnny, patting his shoulder. 'Bill's ower yonder. I think we'll go for a quick one before we follow you down the road.'

# Chapter 14

**Allenheads, Northumberland
Christmas Day 1848**

Outside, the skies were dull and grey, threatening rain, but the atmosphere inside the Dixons' house was joyful and contented. The family sat around the table to eat their Christmas dinner, roast chicken, roast potatoes and vegetables. A good fire burned in the grate.

'You'll have to thank Johnny for that chicken,' Martha said to her husband when she put down her cutlery at the end of the meal.

'Aye, I will,' replied Bill, who had already emptied his plate and was soaking up the leftover gravy with a piece of bread. 'He was grateful for the vegetables I gave him. It's good that we can help each other out. Me with me veg and him with his hens.'

'What did you give him?' asked Martha.

'A sack of taties, half a dozen turnips and a bucket of sprouts.'

Martha raised her eyebrows.

'I know it's a lot at this time of year,' said Bill, 'but it won't go far in their house, will it? Not with nine mouths to feed. And it's Christmas. Anyway, Johnny keeps us in eggs for most of the year. I'd say it's a fair trade.'

'You're right, Bill. They're good neighbours.'

'Aye, they are. We were lucky the day they moved in next door. Can you imagine what it would have been like if the Carrs or the Heslops had got that house?'

Martha laughed out loud. 'We'd have had to mind ourselves with them chapel lot watchin' over us.'

'They're not that bad,' said Bella, getting up to clear the table.

'They're stuck up snobs,' said her father. 'They think they're better than the rest of us just because they don't drink. They don't know how to enjoy themselves. None of them. What they need to do is let their hair down and have a good knees-up!'

Frank chuckled. 'Can you imagine Mrs Carr gettin' drunk and havin' a dance? I don't think I've ever seen her smile. I reckon it would crack her face if she did.'

Bill sat back in his chair and roared with laughter. When he recovered from his outburst, he wiped the tears from his eyes.

Struggling to keep her face straight, Martha said, 'Give over, you two.' She got up and went into the kitchen, taking a pile of dirty dishes with her.

'But seriously,' said Frank, as though he'd given the matter a great deal of thought, 'we couldn't have anyone better than the Lowerys for our neighbours. They'd do anything for us. Like the time I skinned me knee and Mrs Lowery cleaned it up and bandaged it because all of you had gone to Allendale and left me here on me own.'

'And likewise,' shouted Martha, as she served the Christmas pudding. 'We'd do anything for them an' all, wouldn't we?'

As she carried the bowls to the table, everybody nodded in

## CHAPTER 14

agreement.

Bella smiled to herself. She was pleased that her family got on so well with Jack's family and wondered if perhaps one day the two families would be joined by marriage; she secretly hoped that they would be. When Bella first started walking out with Jack, she remembered that her mother had said it would make them all happy if she and Jack got together. Had their parents discussed the possibility of a marriage between her and Jack? It wouldn't have surprised her if they had.

As they ate the rich fruit pudding with white sauce, laced with a bit of brandy, they could hear the sound of laughter coming from next door.

'Sounds like the party's over that way!' said Bill, pointing at the adjoining wall.

The front door opened a few minutes later, and Jack came in.

'Merry Christmas!'

'Merry Christmas, Jack!' The Dixons replied in unison and laughed.

'Do you want to come over to ours?' Jack asked, gesturing to his house. 'We're playing *Throwing the Smile,* and the girls are loving it. It's hilarious!'

Bella saw her family looking at one another, and she decided for them, 'We'd love to, Jack.' It wasn't as if they had any plans for the afternoon.

'You lot go now,' said Martha. 'I'll come over as soon as I've got cleared up in here.'

Bella felt guilty for leaving her mother to wash the large pile of dishes by herself, but she longed to spend time with Jack on Christmas Day. She went next door with her father and Frank and they found the Lowerys sitting around a large table. Johnny had a silly grin on his face and the others were all straight-faced. Seeing his friend looking so daft, Bill chuckled, which set off the girls, and soon everyone was howling with laughter.

'You're all out,' said Johnny gleefully. 'I win!'

'Let's play again,' the girls pleaded. The newcomers joined the group and played frivolous parlour games with the Lowery family, and it wasn't long before Martha joined them too.

Jack whispered to Bella, 'Do you fancy a bit of fresh air?'

'Is that what they call it now?' said Johnny, nudging Bill with his elbow and making the young couple blush furiously.

'Come on,' said Jack.

He took Bella's hand and almost dragged her out of the house. It was raining outside. Bella opened the door of her house intending to get her shawl but quickly realised that there was nobody at home.

'Why don't we go inside?' she asked.

'Good idea,' said Jack. 'Much better than gettin' wet out here.' He followed her into the empty house and closed the door behind them. He turned Bella so that her back was against the door, and he looked hungrily into her eyes before lowering his lips to hers and kissing her gently, teasing her. Soon, his kisses became more insistent and passionate, and his hands moved over her waist to her hips and then to her buttocks, pulling her towards him.

Feeling his body against hers lit a spark in Bella, and she kissed him back eagerly. She was lost in Jack's arms and she had no idea how much time had passed before he stepped back and sighed deeply. Taking her hands in his, he looked earnestly into her eyes, and he said, 'Oh, Bella. I love you so much.'

## CHAPTER 14

She looked up at him adoringly and said, 'I love you, Jack.'

They kissed again with renewed fervour, and when they stopped, Jack said, 'I want to do that every day for the rest of my life,' and then, his voice low, he whispered into her ear, 'and more.'

Bella felt her cheeks flush at his meaning, but she couldn't deny wanting the same. There was nothing more she wanted than to have Jack as her husband and to share his bed. Her voice barely a whisper, she said, 'Me too.'

'Bella, there's somethin' I want to ask you?'

'What is it?'

Jack got down on one knee and looked up to see Bella's eyes widen in surprise.

He cleared his throat and asked, 'Would you – would you marry me?'

Bella hesitated only momentarily before replying. 'Yes, Jack Lowery. I'll marry you!'

He jumped to his feet, picked her up and almost threw her into the air. Then he held her tightly against his body and whispered in her ear, 'Thank you, Bella. You've made me the happiest man alive.'

Stepping back, he picked her up, and they both laughed as he swung her around and around in his arms.

When they finally came to a standstill, Bella said, 'I think I've always loved you, Jack Lowery, and I promise you that I always will, no matter what.'

Grabbing her hand, he said, 'Come on! Let's go. I want to tell everyone!'

'Don't take Christmas away from the bairns. It's their day. Our news can wait until after the holiday. Let it be our secret, just for a couple of days.'

'If you're sure that's what you want? I want to shout it from the rooftops!'

She nodded and said, 'Aye, I'm sure you would an' all.'

Grinning, he shook his head. 'I can't believe it, Bella. We're goin' to be married.'

'I know, it's wonderful, isn't it?' She stepped into his arms again, and after a long, lingering kiss, they went next door to rejoin their families.

On their return, Lizzie took the younger girls upstairs to bed. Eliza went into the kitchen and brought out a bottle of sherry and a plate of sausage rolls while Johnny found a deck of cards. The two families played cards and drank together well into the early hours.

The morning after Boxing Day, the Dixons were sitting at the table eating breakfast when Jack came to their door. He knocked before coming in, which is not something he usually did, and he stood in the doorway, his eyes on Bella.

Bella returned his smile and shyly said, 'Morning, Jack.'

'What's this?' asked Bill, looking back and forth between them. 'Is everythin' alright?'

'Aye, never better,' said Jack. 'I just wanted to tell you that me and Bella are goin' to get married.'

Bill's spoon stopped halfway to his mouth, and the porridge slid off it, back into the bowl, landing with a splash. For a split second, his eyes widened, and then he grinned. Standing up, he went to Jack and slapped him on the back. 'Good on you, lad. Welcome to the family!'

Looking at Bella, he said, 'So, when's the weddin' goin' to be?'

'We haven't talked about that yet. Soon though.'

## CHAPTER 14

Furrowing his eyebrows, Bill shocked them all when he asked, 'There's no hurry, is there? I hope it's not that kind of a wedding. I don't have a shotgun, but I've got one hell of a fist.' He held up his large fist and pointed it at Jack.

Not sure if her husband was joking or not, Martha stepped in and asked, 'How dare you suggest such a thing? Our Bella's a good lass.'

Bill looked sternly at Jack, waiting for confirmation, and Jack replied calmly, 'We're marryin' because we want to, Bill, not because we have to. I've never touched her, and I won't until the day that we're wed.'

'In that case, we'll have to have a celebration,' said Bill, smiling broadly. 'Tell your folks to come round here on Saturday night, an' ask your father to bring his fiddle. We'll have a proper knees-up. You'll do some food, won't you, Martha?'

'Aye, I'll put on a good spread for them.' She smiled at the young couple.

'That's settled then,' said Bill. 'Come on, Jack, Frank, we'd better be off. Them watcher men will have our names on their list if we're late for work, weddin' or no weddin'.'

The men left, and Martha took her daughter's hand and squeezed it gently. 'Congratulations, love. Jack's one of the best. I'm sure you'll be very happy together.'

'Thanks, Mother,' replied Bella. 'I know we will.'

# Chapter 15

**Allenheads, Northumberland**
**New Year's Eve 1848**

When Bella went downstairs, her mother was sitting by the fire, her knitting needles clicking rhythmically, not missing a beat as she looked up to see what her daughter was wearing to go out.

'Did you put some extra layers on?' she asked.

'Aye, I did. I'm not daft.'

'It's just that I don't want you to freeze again, love.'

'I'll be fine, Mother. You needn't worry. Jack's going to be with me.'

As Bella said his name, Jack opened the door and came into the house.

'Are you ready?'

'Aye,' she replied, grinning. 'And I can't wait. I've never been to Allendale for the New Year's celebrations before, but I've heard so much about them. They sound so exciting!'

'We should stay inside until Robbie gets here,' said Jack, peering out of the door. 'It's a cold night.'

Bella slipped her hand into his, and the couple stood and watched for the cart coming along the road.

## CHAPTER 15

'There he is!' said Bella when a lamp came into view. 'Come on!' She almost pulled Jack out of the house.

'Bye, Mrs Dixon,' he shouted before closing the door behind them.

The couple climbed onto Robbie Dodd's cart and sat alongside two other young couples from the village. Robbie's girlfriend sat next to him up front. Jack leaned back against the side panel with his legs stretched out in front of him and his arm around Bella's shoulders. She snuggled into him, her head resting on his shoulder.

The night sky was clear as they headed down the dale towards the market town of Allendale. The half-moon shone brightly, surrounded by twinkling stars. There was little to see on the journey, apart from lamps in cottage windows and a few people walking along the road, on their way to visit family and friends for the New Year.

When they reached the town, Jack jumped off the cart and lifted Bella down, and they made their way to the marketplace, dodging groups of revellers on the streets. The marketplace was busy. Men and women stood in pub doorways, and people lined the edges of the roads to ensure they would have a good view. Jack held Bella's hand firmly as they were jostled by the crowd.

From the snippets of conversation and the bad language she heard, Bella guessed that many of them had spent the evening in the pubs before coming outside for the New Year festivities.

'Would you like somethin' to drink before it starts?' asked Jack.

'No, I'm alright, but you get one if you want.'

'I'm fine. I had plenty of beer last night to last me a lifetime. Me head's still hurtin',' he said, raising his hand to his head. 'It was good of your Mother and Father to put on a party for our engagement. I should thank them again.'

'The pair of them were in their element. I've never seen me Mother laugh as much as she did last night. She had a great time!'

Jack pointed up the street and said, 'They'll be comin' down this way. Let's find a good place to watch them.'

They found a quiet spot further up the road. Long before they saw anything, they heard a brass band playing lively music. They waited patiently for the New Year's procession to come into view. Bella saw them in the distance and grinned up at Jack. Then her eyes were glued to the spectacle in front of her. She had never seen anything like it before.

Around thirty men in flamboyant costumes paraded in pairs through the streets of Allendale, and on their heads, they carried barrel bottoms filled with burning tar. The flames rose high into the air above them and burned so brightly that it looked like the whole town was on fire. Everything Bella could see had an eerie orange glow. The brass band marched behind the fire-bearers, their music almost drowned out by the cheering from the crowd.

Jack and Bella, and the people standing around them, joined the end of the procession and marched towards the marketplace. Jack stopped next to some shop steps, and they climbed up to get a better view. Bella watched in wonder as the men, one by one, threw their burning barrels onto a massive pile of dry wood, setting the bonfire alight.

The people gathered around the enormous fire, which blazed high into the night sky, and as midnight approached, they held hands and formed rings around the fire and sang *Auld Lang Syne,* accompanied by the band.

## CHAPTER 15

Bella looked up at Jack's face. It had a warm glow from the bonfire. He was singing loudly, and somehow she could hear his rich baritone voice above the others. He looked so incredibly happy at that moment that she wanted to jump into his arms. When the song ended, everyone around them began to kiss and hug.

'Happy New Year!' said Jack. 'I can't wait to see what 1849 has in store for us.'

'Happy New Year!' Bella replied. 'By this time next year, we'll be Mr and Mrs Lowery! Can you believe that?'

Jack grinned and said, 'I can't wait.' He held her in his arms and kissed her lovingly, and then they stood together and watched the burning bonfire.

Robbie came over to them a short while later, tapped Jack on the shoulder and shouted, 'Happy New Year!'

'To you, an' all,' said Jack, shaking his friend's hand.

'Sorry to rush you, but we should be headin' home now.'

They walked back to the cart, where the other couples were already waiting, and climbed on board. Jack and Bella sat in silence on the journey home. The lateness of the hour, the comfort of cuddling into Jack, and the rocking motion of the cart made it impossible for Bella to keep her eyes open. She slept for most of the way. When they reached Briar Place, Jack gently woke her and lifted her down from the cart. He said farewell to his friends and then helped Bella to her door as she was still sleepy. Without thinking, he led the way and stepped over the threshold first, holding the door open for Bella to follow.

'Happy New Year!' Jack greeted Martha cheerfully and kissed her on the cheek.

'Jack!' Martha stepped back awkwardly. 'Were you the first

to come through that door?'

In horror, he looked from Bella to Martha and asked, 'Am I your first-foot?'

When Martha nodded, his face fell, and he said, 'I'm so sorry, Mrs Dixon. I haven't brought anythin'.'

'Never mind that,' said Martha, running her hands over her hair and patting the bun on the back of her head. 'There's not much we can do about that now. You're dark, at least. That must count for somethin'. You cannot get hair much darker than yours.'

'That's true,' said Bella, running her fingers through Jack's hair and smiling up at him. 'As our first-foot, you should have a drink. What have we got, Mother?'

'There's a bottle of whisky on the table. Pour us all a tot, would you, love?'

When Bella had filled the glasses, they raised them into the air and toasted the New Year, wishing each other health, wealth and happiness.

A few minutes later, Johnny barged through the front door with a lump of coal in one hand and a whisky bottle in the other. He shouted, 'Happy New Year to you all!'

Bill stopped in the open doorway and looked around the room. 'What's all this? Which of you came in first?'

'I did,' said Jack sheepishly. 'Happy New Year, Bill.'

'Well, that remains to be seen, doesn't it, lad? Your father's been our first-foot for years, and he's always brought us luck. We've had a good year every year that he's been our first-foot. But what'll happen this year remains to be seen.'

Bella thought about the year that her little sister had died of fever. That had not been a good year, but her father seemed to have forgotten all about that one.

## CHAPTER 15

'Lighten up, Bill,' said Martha. 'It's the New Year. I'm goin' over to get Eliza now that we've had a first-foot, and I'll fetch Johnny's fiddle while I'm at it. We should see the year in properly!'

Bill pulled his wife into his arms, saying, 'Come here, lass,' and, to the surprise of Bella and Jack and the cheering of Johnny, he kissed his wife long and hard. 'Happy New Year, love.' When he released her, Martha smiled up at her husband before slipping next door.

When she returned, everyone had a drink in their hand, so she refilled her glass and poured one for Eliza, and then they joined everyone in the front room. The seats were all occupied. Eliza perched lightly on the chair arm next to her husband, her arm resting on the back of his chair.

Bella saw Jack looking at her, and he patted his knee. Knowing what he meant, she said, 'You can have this chair, Mother.' She stepped over to Jack's chair and sat down on his lap, his arm around her waist holding her firmly in place.

It wasn't long before the conversation turned to the bargains that were due to be renewed the next day as they were at the forefront of the miners' minds.

'I'll not set foot in that mine until the watcher men go,' said Bill. 'And I don't mean when we get a promise that they'll go, I mean after they've gone, once and for all.'

'I'm with me father on that,' said Frank. 'I'll not be signin' an agreement tomorrow either.'

'I don't know, man,' said Johnny. 'I can't say that I want a strike, but I do want the watcher men gone.'

'Don't you see,' said Bill, 'that's not goin' to happen unless we do somethin' about it.'

'I'd rather not have a strike,' said Jack.

'Why's that?' asked Frank.

'Because I'm savin' up to marry your sister.' He grinned at Bella. 'And if there's a strike, we might have to put the weddin' back a bit.'

Seeing the disappointment on Bella's face, Martha said, 'That's enough talk about work for the night. Eliza, pass your Johnny his fiddle.'

Within seconds, Johnny was playing a jig, and Bella stood up and asked Jack to dance. Bill and Martha soon joined them, and then Eliza pulled Frank to his feet and danced with the young man.

The New Year's party lasted well into the night.

# Chapter 16

**Allenheads, Northumberland
New Year's Day 1849**

Jack sat opposite his father at the table. They ate their breakfasts in silence, both thinking about the bargains that should be agreed upon that day, bargains that would secure them work for the next three months.

'Have you decided what you're goin' to do yet?' asked his father.

'Aye, I have,' said Jack solemnly. 'I wasn't sure last night, but if the rest of the lads want a strike, I'll stay out. I don't think there'll be many agreements signed today.'

'I don't know,' Johnny sighed. 'A strike means no money and no money means no food. I've got your mother and the girls to think about.'

'It won't be for long. When the lead ore stops comin' out of the ground, Sopwith will get rid of the time-keepers. He'll have to.'

'Mebbe. I don't know.'

'So, what will you do?' Jack asked, concerned that his father intended to work, regardless of what the majority of miners choose to do that day.

'If everybody goes out on strike, then I won't have a choice, will I? I'll have to stay out an' all.'

'Good!' said Jack, relieved that his father had come to his senses. 'We have to stand together. It's the only way that we'll get what we want.'

After breakfast, they met Bill and Frank outside the cottages, exchanged greetings and walked to Allenheads, eager to see if the other miners would follow through with their plans. When they reached the village, crowds of miners stood around, waiting to see who, if anyone, ventured into the mine office to take on a bargain. As the day wore on, the miners grew hopeful of their success.

'Can you believe that?' said Bill. 'There's over four hundred miners work here and only four of them didn't stand with us.'

'And they're incomers. We don't know them and they don't know us,' said Frank. 'They haven't a clue what's been goin' on.'

'We're officially on strike, lads,' said Bill triumphantly.

Johnny leaned back against a fence, crossed his arms, and said somberly, 'Let's hope it doesn't last long, for all our sakes.'

'Don't worry, Father,' said Jack. 'Everything will be fine. You'll see.'

'Hmph! That's easy for you to say. A young lad with no responsibilities.'

'Come on, Johnny,' said Bill, placing his hand on Johnny's shoulder and pushing him forward. 'Let's go and get a pint.'

'Aye, alright,' said Johnny begrudgingly. 'But you're payin'.'

The men laughed and set off down the hill to the pub.

The next morning dawned clear and frosty. All through breakfast, Jack tapped his foot impatiently on the floor.

## CHAPTER 16

'What's up with you?' asked his father, scraping the last bit of porridge out of his bowl with a spoon.

'It's weird just sittin' here. I have nowhere I need to be and nothin' I need to do.'

'You're as bad as me, lad. I cannot sit still for five minutes. Never could.'

'There's a sayin' about idle hands and all that,' said his mother, refilling her teacup from the pot. 'Keepin' busy keeps you out of trouble. So, what are you two plannin' on doin' today?'

'I hadn't really thought about it,' replied Johnny.

'Well, you'd better find somethin' useful to do. I'll be doin' the laundry in here and I don't want you under me feet.' Looking pointedly at her husband, she said, 'And I don't want you spendin' all day at the pub with Bill either.'

Johnny looked blankly at his son.

'We don't know how long this strike's goin' to last,' said Jack, 'or how long the weather's goin' to hold up. Why don't we go to the woods and collect some kindlin' for the fire?'

'That's good thinkin',' said his father. 'And then tomorrow we could go over to Coalcleugh and get some coal. I could show the lasses how to make cats for the fire.'

'That's a mucky job, mixing coal and clay,' said Eliza. 'The lasses won't be doin' it. I'd never get the stains out of their pinnies.'

'But they'd like to go lookin' for hazelnuts,' said Jack. 'That won't mucky up their clothes. Me and Bella could take them up the woods on Sunday, after dinner.'

'They'll not be any nuts left,' said his father. 'The squirrels will have gone with them by now.'

'But there's no harm in us lookin', is there?'

'S'pose not. We've got plenty of time on our hands now.'

A couple of days later, Bella was serving dinner at a gathering to celebrate Mr Sopwith's birthday. While Bella cleared away the dishes from the soup course, the conversation turned to the miners' strike. She hated it when Mr Sopwith and his guests discussed matters relating to the people of Allenheads in front of her as if she wasn't there. The people they were talking about were her family, friends and neighbours.

'They don't know how good they have it here,' said Mr Sopwith. 'They're just making trouble for the sake of it with their petty grievances.'

'And who needs troublemakers?' said a grey-haired woman.

'There's plenty of Irish who would jump at their jobs,' said a small, balding gentleman, 'and they're not afraid of hard graft. I've seen them with my own eyes. They'll work harder than anyone for a pittance and a roof over their heads.'

Bella took out the used dishes and returned with plates for the next course, which she set in front of the diners.

'What do you intend to do about it?' a tall, slim man asked Mr Sopwith.

'I intend to let them stew,' he replied enigmatically.

Bella went to the kitchen, and returned once more, with Mrs Vickers this time, to serve the main course.

'I will leave first thing in the morning,' said Mr Sopwith. 'Jane will stay here with the children. I did hope she'd accompany me, but she prefers to stay in the country, don't you, my dear?'

'Yes, I do,' said Mrs Sopwith emphatically. 'Here, the air is fresh and clean. One can breathe. I can't abide the smoke or the smells in the city, and don't get me started on the fog!'

## CHAPTER 16

'But there's so much to do in the city,' the grey-haired woman protested. 'There are shops, theatres, museums -'

'You'll not change her mind about London,' said Mr Sopwith firmly.

'How long will you stay in the city?' asked the small man.

'Ah, that remains to be seen,' replied Mr Sopwith, raising his eyebrows and then he glanced at Bella.

Back in the kitchen, Bella said, 'They talk as if we're not there.'

'And we should take no notice of what they say,' said Mrs Vickers. 'To them, servants are deaf and blind. Of course, we hear things and see things that we shouldn't, but it stops with us. You'd do well to remember that.'

'I know, I never say a word. It's just when Mr Sopwith says things like that, I wonder if he expects me to pass them on. It feels like he's testing where my loyalties lie - here or at home.'

'I think you're overthinkin' things, lass,' said Mrs Vickers with a chuckle. 'Do you want to finish early? I can manage the desserts. If you head off now, you might still have time to see that nice young fella of yours.'

'Thank you, Mrs Vickers,' said Bella with a grin. 'I'll see you in the morning.'

Bella took off her apron, grabbed her shawl and rushed outside. When she approached Briar Place, she saw Jack peeking out of his door, watching for her returning from work. When he saw her, he walked up the road to meet her, greeting her with a kiss. Then he led her towards the stone wall at the side of the road and leaned back against it. 'Let's stay out here for a bit,' he said. 'I don't see enough of you.'

She put her arms around his waist and cuddled into him. 'Sorry, I had to work late tonight. They're having a party. How are you?'

'I'm fine. It's strange not goin' to work though. I know that stayin' out on strike is what we need to do, but it's strange, all the same.'

'So, what will you do with all of your new-found spare time?'

'Me mother's written me a list of jobs,' Jack laughed.

'Aye, I'm sure she'll keep you busy. You know, now that we're engaged, we could start making plans for the wedding.'

'I cannot ask the company for a house 'til the strike's over, but I don't think it'll last much longer.'

Bella looked down at the ground. After what she'd heard at the dinner party that evening, she doubted that the strike would end any time soon.

'Aw, Bella.' Jack lowered his head to hers and whispered in her ear, 'I can't wait for us to get married, but I want us to have our own place.'

'I know.' She put her arms around his neck. 'I can't imagine us living with my parents, and there's not enough room for us in your house.'

'You're not kiddin',' he chuckled. 'But we could go and see the vicar if you want. We could arrange to have the banns read so we can get married as soon as we have somewhere to live.'

'That sounds like a good plan, Jack Lowery.' She raised her lips to his and kissed him.

# Chapter 17

**Allenheads, Northumberland
January 1849**

The miners waited patiently outside the mine office to collect their pays for the previous quarter.

'How will we get our money if Sopwith's not here?' asked Frank, rubbing his hands together to warm them.

'He has men to do his work for him,' replied Jack.

The clerk opened the door and called for the Dickinson partnership. The team of men moved to the front and followed him inside. Just a few minutes later, the four men came out smiling.

'How did you do, Bob?' Johnny asked his cousin.

'Six pounds! Not bad for a quarter, I'd say. Who wouldn't be pleased with twenty-four pounds a year?'

'Good for you!' Johnny patted him on the shoulder. 'Will we see you later?'

'Aye, I'll be about all day.' Bob walked away, his hands in his pockets, still smiling broadly.

The next group of partners to come out of the office looked far less happy with their remuneration. Jack wasn't at all surprised. He'd heard the Pearsons complaining in the pub that the vein they were working had narrowed to a thread and that they'd not brought up any ore for weeks. Before the watcher men came, the men would not have bothered going into work until after the next bargains because it wasn't worthwhile. Why would anyone choose to work if there was no chance of getting paid? But since the watcher men had started to report their working hours to Sopwith, they'd had to spend their days underground in the hopeless pursuit of lead ore.

'Can we have the Dixon partnership next?' asked the clerk.

Bill and Frank went inside with Jack and Johnny, and the men stood in the office facing a large desk. Mr Metcalf, one of the under-agents, sat in Mr Sopwith's place and counted out their money. He placed it in four neat piles on the desk.

'William Dixon. Here is twelve pounds for you.' He pushed the money towards Bill and repeated the process for the others. 'Francis Dixon. Here is the same for you. John Lowery Senior. Twelve pounds. John Lowery Junior. Here is twelve pounds for you.'

The men were ecstatic with the amount they had earned. All of those extra hours they'd put in at the mine had paid off, and it was the best pay day that they had seen. That's the way it went sometimes, thought Jack. Mining was a gamble, plain and simple. The Pearsons' bargain had failed that quarter, but thankfully for him, theirs had yielded excellent returns.

The men thanked Mr Metcalf and were about to leave when he said, 'You might like to know that your partnership brought out the most ore last quarter.'

'Really!' said Bill proudly. Turning to his partners, he congratulated them. Jack thought the grin on Bill's face could not have been any bigger.

## CHAPTER 17

'It's a pity that your next pays, if there are any, will not be so lucrative,' Mr Metcalf continued smugly.

The men's smiles disappeared at the reference to their strike action, and Bill glared at the man.

'Well, it was your choice to strike,' he said, leaning back in his chair and crossing his legs. 'Nobody forced you into it.'

It was clear to Jack that the under-agent wanted to antagonise them, and he turned away and stood by the door to wait for the others.

Bill looked as though he was about to punch the man. Johnny took his friend's arm and said, 'Don't give him the satisfaction,' and he led Bill to the door, from where they all heard Frank's voice.

'It's our right to strike,' said Frank, standing tall in front of the desk. 'If our employer changes our terms of employment and it's not to our satisfaction, we can strike.'

'And it's our right to dismiss miners who are troublemakers,' replied Mr Metcalf, getting to his feet and leaning menacingly towards Frank.

'It's an idle threat,' declared Johnny. 'They need us experienced miners workin' down there. You heard him. We brought out the most ore. They'd be fools to get rid of us.'

Frank and the under-agent were staring at each other icily. Jack was concerned that Frank might say or do something he'd regret, so he returned to the young man and said, 'Come on, Frank. He's not worth it.'

Slowly, Frank turned away and followed Jack.

'That's my lad!' said Bill, patting Frank on his back. 'Standin' up to the management. I'm proud of you, son. Come on, I'll buy you a drink.'

Robbie Dodd stopped Jack as they stepped outside and said,

'What's up? Did you not get as much as you thought?'

'We got what we expected, but that bastard had to spoil it by sayin' that we wouldn't get much pay next time because of the strike. He's upset Bill and Frank.'

'It doesn't take much to upset Bill and Frank,' laughed Robbie. 'Forget it, Jack. They're just trying to intimidate us into goin' back to work. I'll see you later.'

Jack ran to catch up to his partners, who were walking down the bank towards the village. He usually loved the pays and with pay days only coming around four times a year, that was reason enough to celebrate. Yet, he had mixed feelings about celebrating while there was a strike going on.

The celebrations had already begun, and the village was heaving with people milling around. The local brass band played a march and immediately Jack's mood improved. Music had always cheered him up. He vowed that he wouldn't let the agent spoil his day.

'Jack, are you comin' with us to the pub?' asked his father.

'Aye, I'll get the first round in.'

'Where's Bella?'

'She's workin' today but she'll be comin' to the dance later.'

At the bottom of the bank, two men squared up to each other, their fists raised. A small crowd surrounded them, watching the fight.

'Bill, are you enterin' the boxin' competition?' asked Johnny.

'Aye. I always do.' He asked the organiser to add his name to the list.

'Put mine down an' all,' said Frank.

The men looked at him in surprise.

'But Frank,' said his father, 'have you seen the size of the fellas that compete in the boxin'?

## CHAPTER 17

'Aye, and I've seen how slow most of them are. There's some advantages to bein' young and fast on your feet.'

'I don't know what your mother will say,' said Bill, shaking his head.

'Mother's not here though, is she?'

'No, she's not, but she'll be the one nursin' your wounds tonight, and I'll be the one that gets it in the neck for lettin' you fight.'

'I'm enterin', Father, whether you like it or not.'

'Calm down you two,' said Johnny. 'Our Jack just said he'll get the first round in. We'd better get to the bar before he changes his mind.'

Lining the road, traders had set up their stalls and tried to talk the men into buying their wares as they passed. The village shopkeeper approached them, a ledger under his arm. 'Good afternoon, gentlemen. Now is as good a time as any to settle your accounts.'

Bill and Johnny paid the man what they owed, and cynically, Jack wondered how much of their twelve pounds would be left by the end of the day once they had settled their debts, placed a few bets and drank their fill. They continued towards the pub, where men and boys circled a pair of wrestlers, cheering them on.

'Cumberland wrestling. That's more your thing, Johnny. Are you puttin' your name down?'

'I might as well,' he took a pen and wrote his name in the notebook.

'Put my name down an' all, Father,' said Jack. He didn't want to spend all day drinking in the pub with his partners, and he reckoned they'd have less time for drinking if they entered more events.

# Chapter 18

**Allenheads, Northumberland**
**February 1849**

After the church service on Sunday, Bella and Jack wandered around the churchyard leaving footprints in the shallow snow that had fallen overnight. After the last of the parishioners left the church, they approached the vicar who was standing at the church door.

'Good morning, Reverend.'

'Good morning, Miss Dixon, Mr Lowery. It's a beautiful day, but it is rather chilly. Please, come inside.'

The couple followed him into the church.

'What can I do for you?' asked the vicar.

'Me and Jack would like to get married,' said Bella, smiling at Jack. 'But we're not sure what we need to do and we wondered if you could help us, please?'

'Of course, Miss Dixon, it would be my pleasure. Have you considered if you would like the banns to be read out in church or do you intend to obtain a marriage licence? The reason I ask is because the procedure is different in each case.'

'Banns, I think. I don't know anyone who's got married with a licence.'

## CHAPTER 18

'That's fine. Most church-goers marry by banns. It tends to be the Methodists and Quakers who apply for a licence or those who want to keep their business private. So, when would you like the wedding to take place?'

'As soon as the strike's finished,' replied Jack.

'Yes, that's very sensible, but for the banns to be read, I need to know the actual date that the wedding will take place.'

Jack looked at Bella and felt gutted when he saw her disappointment.

'The eighteenth of May,' said Jack, thinking that surely the strike would be over and done with by then. 'I think that's a Saturday.'

Bella grinned at Jack and slipped her hand into his.

'You're right, it is. And that gives us plenty of time to prepare. Come and see me at the vicarage for a little chat. I must be sure that you're both aware of what the institution of marriage entails and that you're entering into it for the right reasons because it is a binding agreement. Once you're married, there's no changing your mind or turning back. Anyway, after we've had a chat, we can make the arrangements. Would Saturday morning be convenient?'

'I work on Saturdays,' said Bella. 'I don't know if they'd give me the time off.'

'Well, on Sunday then, right after the morning service. How does that sound?'

'Perfect,' said Bella, smiling broadly. 'We'll be there.'

'Thank you, Reverend,' said Jack, holding out his hand.

'You're very welcome, Mr Lowery,' said the vicar sincerely, shaking Jack's hand firmly. 'It's lovely when a young couple come together to be husband and wife. You've made my day!'

Bella left the church feeling elated. As soon as they were out of the gate, she turned to Jack and said, 'It's really happening, isn't it? We're going to get married!'

Jack embraced her. 'Aye, love. It's really happening. We won't have much longer to wait.'

They walked back to Briar Place, thrilled that soon they would be man and wife.

When Jack returned home, his mother was making dinner in the kitchen and when she heard the door, she popped her head around the door.

'I wasn't expecting you back, Jack. Will you be stayin' for dinner?' she asked.

'Aye, where else would I be goin'?' he replied sarcastically and regretted his words when he saw his mother's face fall. Going into the kitchen, he asked, 'Why did you ask?'

He saw the rows of plates lined up with just a small amount of food on each.

'Ah! I see. There's not enough to go round again.'

'I'm tryin' me best, Jack, but that's all I've got. And there's no end to the strike in sight. '

She took another plate from the rack and spooned some food off each of the plates to make up another portion for her son.

Jack carried a couple of the plates to the table in the living room and shouted upstairs, 'Dinner's ready!'

He smiled at the sound of little feet running down the stairs and watched his sisters sit around the table.

His mother put the plates in front of them and he saw the disappointment on their faces, as did his mother but she pretended not to notice.

'Jack, go and get your father. He's in the garden.'

When everyone was present at the table, they began their

## CHAPTER 18

meal, which took about a minute to eat. Jack had eaten two spoonfuls of stew and half a potato.

'Mother, is there any more, please?' asked Catherine.

'No, that's your lot.' Eliza stood up abruptly and began to clear the table.

'Is there a puddin'?' asked Mary hopefully. 'I love treacle puddin'.'

'No, there's no puddin' today.'

'But I'm still hungry,' moaned Deborah, picking up her plate and licking it clean.

'Don't do that!' said her mother crossly. 'It's very unladylike.'

'Let her be, Mother,' said Jack, who was tempted to lick his plate too. 'She's not being wilful. She's just hungry.'

'I'll get another jug of water,' said Lizzie.

'They'll be up all night if they have any more water,' said Eliza sharply.

'They need somethin' in their stomachs.' Lizzie picked up the jug and went to the kitchen to refill it.

Johnny had been silent throughout the meal. He looked around the table at his children's thin faces, and then he got up and went back out into the garden, but not before Jack noticed a tear in the corner of his father's eye.

After Lizzie had returned and poured more water, her mother said, 'Lizzie, you can help me with the dishes. Hannah, you take the girls upstairs to play. Keep them occupied, will you?'

'Aye, of course.'

'But it's cold upstairs,' complained Catherine. 'Can we have the fire on?'

'No, you can't. It's warmer upstairs than it is outside, but you can play outside if you want?'

'No, Mother. It's alright. We'll play in our bedroom.'

Hannah led the way upstairs, closely followed by her younger sisters, and Lizzie finished clearing the dishes and went into the kitchen to help her mother. Jack was left at the table alone. His stomach rumbled; he was still hungry too. Damn the strike, he thought, when would it end?

His father came back indoors carrying a dead chicken, which he handed to his wife. 'That's the last of me hens. Make the bairns a decent meal with it tonight.'

# Chapter 19

**Allenheads, Northumberland**
**March 1849**

Johnny Lowery was determined to put things right. He couldn't spend another day watching his bairns go hungry and beg for food. His wife had always been slim, but now she was skin and bone, there was nothing on her, and it was all his fault.

He wouldn't be in this mess if he had done what he thought was right and refused to join the strike. But he'd been swayed by Bill and Jack. He recalled Jack saying that it wouldn't be for long. Well, his son had been wrong. They'd not worked for three months, which meant three months without any subsistence pay, and who knew how much longer the strike would continue?

The wages he'd received in January were long gone. He'd paid his debts, Eliza had stocked the kitchen with supplies, and he didn't know how she had managed to eke out the food for this long. She was a marvel, his Eliza, but she couldn't perform miracles.

Johnny walked into Allendale town and approached the magistrate's house. A serving girl answered the door, and he asked to speak with Mr Atkinson. She invited him inside, and he sat on a chair in the hall and waited.

A few minutes later, Mr Atkinson appeared, wiping his mouth with a napkin.

'I'm sorry if I've disturbed your dinner, sir,' said Johnny.

'It's quite alright, Mr Lowery. I had finished eating. Please, come into the parlour.'

Johnny followed the older man into a well-furnished room with pictures on every wall and a tall potted palm in the corner. He sat on a chair at a polished table, and the magistrate sat opposite.

'So, Mr Lowery. May I ask why you've called on me today?'

'I know that you're on the Board of Guardians, Mr Atkinson, and I was hopin' you could put in a good word for me and me family. I hate to say this, but we're sufferin' badly. We haven't any money, and there's no food left in the house. Me bairns are hungry, and it breaks me heart to see them like that. I know that gettin' outdoor relief means we'll all have to wear badges, but we're desperate, sir. I wouldn't be here if it was otherwise.'

'I'm sorry to hear of your dire situation, but I'm afraid there's nothing I can do to help. The poor laws were changed about five years ago, and outdoor relief was stopped. However, as your poverty is self-inflicted, you would not have qualified for it anyway.'

Johnny's face fell.

'You chose to join the strike, did you not?'

Johnny looked down at the floor.

'As I see it, you have two choices, Mr Lowery. You can take your wife and children to the Poor House at Hexham, where you will be given food and shelter in exchange for your labour,

## CHAPTER 19

or you can return to work.'

'I cannot take them to the Poor House,' said Johnny. 'I've known people who've gone in there and never come out again, and they separate men from their wives, and mothers from their bairns.'

'In that case, you must go back to the mine. Granted, the circumstances are difficult, but there is work available for you, and Mr Sopwith is known to pay a decent wage.'

'I cannot go back before the strike finishes, Mr Atkinson. I cannot.'

'That's up to you, but in my mind, it's the lesser of two evils. I wish you well.'

Mr Atkinson stood up, shook Johnny's hand and showed him to the door.

Johnny strolled back up the road to Allenheads, burdened by his troubles. He had a decision to make, one that could have far-reaching consequences, and he had to be sure that he made the right choice. Either one would make life difficult for him and his family, but both would ensure that they had food to eat, and that was the most important thing to him at that time. As long as they had full stomachs, he was certain that they could cope with anything that came their way.

As Bella prepared to leave Allenheads Hall at the end of the day, Mrs Vickers handed her a basket covered with a white tea towel.

'What's this?' Bella asked.

'Just a few leftovers I've put together. I'm sure you can put them to good use.'

'Thank you,' said Bella sincerely.

It was three months since the miners had started the strike.

Bella knew that her family was managing better than most, but there were only four mouths to feed in their house, and they still had her wage coming in. Bella sometimes took her meals with Mrs Vickers at the Hall which had helped too. She thought it was unfortunate that the strike was in the middle of winter when her father couldn't grow anything in his garden and there was little in the surrounding countryside to forage. She knew that most of the money her father and Frank had collected in January had been spent because her mother had confided that she was using her savings to buy groceries.

The local shops and pubs would no longer allow mining families to buy supplies on tick because the owners were worried that the bills would not be paid.

If the situation was bad in their house, what must it be like in Jack's? There were nine of them living in there, and they had less money coming in than the Dixons.

Bella hesitated outside the Lowerys' house, and then she opened the door. 'Anyone home?' she asked as she went inside.

'Come on in, love,' said Eliza. 'By, you're looking well.'

'Thank you.' Looking around the house, Bella said, 'It's quiet in here. Where is everybody?'

'Jack's gone up the woods to collect kindling for the fire. He took the lasses with him. The fellas hate sittin' around doin' nothin'. I don't know where Johnny's got to. I haven't seen him since breakfast.'

'Mrs Vickers gave me this,' said Bella, 'and I want you to have it. Just don't tell me mother. Alright?'

Lifting off the cloth, Eliza's eyes filled up when she saw a large loaf of bread, a meat pie, a sweet cake with jam in the centre, and a rhubarb crumble. 'Shouldn't you be givin' this

## CHAPTER 19

to your mother?'

'Like I said, I want you to have it. Your need is greater than ours.'

'Bless you, Bella! Thank you so much.'

'You're welcome.' Bella smiled. 'I thought I'd be working late today, but I finished early. Would you tell Jack when he gets back?'

'Of course, I will.'

Bella went home and was immediately confronted by her mother, who said, 'What were you doing next door?'

'I went to see Jack, but he's gone up to the woods to collect firewood.'

'I could have told you that. Your father and Frank have gone an' all,' said Martha. 'I saw Eliza hangin' out her washing earlier. She's never had much weight on her, but she's as thin as a pin these days.'

'You know what she's like,' replied Bella. 'She's probably giving her share of the food to the bairns.'

'It's hard enough to make ends meet in this house. I wouldn't like to be in her shoes.'

'No, it must be hard for her.'

'Eeh! You'll never believe this. The Martindale lads have been knockin' on doors and beggin' for food? I can't think they'll have had much luck. There's none of us got anythin' to spare.'

'How much longer do you think the strike will last?' asked Bella.

'You're askin' me? You're the one that works for the boss.'

Shifting slightly, Bella said, 'Mr Sopwith went to London after the New Year and he's not been back since. There's not even been any talk of him coming home, not that I've heard

127

anyway.'

'Well, nothin' will get settled 'til he's back, I can tell you that for nowt.'

After dinner, Bella read her library book for an hour or two until Jack came to the door.

'Do you fancy goin' out?' he asked.

'Aye, I do.' She grabbed her shawl, wrapped it around her shoulders and followed Jack outside.

'Come on,' he said. 'Let's get away from here.'

It was a cold evening. Jack put his arm around Bella, and they walked slowly towards the village.

'I wanted to thank you for givin' me mother that food. That was very thoughtful of you.'

'It was nothing.'

Stopping, he turned to face her and said, 'It wasn't nothin', Bella. We've not had enough to eat in our house for weeks.' Pulling his trouser waistband out to the side, he said, 'Our clothes are fallin' off us. Father's got no hens left. Your father's got nowt left in his garden. You givin' me mother that basket of food today meant the world to her. And you should have seen the girls' faces when they had a bit of cake.' His eyes softened as he looked at her and whispered, 'I love you so much.'

'And I love you, Jack Lowery.' She grinned at him cheekily and nudged him with her elbow. She wanted to kiss him so badly, but there were too many people out and about in the centre of the village for a public show of affection.

As they passed by the mine yard, Jack said, 'I'm worried about me father. I don't know how much longer he'll be able to stay out on strike. He's started to leave the house at mealtimes. He can't bear to see the bairns hungry and hear them askin' for more food. You know, he wasn't keen on strikin' in the first place. We pressured him into it. Me and your father.'

'He can't go back to work,' said Bella. 'If he did, his life wouldn't be worth living.'

'But, is it now? Watchin' his wife and bairns wastin' away. There's nothin' on any of them.'

'Come on, it can't be that bad.'

'Aye, Bella. It is,' he said, deadly serious.

Bella looked down at her feet. She had known that the Lowerys were struggling because of the strike, but hadn't realised to what extent. She wished that she'd done more to help them. With tears in her eyes, she said, 'I'm sorry, Jack. I'm so sorry.'

They continued walking in silence until they were nearly home. Then, Jack playfully pulled Bella behind the large tree.

'What was that nudge about earlier, eh?' he asked, his eyes glowing as he lowered his face towards hers.

'I think you know,' she said coyly, looking at him through her lashes.

'Was there somethin' you wanted, Miss Dixon?' he whispered, his lips almost touching hers.

She put her arms around his neck and reached up to kiss him.

# Chapter 20

**Allenheads, Northumberland**
**March 1849**

The following day, Johnny came downstairs in his work clothes. Without a word, he left the house and set off for the mine. Eliza and Jack followed him to the door and watched him walk up the road. Jack was about to go after him, but his mother put her hand on his arm and said, 'Let him go. He's made his choice.'

Frank saw Johnny leave and shouted urgently for his father. Martha and Bella came to the door to see what was going on, and moments later, Bill barged out of the netty, pulling up his braces. When he saw Johnny walking towards the village in his work gear, he ran up the road to catch up with his friend.

'What are you doin', man?' Bill took hold of Johnny's arm and practically spun him around on the spot.

'What's it look like I'm doin'?'

'Aw, Johnny, you cannot. Not after all this time.'

Johnny stood with his head down and his shoulders slumped, and said, 'A man has to feed his family, Bill. Believe me, if there was any other way, I'd take it. Either I watch me family starve, take them to the workhouse, or I go back to work and put food on the table. I don't have a choice. Come on, Bill. You must be able to see that?'

Bill stood staring at his friend, and then, wagging his finger, he spitted, 'I'll not have anythin' to do with a blackleg, Johnny! If you go back to work now, that's us finished. It's up to you. That's your choice!' He slapped Johnny hard on the shoulder, before marching away in disgust.

A look passed between Bella and Jack. They both knew that Bill was a man of his word. His ultimatum meant that if Johnny returned to work, the relationship between the Dixons and Lowerys would never be the same again.

Bill passed the Lowerys' door and shouted at Jack, 'This is your fault! Nothin' like this ever happened when your father was our bloody first-foot.'

Johnny was out all day, and everyone at Briar Place presumed that he must have gone back to work as he'd intended. Late in the afternoon, Jack sat in the front room, tapping his fingers on the table, waiting for his father to come home. He understood his father's reasons for returning to work, but since hearing Bill that morning, he hadn't been able to get the word *blackleg* out of his mind. On every occasion that he'd ever heard the term, it had been used as a curse. He'd been brought up to believe that blacklegs were the scum of the earth.

Since he was a child, he'd been told that miners had to stick together to make the bosses listen to them and that there was strength in numbers. He knew it showed weakness if some of the men went against the rest and continued to work. They were the ones that undermined the cause. Sighing, he knew that his father was one of those men now. A blackleg.

The door opened, and Johnny came into the house. The

men's eyes met.

'What are you lookin' at?' said Johnny.

'I don't know.' Jack shook his head. 'You tell me! Did you go to work today?'

'Aye, I did,' he said, looking his son in the eye. 'I had to for your mother and the bairns. Seein' them hungry, Jack, what was I supposed to do? Watch them waste away to nothin'? I got me subsistence pay today and I've been to the shop. From now on, they'll have food in their bellies.'

Johnny removed his jacket and hung it on a hook. Turning back to his son, he asked, 'What are you plannin' to do?'

'What do you mean?' Jack asked, puzzled. 'Are you askin' me if I'm goin' to go back to work an' all?'

'Well, are you?'

'Not a chance!'

'In that case, you can find somewhere else to stay. If you're not willin' to contribute to this household, you're not welcome here! I didn't go back to work so I could support a grown man who's capable of supportin' himself.'

Jack stood up and looked at his father, hardly recognising the bitter, broken man who stood in front of him.

'If that's what you want, I'll get me things and I'll go.'

The house had two bedrooms. His parents shared one and his sisters the other. Jack had always slept on a pull-down bed downstairs, and his few belongings were piled up in the corner of the room. He gathered them together and walked out of the door without looking back. Jack walked towards the village, deep in thought. If his father hadn't told him to leave, he wondered if he might have left anyway. Could he have stayed in the house with a blackleg? But then he reckoned that he probably would have stayed, even if it was only to protect

## CHAPTER 20

his mother and sisters. Now that his father had broken the strike, he would be an outcast, and so too would his family by association.

Bella had heard the heated exchange between Jack and Johnny next door, and when she heard the thud of their door, she went outside and saw Jack walking up the road towards the village. She ran to catch up with him.

'Jack! Wait!'

He stopped and turned to face her.

'What's goin' on?' she asked when she reached him.

'Me father threw me out.' Jack continued to walk with long strides, and Bella had to run to keep up with him.

'But why?'

'He has a short memory,' said Jack angrily. 'He seems to have forgotten that all me wages since I was ten years old have gone into that house.'

Bella realised that Jack must have refused to return to work.

'Did you know he was going back this morning?' she asked.

'Not until he went. He never said a word to any of us.'

'My father is so mad at him.'

'I am an' all!' Jack fumed. 'He says he's doin' it for the family. Yes, there will be food on the table, but has he given a thought as to what will happen to them now?' Slowing down, he turned to Bella, his voice quivering, and said, 'He's a blackleg, Bella. Me father's a bloody blackleg!'

'It'll be alright, Jack. The strike will be over soon, and all of this will be forgotten.'

'Blacklegs are never forgotten, Bella. Never!'

Bella knew Jack was right. Johnny had solved one problem by going back to work, but at what cost? She took Jack's hand

and asked, 'Where will you stay?'

'I'm hopin' Robbie will put me up. Just 'til the strike's over.' His face softening, he said, 'And then we can get a place of our own.'

'I could ask me father if you can stay with us, if you want? That way, you could keep an eye on your place when your father's out.'

'Do you think he'd let me?'

'Aye, I think he might,' said Bella, with more confidence than she felt. 'You could share the front room with our Frank.' Her father was a strong man and set in his ways, and she hoped that she could persuade him to take in Jack.

'Thanks, Bella. I'll walk back that way with you, but I'll wait on the roadside. I'm not goin' anywhere near our house.'

When Bella went home, Bill was seated by the fire polishing his Sunday shoes. 'Father, there you are.'

'Where else would I be?' he asked, frowning.

Standing in front of him, she said, 'There's something I'd like to ask you.'

He put the shoe and the polish-covered brush down onto a sheet of newspaper and looked up at her.

'It's about Jack. Well, you know Mr Lowery went to work today. He wanted Jack to go back an' all, but Jack refused. Anyway, Mr Lowery has thrown him out and I wondered if he could stay here with us? Just until the strike's over. Then we'll get married and move out.'

Bill rose to his feet, towering above his daughter, but his eyes never left hers. 'I cannot believe what you've just asked me.'

Bella was puzzled by his response, but she didn't question it. She stood in silence and watched his face turn red.

## CHAPTER 20

'Jack's not welcome here anymore. His father's a strike-breaker. You are not to have anythin' to do with Jack anymore. The weddin's off!'

'But Father -'

'This is not up for discussion, lass. You're not to see him. Do you understand me?' Bill's face was just inches from hers, and she cowered away from him.

'But the banns have already been read at the church,' she said feistily. 'We could get married now if we wanted. You cannot stop us.'

'You not old enough to marry without my consent, Bella, and that weddin' will take place over my dead body!' Bill stared at his daughter, daring her to contradict him, and then he stormed outside and went into his garden.

Bella walked with her head down as she returned to where Jack waited at the roadside.

'What did he say?'

Bella stood in front of him and didn't say a word.

Jack lifted her chin, saw the tears on her face, pulled her into his arms and held her close. 'It's alright, love,' he said. 'I'm sure Robbie will put me up.'

Bella began to sob even more.

'What is it?' asked Jack. 'What's wrong?'

When Bella could speak, she said, 'Me father doesn't want me to see you again. He said he won't let us get married.' She turned and ran back to the house, leaving Jack standing alone in shock.

Bella ran upstairs to her room, threw herself onto her bed, and sobbed. She loved Jack, and she wanted to marry him so much. She'd already pictured their future together. Their wedding would take place at their local church, with their family and friends around them. She'd wear the beautiful blue dress that Mrs Sopwith had given her. She was sure that Mr Sopwith would let them rent one of the lovely new houses in Allenheads, the honey-coloured sandstone ones that she'd secretly admired every time she passed them. Of course, she'd have to give up work when she was expecting their first baby, and then they'd have many more children. She wanted nothing more than to be Jack Lowery's wife and to bring up a large, happy family with him.

When she finally came to her senses, Bella thought about her predicament in a more practical light. If she wanted to continue to see Jack, which she did, she'd have to do it secretly, behind her father's back, and he could never know that she had defied him.

# Chapter 21

**Allenheads, Northumberland**
**March 1849**

Lizzie Lowery stood frozen to the spot, but when she heard the almighty scream for the second time, she leapt up the staircase faster than she had ever done so before and burst into the girls' bedroom. Looking around she saw Jane was sitting on the floor sobbing and Catherine was standing by the bed staring down at it. Hannah and Mary had just woken up in the other bed and looked around, trying to figure out what was going on.

'Whatever's the matter?'

But even as Lizzie asked the question, she knew the answer. Deborah was lying on the bed, her gaunt face as white as the pillow on which her head rested, and her chest was still. Lizzie ran over to her and shook her, hoping that she was just sleeping, but her sister's body was cold and stiff. There was no doubt that she was dead and that she had been for some time. With a lump in her throat, Lizzie pulled the sheet over the small body. Despite the pain in her chest and the strong emotions that threatened to overcome her, Lizzie knew that she had to keep calm for the sake of the girls. She looked around the room and saw that Mary was the only one who was unaware of Deborah's death.

'Hannah, take Mary downstairs and start on breakfast,' commanded Lizzie.

Hannah didn't move. Lizzie went over to her and put her hand on her sister's shoulder, saying firmly, 'Hannah, please take Mary downstairs. Now.'

Hannah lifted Mary out of the bed and carried her out of the room.

Catherine stood like a statue by the bedhead, unable to comprehend what had happened. Lizzie took her into her arms and held her until the shock gave way to sorrow and Catherine crumpled to the floor, where Jane wept silently. Lizzie sat down on the rug with them and they clung to her for comfort.

'Hush, girls,' Lizzie said, soothingly. 'Hush, now. Deborah's gone to a better place. Heaven's lovely. Haven't you heard the vicar say so? And she'll have Granda and Granny Lowery to look after her, and Grandad and Nana Walton, as well. She'll not want for anything anymore.' But all the while, Lizzie wondered how this dreadful thing could have happened, and silently cursed the miners and their strike, and the bosses who were too stubborn to cede to their demands. If they hadn't all been so pig-headed and had sorted out the dispute sooner, their Deborah would still be alive. It was so unfair that an innocent child had suffered the consequences.

The sound of someone shutting the door downstairs roused Lizzie from her bitter thoughts. It was her mother returning to the house from the netty. How could she break the news to her? She heard her mother greet Hannah and Mary, and wondered if perhaps Hannah would say something.

## CHAPTER 21

'Lizzie!' Eliza shouted. 'Are the others up yet?'

Lizzie didn't reply. She left her sisters to comfort each other and went downstairs to face her mother.

Eliza only had to take one look at Lizzie's face to know that something terrible had happened in the short time that she'd been outside.

'Oh, God!' she said, with a feeling of dread. 'What is it?'

'Sit down, Mother.'

Eliza sat in the chair closest to the fire, not taking her eyes off her eldest daughter.

'It's our Deborah,' said Lizzie.

Eliza's eyes were wide, her mouth open, needing to know, but not wanting to hear what Lizzie was about to say.

'She went in her sleep. She's gone, Mother. She's gone.'

With the weight of the news, Eliza sank into the chair and for a few seconds her face contorted with pain before any sound escaped from her mouth, and then she began to wail loudly. Lizzie got to her knees and held her mother, finally giving in to her tears too.

The sound carried next door, where the Dixons were eating breakfast.

'What a racket!' said Bill.

'I wonder what's happened,' said Martha, feeling uneasy. She glanced sub-consciously at the space where her late daughter used to sit. 'Maybe I should go over and see if they're alright?'

'You are not goin' next door, Martha, do you hear me? Not under any circumstances.'

'Aye, I hear you, but I don't know what's happened to you. You've become heartless, Bill. The Lowerys have been like family to us for years. Johnny was your best friend. I don't know how you can sit there and listen to that.' Martha pointed to the wall, her voice breaking as she said, 'That's a cry for help if ever there was one.'

She stood up and flounced into the kitchen, filled with anger and sadness. In all the years that she'd been married to Bill, she'd never spoken to him in that way, but the sound of Eliza howling like that had brought tears to her own eyes. She remembered fine well that it had been Eliza who'd comforted her when she'd lost Lucy. She desperately hoped that she was wrong, but in her gut, she knew that something dreadful had happened to one of Eliza's children. Yet, as much as she wanted to comfort her friend, she couldn't go against her husband's wishes; he'd made them plain enough.

All that day Martha worried about Eliza and wondered what had occurred that morning, but it wasn't until later that evening, when Bill went out to work in his garden, that she had an opportunity to find out. She leaned across the table and whispered to Bella, 'Do you know what's happened next door?'

Bella shifted uncomfortably in her chair. If she admitted that she did, her mother would know that she'd spoken to Jack, but her mother's eyes were begging her for news about their estranged friends.

'Deborah died last night,' confided Bella. 'They found her this morning.'

Martha clutched at her chest. 'Oh, no! Poor Eliza, and those poor girls.'

'Lizzie went over to Robbie's place this afternoon to tell Jack. Her father had forbidden her from going, but she went anyway. Jack wouldn't have known about it otherwise. They're all very upset as you would imagine.'

## CHAPTER 21

'What was wrong with Deborah?' asked Martha.

'The doctor said she hadn't been eating enough. Lizzie thought Deborah must been giving her food to the others, probably copying her mother.'

'The poor little love.'

'You won't tell Father that I've seen Jack, will you?'

'No, lass. Your secret's safe with me.'

The next afternoon, Bella and Jack watched Johnny carry Deborah's coffin to the churchyard, with the help of his wife and children. Eliza, Lizzie and Hannah took turns carrying one end of the small wooden box. Jack was annoyed that nobody had lent his father a cart to take his child to her final resting place, or at least offered to help him carry the coffin.

'Shouldn't you go and help him?' asked Bella.

'He'll not take my help,' Jack said sadly. 'Me and me father should have been the bearers, or maybe your father, with him being his best mate. It's certainly not a job for me mother and me sisters. It's disgustin'. How can people be so heartless?'

'Me mother wanted to go to the funeral, but me father wouldn't hear of it. I wouldn't be surprised if he stays in today to stop her from leaving the house.'

'Why did it have to be our Deborah?' asked Jack quietly, his eyes glassy. 'She was such a lively bairn, full of fun, and she had the kindest heart of them all. Maybe except for our Lizzie, that is. She's like a saint, our Lizzie.'

Bella took Jack's hand and held it firmly, and he smiled down at her. They stood on the roadside, keeping their distance from the church, and watched the family disappear inside the building. They spoke quietly until the service was over and the family moved into the churchyard for the burial. Mr and

Mrs Lowery, Lizzie, Hannah, Jane, Catherine and Mary stood around the grave, the girls holding hands, while the minister performed the committal. There were no mourners from outside the family in attendance as little Deborah Lowery was laid to rest.

Jack swallowed and sniffed loudly, trying his best not to cry in front of Bella. He couldn't remember being this upset about anything before, ever. The needless loss of his little sister. The exclusion from his family. He felt helpless. Gripping Bella's hand tighter, he watched as the small coffin was lowered into the ground by his father and the gravedigger. A choked sound escaped from his throat, followed by a sob, and he sat down on the grassy verge, his arms around his knees. Bella knelt next to him and held him as he cried.

Shortly after the Lowery family wandered home, Jack and Bella went to the open grave. They threw some soil down onto the coffin, and each of them said a silent prayer for Deborah to rest in peace, and for an early end to the strike that had caused her death.

The gravedigger stood at the corner of the church, his head bowed, patiently waiting for them to leave so that he could backfill the grave and complete his task.

Bella took Jack's hand and they walked back to Allenheads together.

'This strike has a lot to answer for,' said Jack. 'By God! I wish we could go back to how things were before.'

'Me too,' said Bella. 'I hate that our families are at each other's throats. I hate sneaking around to meet you in secret. And if it hadn't been for the strike, your Deborah would still be with us.'

'Aye, don't I know it!' Jack's anger changed to melancholy

as he said, 'You know, it was me that persuaded me father go out on strike with the rest of us. He must hate me for it. Now, more than ever. If he had followed his conscience, he would have been gettin' paid all this time, and the bairns would have had plenty to eat. It's my fault that our Deborah died.'

'Oh, Jack! You can't blame yourself for what happened.'

'But I do,' he said.

'So, what are you going to do now? Are you going back to work an' all?'

'No! I cannot. I could never break the strike.'

'Even after what's happened?' asked Bella incredulously.

'Aye, even after what's happened. We'd never live it down, Bella. I'm stayin' out with the rest of them until this fight's over, one way or the other.'

'I don't know what's going to happen with us,' said Bella, sadly. 'Ever since your father went back to work, me father's been dead set against us getting married.'

Jack stopped, pulled Bella into his arms, and whispered, 'Don't worry, love. I know that we're meant to be together. Somehow, we'll find a way.'

# Chapter 22

### Swinhope Chapel, Northumberland
### March 1849

'We must stand together and work together to do everythin' in our power to harm the strike-breakers, be it in words or in actions.'

Jack sat with Robbie Dodd at the front of the chapel, aware that Bill and Frank sat a few pews behind them. He listened to the chairman of the miners' meeting and was shocked by his tirade, but he knew that the only way that they'd reach an agreement was for the miners to stand together. By going back to work, blacklegs threatened everything that they'd worked for so far. And if an agreement were not reached, the poverty, the suffering, the starvation, and the loss, all of it would have been for nothing. But a deal wasn't likely any time soon, not when Sopwith hadn't set foot in Allenheads since January. He'd been away for over two months now, and there was no hope of an end to the situation until he returned.

'If they are sick do not visit them,' continued the chairman, 'if they are in need of a doctor do not seek them one, if they die do not bury them, if they are fastened underground in the mines do not assist in seekin' them out but let them die or be

## CHAPTER 22

killed in the dark!'

Jack wiped his clammy palms on his trousers. He could feel the tension building in the room, and he feared for his father's safety. He thought it was strange that this meeting had started with a hymn and a prayer because the meeting was being held in a chapel, but then the chairman had gone on to incite violence towards men who had been friends and neighbours and workmates such a short time ago. And not just towards the men either, but against their families, innocent women and children. He prayed that his mother and sisters would be safe.

The chairman continued, 'I would not give one of them a mouthful to save their lives if I saw them dying of want.'

The men got to their feet, Bill and Frank among them, cheering the chairman's call to arms. Nelson Kidd and his workmates stood on the pews and whooped loudly, and others followed their lead. Jack stood up and walked out, leaving Robbie there alone.

Walking back to Allenheads, there were tears in Jack's eyes. It was just days since his sister had died of want. He wondered how a man could stand in the pulpit of a chapel and say that he would allow a fellow human to die from starvation when he was in a position to help. And how could the miners applaud his words? Where was their Christianity? Where was their humanity?

As he passed Briar Place on his way back to the village, Jack stopped and looked towards his family home, wondering what he should do. He knew that he wouldn't get a warm welcome there, but he had to warn his family about the trouble that would undoubtedly come their way after the speech that night. He went to the door and knocked loudly. Someone moved a curtain and peered out, then he heard voices inside, but nobody came to the door. Jack suspected his father had forbidden it.

Jack was about to walk away when he heard the Dixons' door open and Bella stepped out.

'What are you doin' here?' she whispered.

They went to the side of the house so they couldn't be seen, and he explained what had been said at the chapel meeting.

'I need to warn me father about what's in store. I'm scared for them, Bella.'

'Why don't you wait until your mother comes out to use the netty at bedtime. Catch her then.'

'That's a good idea. Thank you.' Looking into her eyes, he said, 'It's good to see you.'

Even though they could be disturbed at any moment, Jack lowered his lips to meet hers and kissed her longingly. Breaking away, he said, 'I hate to say it, but you'd better go back inside. Your father and Frank will be back soon.'

'Will I see you tomorrow?' she asked hopefully.

'Aye, I'll come to the Hall when you finish work.'

He kissed her on the brow and then went to hide over the wall on the opposite side of the road until he could warn his mother of the impending danger.

The sun was low in the sky the following day when Jack walked past the mine yard. He saw his father standing outside the gate, covered in broken eggs, the yolks dripping off him. Johnny picked bits of eggshell off his clothes and threw them to the ground.

'Who did this to you?' demanded Jack.

'It's got nothin' to do with you, lad.'

## CHAPTER 22

'What! You won't tell me who did it?'

Johnny continued to clean his jacket in silence.

'Don't you understand?' asked Jack. 'Today, it's you they've pelted with eggs, but tomorrow they could target Mother or our Lizzie or the little uns.'

'They wouldn't hurt the lasses.'

'And how do you know that? At the chapel last night, that's exactly what they were tellin' folks to do.'

Johnny looked up at his son, his face contrite.

'I wish I was at home so I could take care of them,' said Jack. 'There's not much I can do to help them when I'm stayin' in the village.'

'So, that's what this is about,' said Johnny, shaking his head. 'You're tryin' to scare me into lettin' you come home.' Pointing his thin finger at Jack, he said, 'The only way you'll get back through that door is when you start bringin' in a wage. Do you hear me?'

'Aye, I hear you. Let's hope that you're right and that they don't carry out the threats on me mother and the lasses, because if they do, you'll have me to answer to. You're too stubborn for your own bloody good!' Jack turned away and marched off.

He heard his father call after him, 'I wouldn't be surprised if it was you who threw the eggs at me. It's funny how you appeared just after. The first eggs of the year. What a bloody waste when bairns are starvin' to death!'

Jack kept walking. There was no point in talking to his father when he was behaving like that, and he wondered what effect the unrest was having on his father's mind. Was it rational to turn against your own son and throw him out of the house? Or to refuse protection for your family in times of trouble?

A carriage came up behind him at a rapid pace. Jack stepped to the side of the road and watched it pass, and he saw that the occupant was Sopwith, returned to Allenheads at last. He sincerely hoped that now the boss was back, the situation might be resolved, and the strike ended.

After the confrontation with his father, Jack decided that he would keep an eye on his sisters. He could watch them when they walked to school and back, and his father need never know.

Either Lizzie or Hannah had always accompanied the younger girls in the morning so that they didn't get distracted on the way and lose track of time, for the consequences were unthinkable. Sopwith abhorred tardiness, and he had ordered that any child who arrived after nine o'clock was to be punished severely. Since he had warned his mother that night after the chapel meeting, Jack was pleased to see that they were collecting the girls after school too.

Jack watched from afar for a few days, ensuring that they went to school without incident. Then, one afternoon, when Jack leaned against a dry stone wall watching Hannah from a distance, he sensed trouble. Hannah stood outside the schoolhouse waiting for her sisters to finish their classes and a couple of young men were loitering nearby. Jack thought they were up to no good. Stealthily, he moved closer so he could see more clearly.

He saw one of the lads bend down, pick up something from the ground and hurl it at Hannah. He heard his sister yelp and saw her take a step back, and then she turned to see who had thrown the stone. The youths laughed and gathered more

## CHAPTER 22

stones, which they promptly threw at her before she had time to react.

Jack leapt over the wall that he'd been hiding behind and stood in front of Hannah.

The lads' faces fell when they saw him.

Mocking them, Jack said, 'Look at you, big fellas! Picking on a bit lass. You should be ashamed of yourselves.' Pointing at himself, he continued, 'But, if you're man enough to take on someone your own size, I'm game.'

'It's alright, mate. We didn't mean no harm,' said the taller of the two, and they walked briskly down the hill towards the village.

Turning to his sister, he noticed a streak of blood on her brow. He took a handkerchief from his pocket and held it to her head. 'Are you alright?' he asked.

'Aye, I'm fine. But I'm glad you showed up when you did.'

Removing the handkerchief, he was relieved to see that the small wound wasn't deep. 'It's just a scratch,' he said. 'You'll live.'

Hannah giggled.

'Do you want me to walk you back? They might be hangin' around the village.'

'Thanks, Jack, but better not. If Father sees us with you, he'll go mad. He's told us not to talk to you.'

'He what?' Jack shook his head in disbelief. 'For God's sake, I'm your brother!'

'I know. It's not right,' said Hannah, smiling up at him. 'But you needn't worry, Jack, he'll never turn us against you. You're our big brother!'

Jack hoped she meant what she'd said. What was his father playing at, stopping his sisters from seeing him or talking to him? It wasn't right to keep his family away from him just because he'd stayed out on strike. He couldn't understand his father's behaviour, and Jack wondered if this was just a temporary disagreement as he'd thought, or if there was something more deep-seated behind it.

The younger girls rushed out of the door and ran over to Jack, wrapping their arms around his legs and hugging them. He had missed them, and they'd obviously missed him too. Despite Hannah's concern about them being seen together, Jack walked his sisters through the village and back to Briar Place. The girls chattered non-stop, fighting over who would hold his hands, and they must have asked him at least a hundred questions by the time they got home, which he had answered with good humour. He loved the lot of them, and he vowed to himself that he would do his best to keep them safe, come what may.

# Chapter 23

**Allenheads, Northumberland
April 1849**

When Jack walked through the village a few days later, he saw Lizzie standing outside the village shop, and she looked vexed. Crossing the road, he went over to her.

'What's the matter?' he asked.

'The stupid shopkeeper won't serve me,' said Lizzie.

'Why not? What did he say?'

'He said he won't serve me 'cos I'm the whelp of a blackleg.'

'The cheeky sod!' exclaimed Jack. 'What is it that you want?'

'Just yeast for bread and half a pound of butter will do. Father bought a dozen hens on Saturday, so I don't need eggs.'

Jack marched into the shop with Lizzie by his side and slammed the door shut behind them, startling the shopkeeper who was stacking the shelves.

'What's this I hear about you not servin' our Lizzie?' asked Jack sternly.

'You were there the other night, Jack. You heard them. I can't be seen to serve blacklegs or their families. It's not worth the bother.'

'I'm not a blackleg, so as long as I'm around, you'll give my sister what she asks for. Do you hear me?'

'Aye, alright, but it's not goin' on tick. Whose payin' for it? '

'No, it's not goin' on tick.' Lizzie opened her hand and showed him the coins she held. 'I can pay for it.'

The shopkeeper looked as though he was about to answer back, but a severe look from Jack made him think better of it, and he got the groceries for Lizzie. She put the items in her basket and gave him the correct money.

When they left the shop, Lizzie said, 'I was hopin' I'd bump into you. Gettin' a bit of shoppin' was just an excuse for comin' out really.'

'Why?' asked Jack, looking puzzled.

'It's Father,' replied Lizzie. 'He went to work yesterday mornin' and didn't come home last night. Mother's worried. She thought he might have fallen asleep in the mine 'cos he's findin' it hard doin' all the work down there on his own. Could he have slept down there and carried on workin' this mornin', do you think? Would he do that?'

Jack felt panic rising in his chest and took a deep breath to calm himself. Even if his father had fallen asleep underground, as Lizzie suggested, he wouldn't have enough food and water to stay in the mine and work for two days. He would have come up this morning to get some more bait.

'He might have,' said Jack. 'It's dry enough on the stope where we were workin' for him to kip down. He could have used his jacket as a pillow and made himself comfortable.'

'But you don't think he did, do you? I can tell by your voice.' Lizzie's face started to crumple. 'What do you think has happened to him?'

'I don't know, Lizzie. I suppose he could have had an

## CHAPTER 23

accident. If he was injured, he might not have been able to get back up.'

'You mean he might be stuck down there?' Lizzie put her hand on her head as she contemplated all the awful things that could have happened to her father. 'There's hardly anybody goin' down the mine now,' she said, 'so nobody would know if he was hurt.'

'I'll go down and check that he's alright,' said Jack reassuringly.

Lizzie put down her shopping basket and hugged her brother. 'Thank you, Jack. He's been so mean to you, but I knew you wouldn't bear a grudge against him if he was in trouble. Thank God, you're nothin' like him.'

Lizzie grabbed her basket and walked quickly in the direction of Briar Place to tell her mother that Jack was going in search of his father.

Jack went back to Robbie's place to enlist the help of his friend. Robbie was more reluctant to go into the mine than Jack had expected.

'You were there and you heard what they said,' said Robbie. 'We're not to help anyone if they're stuck down the mine.'

'Aye, I heard. We're to leave them to die in the dark on their own. But Robbie, man, he's me father. I cannot leave him down there. If anythin' happened to him, I wouldn't be able to live with meself. I've got to at least try and help him. What would you do if it was your father that was missin'?'

'My father's long gone,' said Robbie sadly, 'but I'd have done anythin' to have had more time with him.'

'Right, let's get goin', then.'

The men put on their work clothes and stuffed some candles and matches into their pockets. There wasn't much food in the house, but Jack found some bread and jam. He made a sandwich, wrapped it in paper and put it in his pocket, along with a flask of water, and then they set off for the mine.

A few striking miners hung around the mine entrance to deter men from returning to work. As they approached, Tommy Ritson shouted, 'Jack, what do you think you're doing?'

'It's not what you think, Tommy. We're not goin' back to work. Me father didn't come up last night, and me mother's worried sick about him. We're only goin' down to see that he's alright, that's all.'

Some of the men had tools by their sides, and their hands menacingly moved to the handles. Nelson Kidd lifted his pick-axe and held it in front of him, not taking his eyes off Jack.

'You're not goin' in,' said Tommy. 'Your father's a blackleg. He doesn't deserve anyone's help.'

More worried for his father's safety than he had been before, he and Robbie left the yard and stopped on the road outside.

'There's always the horse level,' whispered Robbie. 'I doubt they'll be guardin' that.'

'Good idea!' Jack slapped him on the back.

The two men walked up the road to the horse level, near the gates of Allenheads Hall. Robbie was right - nobody was guarding it. They disappeared through the arch, following the steep curve of the tunnel as it spiralled down into the depths of the mine. They branched off into a cross-cut, where they had been working before the New Year and approached the stope.

Jack shouted, 'Father, are you down here?' His voice echoed around the subterranean maze, but there was no reply from

## CHAPTER 23

Johnny. It was eerily quiet. The only sounds they could hear were the clunking and splashing of the waterwheels that pumped water from the mine. There were no hammers hitting chisels against the rocks, no shovels scraping stones off the ground, no tubs pulled by ponies rattling on the rails, and no voices or laughter. He had never known the mine to be so silent.

The passageway veered left at a sharp angle, where the vein intercepted another. When Jack and Robbie reached the corner, they stepped back in horror. Fallen rocks completely blocked the tunnel ahead. Cracked timber stuck out at precarious angles, like a lethal barricade preventing them from advancing.

Beyond the blockage was a dead end. Jack and Robbie realised that if there were no gaps between the rocks, the air supply would have been cut off at the time of the collapse. But when would that have been? Before he had time to process the situation properly, Jack reached up and passed the loose stones to Robbie, who stacked them neatly against the wall of the tunnel as if he were building a dry stone wall.

As Jack moved stone after stone, being careful not to skewer himself on the splintered wood, he wondered how long a man could survive with only the air that had been trapped with him. Was his father still alive? Jack didn't waste any time or energy trying to contact his father. He knew that every minute could make the difference between life and death.

Sweat poured off Jack, and he wiped his brow with his dusty sleeve.

'Should I go and get help?' asked Robbie. 'We can't move all this ourselves.'

'We have to! Nobody will come down to help the poor sod.

Not now that he's a blackleg.'

They resumed their gruelling work. Jack passed rocks back to Robbie until there was a slight gap at the top of the blockage. At last, air could penetrate the chamber.

Jack put his mouth to the hole and shouted, 'Father, are you in there?'

A weak voice replied, 'Aye.'

Knowing that his father was still alive, Jack continued his efforts with renewed vigour. Up until then, he hadn't given a thought as to how the roof had collapsed. He'd just concentrated on getting through the blockage. But thinking about it now, he remembered that the roof had been a solid layer of limestone. None of the partners had been concerned about it collapsing, or they would have put in wooden props to support it. So why had it given way now, at a time when only his father was working there?

'Robbie, it won't be long before I can get in,' said Jack. 'Go and fetch a stretcher so we can carry him out.'

His friend nodded and rushed towards the bottom of the shaft where he knew a stretcher was kept for emergencies.

When the gap was large enough for Jack to squeeze through, he lifted himself up with the help of the broken timbers embedded in the rocks. He went headfirst through the hole into the chamber beyond and slithered down the other side. His candle had fallen off his hat, so he took another from his pocket, struck a match against the wall and lit it. In the flickering candlelight, Jack could see his father lying on the stope about six feet above the ground. With great agility, Jack leapt up onto the wooden platform and knelt beside his father.

'Jack?' croaked Johnny, reaching for his son's hand.

'Aye, Father. It's me. Are you hurt?'

## CHAPTER 23

His father shook his head. At least that was a blessing, thought Jack.

'Come on, let's get you up.' Jack lifted his father's shoulders. 'That's right, lean back against the wall.'

Jack fished in his pocket and brought out the canteen of water, which Johnny took from him and drank greedily. Water ran over his grimy beard and dripped onto his clothes.

'What happened?' asked Jack.

Johnny shook his head again, and then he opened his eyes wide and said, 'I heard some voices.'

'There was somebody else down here?'

'Aye, I reckon there must have been,' Johnny took another long swig of water. 'I was drillin' and makin' quite a racket. I heard voices, and I stopped to listen - and then there was a blast. I fell against the wall and hit me head. I think I heard someone laughin' after that, but I might have been imaginin' it, I don't know. I'm starvin' hungry, lad. Did you bring us anythin' to eat?'

Jack passed him the jam sandwich and watched him eat it, all the while thinking that his father hadn't imagined anything. He recalled the words spoken at the miners' meeting and knew that the miners had taken things a step further. Some of them must have come into the mine and deliberately brought down the roof to trap his father underground, leaving him to die a slow death from lack of air or water. How cruel could they get? Johnny Lowery was one of their own, born and bred in the village, and he'd worked all his life at the Allenheads lead mine, as had his father and grandfather before him. These men had tried to murder him, and for what? All he'd done to deserve this treatment was to provide for his family. That must be one of the most basic human instincts, thought Jack.

Thinking about Bella, he looked forward to when they would be married and have a family together. He would enjoy providing for them and protecting them. There was no way he would be able to stand by and watch Bella and their children suffer needlessly, and for the first time, Jack really understood his father's actions.

When Robbie returned with the stretcher, he shouted, 'I'm back, Jack.' His voice sounded strange coming from the other side of the rockfall. 'Is your father alright?'

'Aye, thank God, he is,' replied Jack.

'Now, I need you to get out of that hole,' Jack said to his father, pointing out the narrow gap that he'd come through. 'That's all you need to do. We'll carry you out after that. Do you think you can manage?'

Johnny looked at the steep pile of rocks and the small gap near the roof and said, 'I'll give it a go.'

Jack jumped off the stope and assisted his father down the wooden ladder. Johnny was wobbly on his feet, so Jack supported him until he was steady and they stepped slowly towards the rockfall.

'Robbie,' Jack shouted, 'when you see his hands, pull him through.'

Leaning back against the rocks, Jack said to his father, 'Stand on me shoulders and put your arms through first.' Jack groaned with the effort of lifting a man who was about his own weight. Gradually, the weight lessened as Robbie pulled Johnny through the gap and helped him down the other side.

When Jack joined them, his father was lying on the stretcher. He and Robbie carried the stretcher through the mine, occasionally stumbling on the wooden rails that ran through the tunnels. As they rounded a corner and natural light appeared,

## CHAPTER 23

Jack spotted a tear in his old man's eye, and at that moment, Jack realised that his father had not expected to see the light of day again.

Outside, Jack said to Robbie, 'Stay with me father,' and he ran off in the direction of the mine yard. There were pickets at the gates, and he headed straight for them.

Nelson Kidd stepped forward and said, 'Back again, Jack? We're still not lettin' you go in.'

Anger at what had happened to his father flooded Jack's veins. He rushed at Nelson and headed him hard in the stomach, knocking him back and winding him. Nelson doubled over.

'I've already been in, and I know what you were hiding, you bastards! I've come to get a barrow to take me father home. Does anyone else want to try and stop me?' Jack looked wildly at the other miners, who moved aside to let him pass. 'And if I find out who did this to him,' said Jack, in a low voice, glaring at each of them in turn. 'I'll hang for them!'

Jack went through the gate and onto the washing floor, where he found a wooden wheelbarrow. He pushed it up the hill to the horse level. Robbie helped him lift his father into the contraption, and then Jack wheeled him home.

As they approached Briar Place, Jack saw Bill and Frank standing outside the door of their cottage, smoking their pipes, but the men disappeared indoors before they reached the houses. Jack helped his father out of the barrow and put an arm around him to help him through the front door.

'Mother!' shouted Jack.

Eliza ran into the front room from the kitchen and gasped when she saw that her husband could not stand without Jack's help.

'Oh my God! What happened?' she asked as Jack lowered his father onto a chair at the table.

'He'll be alright, Mother. He just needs some food and rest.'

'Lizzie, make a cup of sweet tea, will you? Very sweet.'

Lizzie nodded and went into the kitchen.

Eliza sat next to her husband and said, 'Johnny, love. You are alright, aren't you?'

'Aye, hinny. I had a bang to me head but I'm alright now. I could do with a good feed, like Jack said, but otherwise, I'm as right as rain. They'll have to try harder than that if they want to get rid of me.'

Nobody in the room laughed at his joke.

Lizzie put the cup down in front of her father, and he immediately gulped down the sweet liquid.

'You mean it wasn't an accident?' asked Eliza, her face full of concern.

'No, Mother,' replied Jack. 'It was no accident.'

'Get him a bowl of that broth, Lizzie,' said Eliza, 'and a hunk of bread.'

While Lizzie fetched the food from the kitchen, Jack told his mother what he suspected had happened. She sat there with tears in her eyes and a hand over her mouth.

'I wish you'd never gone back to work, Johnny,' said Eliza, holding her husband's hand. 'They'll never let it rest, will they?'

Johnny sat straight-faced, without any outward sign of emotion, dipping his bread into the bowl of broth. Something his mother used to say had been going around in his head since the blast in the mine. 'You've made your bed, Johnny, lad. Now, you'll have to lie in it.'

'Jack,' said his father. 'Thank you. If you hadn't come down

## CHAPTER 23

when you did, I know I wouldn't have got out alive.'

Jack squeezed his father's shoulder, not sure what to say. The fact that he'd saved his father's life was only just starting to sink in.

'You should move back home,' his father continued. 'This is where you belong. You will come back, won't you?'

Jack considered the question for a few seconds before he replied. 'Aye, I will. I'll stay at Robbie's tonight, let him know what's happenin', and I'll bring me stuff over tomorrow.' He saw his mother smile.

'That's good,' mumbled Johnny as his eyes closed, and he fell asleep at the table.

# Chapter 24

**Allenheads, Northumberland**
**April 1849**

Lizzie Lowery banked up the fire at ten o'clock before going to bed. She picked up a candlestick and looked to the corner of the room where Jack used to sleep out of habit. She'd been about to say 'Goodnight', but stopped herself. Jack wasn't there, but he would be tomorrow. She smiled; she was glad that her father had asked him to come home.

Lizzie climbed the stairs quietly and tiptoed past her parent's bedroom so as not to disturb them. All was quiet in the girl's room; her sisters were sleeping soundly. She undressed quickly and pulled on a nightdress, and then moved Catherine over a few inches to allow her to join her sisters in the bed. She blew out the candle and climbed in, pulling the blanket up around her neck.

Almost as soon as her head hit the pillow, Lizzie drifted off into a light sleep, but not long after, she was disturbed by an unfamiliar noise. She sat up in bed. It didn't appear that any of her sisters had heard it, whatever it was, because none of them had stirred. They were still sleeping peacefully. Lizzie listened intently. There it was again. It sounded like

## CHAPTER 24

somebody tapping. She thought her parents would be asleep by now, and she didn't want to wake them unnecessarily. Her father needed to rest after his ordeal at the mine. But her curiosity had been piqued, and she wanted to know what was making the sound, so she lit the candle and went downstairs. Outside the house, she heard men speaking in hushed tones. She fled back upstairs and loudly banged on her parents' bedroom door before pushing it open.

'Father, there are men outside our house!'

'It'll just be them next door.' Johnny said dismissively, rolling over onto his side.

Eliza nudged him with her elbow. 'Our Lizzie wouldn't wake us up for nothin'. Don't you think you'd better go down and see what's goin' on?'

With a large sigh, Johnny said, 'Get out, lass. I need to put me trousers on. I'm not goin' outside in me nightshirt.'

Lizzie retreated from the room and waited impatiently on the landing for her father. She heard a thud and then the sound of footsteps above her.

'They're on the roof!' she shouted.

Her father joined her on the landing and cocked his head to listen. 'My God! You're right. There is somebody up there!'

Johnny stumbled downstairs and tried to open the front door, but it wouldn't budge. He fiddled with the key in the lock, but it made no difference. He turned and went into the kitchen, followed by Lizzie, and tried the back door, but it too refused to open.

Through the window, Lizzie could see the silhouettes of men moving around, and then suddenly the window was covered with something, and she heard the sound of hammering, which she recognised as the tapping sound that had woken her.

'What are they doing?' she asked, her voice tense with fear.

Before her father could reply, they noticed smoke coming into the kitchen from the front room, and they went to take a look. Smoke and fumes spewed out from the fireplace. Johnny ran into the kitchen and grabbed a towel, which he soaked in a bucket of water, and he tried to smother the fire with it, but it didn't work. If anything, it seemed to Lizzie that the fire was producing even more smoke than before.

'We have to get out!' shouted her father. 'Get everyone up! I'll break the door down.'

When Lizzie rushed back upstairs, she found her mother sitting on the edge of her bed, pulling on her boots,

'There's smoke everywhere!' said Lizzie. 'We have to get them out. Now!'

Lizzie went into the girls' room, deciding in a split second that she didn't have time to dress them. She had to get them out of the house as quickly as possible. Shaking them awake, the girls soon realised that they had to follow Lizzie downstairs, where they saw their father trying to break through the door with a small hammer and a carving knife.

'Damn it! I wish I had me work tools here. They've fastened the doors shut and covered the windows. What are we goin' to do?' he asked, his voice full of despair. He was still weak and exhausted after being trapped in the mine.

The smoke was so thick that it was difficult to see one another, and Catherine and Mary began to cough.

'The upstairs windows aren't blocked,' said Lizzie. 'We can jump out.'

'No!' Lizzie heard her mother shout. She was shaking her head wildly, and her eyes were wide with fear.

## CHAPTER 24

'Mother, the smoke's gettin' thicker. Father cannot open the door. We don't have a choice. Come on upstairs, all of you!'

Obediently, the children went upstairs again, followed by their mother, who was still shaking her head. Lizzie took her father's arm. 'Come on. You'll not get the door open in time.'

Her words must have struck a chord with her father because, despite his weakened state, he practically shoved Lizzie up the stairs. Even upstairs, the air was foul. Eliza had opened the window on the front of the house and stood looking out at the hard surface of the road beneath them.

'We'll not make it,' said Eliza. 'We'll be killed.'

The girls were crying now, as well as coughing.

'Shush, Mother', said Lizzie. 'You're frightenin' the bairns. The window on the back will be better. The garden will be a softer landin', and the drop isn't as far.'

'Really?' said her mother, rushing to the back of the house.

A look passed between Lizzie and her father. They both knew that the drop was the same on both sides of the house, but Johnny nodded at her, acknowledging her ingenuity. They followed the family through to the other bedroom.

Eliza opened the back window, looked out, and shook her head. 'There's no way I'm goin' out of there.' She backed away from the window and looked on in horror as she saw her husband pick up Mary and move towards the window.

'What's goin' on up there?'

Johnny hesitated with his daughter still in his arms and peered outside. 'Bella, is that you?'

'Aye. Why are your windows covered with wood?'

'Bella,' said Johnny, sounding surprisingly calm. 'Go to the door. What's stopping it from opening?'

A moment later, she shouted, 'There's a bolt on the outside.

I've undone it and opened the door. My God! There's so much smoke coming out!'

'Right!' said Lizzie. 'We're all goin' to run to the back door and out into the garden. It's a race. Let's see who can run the fastest, alright?'

Wide-eyed, the girls nodded.

'Hannah, you go first.'

The family made their way downstairs and out of the house into the garden, where they took deep breaths of cold, fresh air, and then they sat on a low stone wall that edged the hen run.

'Thank you, Bella,' said Eliza sincerely. 'Thank you so much. I thought we were goin' to die.'

'Don't tell me father that I've helped you, mind,' whispered Bella. 'He's forbidden us all from having anything to do with you.'

'Was it him that did this?' asked Johnny. 'Was it Bill?'

'No, it had nothing to do with him. He's been in bed for hours. I'd better get back though.'

'Goodnight, Bella,' said Johnny, 'and thank you.'

Johnny pulled down the planks of wood that had been used to block the downstairs windows and removed the bolts from both doors. He opened all of the doors and windows to release the smoke from the house. Then, he brought out some blankets, returned to his family, and wrapped everyone up to protect them from the cold night air.

He sat down next to Lizzie and said, 'We'll have to wait for the smoke to clear before we can go back in.'

'Aye, I know. Do you know what caused so much smoke?'

'Hmph!' Johnny shook his head. 'I've heard of this happenin' before. People bein' smoked out of their houses. When we

## CHAPTER 24

were bairns, there was a fella that lived up near Ninebanks. A blackleg. They tried to smoke him to death.'

'Smoke him to death?' Lizzie asked, shocked.

'Aye, they bolted his door and blocked his chimney with peat. The house filled up with smoke, and he couldn't get out.'

'Oh, my God! That's awful.'

'He managed to get out of a window in the end, but not before the smoke had burnt his lungs. He broke his leg from the fall an' all. He survived it, but he was never well enough to work again.'

'It's hard to believe that people can be so evil,' said Lizzie, wondering if whoever had done this to her family had intended for them to die.

# Chapter 25

**Allenheads Hall, Northumberland**
**April 1849**

As Bella set off for work the following morning, every member of the Lowery family, apart from Jack, was engaged in cleaning their house. Eliza was managing the operation. Lizzie cleaned the windows with vinegar, Hannah beat the mats, and the younger girls washed crockery and cutlery in buckets of soapy water.

Johnny stepped outside, and when he saw Bella, he smiled. 'Thank you again for what you did last night, Bella. I hate to think what would have happened if you hadn't come to our rescue.'

'Anyone would have done the same, Mr Lowery.'

'Now, you're just bein' modest, lass.' With tears in his eyes, he said, 'We owe you our lives. If there's ever anythin' we can do for you, just ask.'

Bella heard her father's voice behind her, 'Bella, what are you doin' talkin' to them lot. Shouldn't you be gettin' to work?'

'I'm on me way, Father.'

She nodded to Johnny as she left. When she reached the village, she went to Robbie's place and knocked loudly at the

## CHAPTER 25

door. Jack opened it.

'I didn't expect to see you this mornin',' he said, beaming at her.

'Jack, there's something you need to know.'

Jack stepped outside, and Bella told him everything that had happened the night before.

'No!' said Jack, rubbing his hands through his hair. 'They did that to me mother and the girls! Nobody deserves that. Especially not them. Who did it, Bella? Did you see anybody?'

'No, I didn't. They were probably long gone by the time I went outside.'

Through gritted teeth, Jack said, 'I'll strangle them with me bare hands if I find out who did it.'

'And I wouldn't blame you,' said Bella.

'I should have been there,' Jack said, his voice full of despair. 'Yesterday, me father asked me to move back in and I should have been there last night. I only came back to Robbie's place because I wanted to thank him for helpin' us to get me father out of the mine. I took him out for a drink, and to think that while I was in the pub, they could have been killed.'

'Oh, Jack! It's not your fault.'

'But don't you see, if I'd been there, I would have been strong enough to break down the door. Me father was trapped in the mine with no food and water and very little air for two days. You should have seen him, Bella. He couldn't even stand up without holdin' on to us. He would never have been able to get them out on his own.'

Bella grimaced. It was the first she'd heard about the incident in the mine.

'My God!' exclaimed Jack. 'I bet it was the same fellas that trapped him underground that smoked them out of the house.'

'Aye, Jack. There's a good chance it was. It's one thing to shun people on the street or call them names, but to want to hurt people, that's a different thing entirely. Not many would do that.'

'Thank God you were there, Bella.' He took Bella in his arms, hugged her tightly, and said, 'I'll never be able to thank you enough for what you did. You saved them all. My whole family. Thank you.' His voice wavered as he finished speaking, and Bella could feel him sobbing. She held him for a long time before his tears subsided.

Jack kissed Bella and said, 'Thank you for everythin'. I should go and see them.'

Jack collected his belongings from the house, told Robbie what had happened, and then set off for Briar Place. Bella went to the Hall to begin work, where she had to explain to a very worried Mrs Vickers why she was over an hour late.

After sweeping the floor in the hallway, Bella filled a bucket with water and added a little soda, picked up a scrubbing brush and began to scrub the floor tiles. She had done about half of the room when she heard the sound of children's voices outside. The front door opened and the nanny entered with the children, the baby in a pram and the others following behind.

'Be careful,' said the nanny. 'The floor is wet. It will be slippy.'

They walked across the hall and climbed up the stairs, leaving trails of little muddy footsteps on the newly cleaned floor.

Rolling her eyes, Bella returned to the front door, retraced their steps with a floor cloth, and continued her work down the hall. When she was outside Mr Sopwith's office, she heard his voice. She didn't hear what he said at first, but he sounded vexed. She was surprised to hear Mrs Sopwith reply, for it wasn't often that she went into her husband's study.

'Let me read it. It can't be as bad as you say.'

After a short silence, Mrs Sopwith said, 'Oh dear! How could they embarrass you like this after all that you've done for them?'

'Clearly, they don't appreciate it, Jane. None of it. All I want to do is make the mines as profitable as I can and improve the lives of the miners and their families. I changed the payment system so they could avoid being in debt all the time. I saw that the school, the library and the reading room were built for their benefit. I put up better housing and even a church, for God's sake! Change is good when it's for the better. Improvement is good. And this is the thanks I get for my efforts. Public humiliation!'

'Oh Tommy, don't take it to heart. What you are doing here in Allenheads is wonderful. You love to show off the village to your friends when they visit, and they all applaud your achievements.'

'You're right, my dear. You're always right. Already, several men have seen the error of their ways and have returned to work.'

'You must write a reply to the newspaper. I'm sure they'll publish your response.'

'That's a good idea. An excellent idea, indeed. One should defend oneself. I will write a reply immediately.'

At this point in the conversation, Bella moved on and could no longer hear what was said. Of course, she had been aware that the miners had written to the *Newcastle Guardian* to tell the world about their plight and hopefully to drum up support.

Her father had helped to draft the letter.

Her thoughts turned to Johnny Lowery and all that he had gone through since he returned to work. The image of his shivering children with sooty faces came to mind, and she shook her head. What if she hadn't heard the commotion and gone outside? The whole family would have perished, and if that had happened, Jack would never have forgiven himself for not being there to save them.

Later that same day, Bella was dusting the ornaments in the drawing-room when she heard a knock at the front door, and she went to open it. Johnny Lowery was standing there, looking as uncomfortable as he had done the first time she'd opened the door to him.

'Mr Sopwith has sent for me, Bella. Do you know what it's about?'

'I'm sorry, Mr Lowery, I've no idea. You'd better come in.'

She showed Johnny to Mr Sopwith's office, where a parish constable was seated. She saw a brief look of horror on Johnny's face when he saw the officer, and as she turned to leave, she heard her master say, 'Bella, please stay.' Her surprise must have been evident because he continued, 'I know this is an unusual request, but so is the predicament in which we find ourselves. Please take a seat, both of you.'

Johnny and Bella sat in the chairs that he indicated.

Mr Sopwith said, 'I've invited you here today because it has come to my attention that Mr Lowery and his family have been victimised by his fellow workmen for breaking the miners' strike and returning to work. In my opinion, to turn on one's peers is a very low act indeed. What they did is not only immoral, it is also illegal, and that is why I have asked Constable Heaviside to join us today.'

## CHAPTER 25

The constable nodded to Johnny and Bella.

'Who told you?' asked Johnny. 'None of me family would have said a word.'

'Ah! That's where Bella comes into this.'

Johnny looked daggers at Bella. 'What did you tell him for?'

'I never said anything to him, Mr Lowery. I promise you.'

'No, Mr Lowery,' said Mr Sopwith. 'Bella did not breathe a word of it to me. I only wish that she had, and then perhaps we could have prevented some of the unfortunate events that you've encountered from happening. Bella confided in Mrs Vickers, our cook, who had the good sense to come to me. The dear lady couldn't bear to think of anyone suffering, especially children.'

'What can be done about it?' asked Johnny. 'I went back to work. I'm a blackleg. Miners detest blacklegs. There's nothin' you can do to change that.'

'Mr Lowery,' said the constable. 'Mr Sopwith has asked me to track down the men responsible for trapping you in the mine and for barring you and your family in the house while they filled it with smoke. I believe there's a good chance that the same people were involved in both incidents. If I can find these men, they will be tried for the attempted murder of not only you but of your wife and children as well.'

'Attempted murder!' exclaimed Johnny. 'They'd be transported for that.'

'Not many convicts are transported anymore,' said Mr Sopwith. 'A more likely punishment would be life imprisonment. A serious crime has been committed here.'

'I need to know what happened on those two occasions in as much detail as possible,' said the constable.

As Johnny answered the man's questions, Bella sat there

feeling guilty for telling tales, annoyed at Mrs Vickers for sharing them, and embarrassed that her actions had been responsible for getting the constable involved. If the men who had tried to kill Johnny found out that the constables were looking for them, they'd think Johnny had informed on them, and she was afraid of the consequences for him and his family. What would they do to him next?

When Constable Heaviside closed his notebook, he thanked Johnny for the information he'd given and looked at Mr Sopwith.

'Is that all you need from Mr Lowery?' asked Mr Sopwith.

'Yes, sir. We'll begin our enquiries right away.'

'Please make it your highest priority. I want those men brought to justice.'

The constable and Johnny stood up to leave, so Bella rose from her chair.

'Just one moment, Bella, please.'

When they were alone, Mr Sopwith said, 'If there is any further trouble in the village, with Mr Lowery's family or any other family for that matter, please come and tell me. I can't do anything to help if I am not aware of it. Will you do that for me?'

Her master was asking her to inform on her friends and family, and, once again, it felt as though Mr Sopwith was testing her loyalty. She hesitated, wondering if she should agree to the request.

'I know this is difficult for you,' he said, 'but you must believe me when I say I only want what is best for my men and their families. If I can't protect them, who can?'

'Yes, sir,' she said, thinking that the poor Lowery girls needed all the protection they could get. 'I'll let you know if anything

## CHAPTER 25

else happens.'

'Thank you, Bella. I knew I could rely on you.'

# Chapter 26

**Allenheads, Northumberland**
**May 1849**

At precisely nine o'clock, the bell rang loudly to herald the start of the school day. Jack watched the excited children file into the new school for the first time while their parents stood outside admiring the building.

He overheard Thomas Sopwith talking to a gentleman; his voice raised so that those around him could easily hear his words. 'The children of Allenheads respond so well to timekeeping, unlike the miners who do not commit to punctuality or to keeping their agreements'.

Jack bristled at the comment but realised that Mr Sopwith had intended to antagonise the striking miners who had accompanied their children to school. He noticed a few of the men looked uncomfortable, sharing furtive glances with one another. Still, none of them gave Mr Sopwith the satisfaction of a reaction.

As he walked home, Jack contemplated the complete hold that Mr Sopwith had over their lives. The miners of Allenheads were indebted to him for the new school. He had sought funding from Mr Beaumont and commissioned it to be built to educate their children. They depended on him for their jobs, homes, and social lives, for Mr Sopwith had commissioned the library and reading room in the village too.

Yes, he thought, the miners had some say in their jobs. There were bargains every quarter where they met with the agents to agree on a price for their work. But if the price they were offered wasn't good enough in the miners' estimation and they walked away from the negotiation, they would be unemployed. So, in reality, what choice did they have?

He reckoned that most of the men who lived in Allenheads and the surrounding villages were utterly reliant on Mr Sopwith and the mining company, WB Lead, and they didn't even realise it. And that brought the strike to mind.

Walking down the road towards Briar Place, Jack felt bitter. The men had been on strike for far longer than they'd expected, and it had been tough. Very tough. His family had suffered sooner than most because they were one of the larger families in the village, and poor Deborah had paid the ultimate price because they had run out of food. His father had been lucky to survive the attempt on his life in the mine, and the whole family was very fortunate that Bella had gone outside that night and opened the back door for them to escape from the smoke-filled house. If she hadn't, Jack had no doubt that they would have suffocated or been seriously injured jumping from an upstairs window. He reckoned that it wouldn't have made much difference if his father had gone back to work or stayed out on strike. Either way, the Lowery family had been destined to suffer.

Jack had heard the men talking lately, and the optimism and fight that was in them at the start of the dispute had dwindled away to nothing. Mr Sopwith had not budged an inch, and there was no indication that he would. It looked like he would win. All of the want and the loss had been for nothing, after all. Jack vowed that he would never agree to another strike again in his life, no matter what the circumstances.

But it wasn't only the strike that had everyone in the village on edge. Constable Heaviside had visited the miners' homes and asked questions about the strike and who had been responsible for bullying the strike-breakers. The investigation had resulted in even more trouble for the Lowerys because everyone thought that it was his father who had reported the incidents to the authorities. Nobody trusted anyone in the village anymore.

After making his enquiries, Constable Heaviside returned to Allenheads Hall, and Bella showed him into her master's study.

'Perhaps you should stay, Bella,' said Mr Sopwith.

After taking their seats, the constable began a lengthy explanation of all the houses he had visited and the men he had questioned.

'And what have you found out about the incidents?'

'Very little, sir.'

'You've been investigating these crimes for two weeks now. What exactly do you know?'

'A few people confirmed what happened to Mr Lowery and his family.'

'Do you have any clue as to who was responsible?' asked Mr Sopwith.

'No, sir. Nobody has given me any names, but I suspect that Nelson Kidd may be involved somehow.'

'Why do you think that?'

## CHAPTER 26

'He's the only one I spoke to who didn't look ashamed or sorry for what had happened to the Lowerys. If anything, he appeared to gloat.'

Mr Sopwith looked disgusted. 'Will you arrest him?' he asked.

'There's no evidence, sir. It's just a hunch. No jury would convict him for gloating.'

'I guess not.'

Bella had never liked Nelson Kidd. He'd always been a bully, but was he capable of trapping Mr Lowery in the mine and leaving him to die? Or of blocking the doors, windows and chimney of his house so that his wife and children would die?

'What evidence do you need to convict him?' she asked the constable.

'A witness. Someone who saw what he did. Or a confession. But he doesn't look like the kind of man who would confess.'

'Do you know if there are any witnesses, Bella?' asked Mr Sopwith.

'I'll ask around and let you know if I find anything out. If Nelson Kidd was responsible, he should be locked up so he can't hurt anyone else.'

'I agree,' said Mr Sopwith. 'May God help you in your search.'

The constable stood up and shook Mr Sopwith's hand. Turning to Bella, he said, 'Please, miss, if you find out anything that could be of use, tell Mr Sopwith, and he'll let me know.'

She smiled at him and nodded.

Bella knew that a miner would never inform on another miner. The constable's enquiries would lead nowhere. She had to do whatever she could to help put the people who did these terrible things behind bars.

On her way home, she called at the Lowerys' house, and Lizzie opened the door.

'Bella! What are you doin' here?'

'I need to speak to you all. Are Jack and your father in?'

'Yes, they are. Come on in.'

Jack rose from his chair when he saw Bella and walked over to her. 'Does your father know you're here?' he asked.

'No, and I hope he doesn't find out or I'll be in trouble.'

'Sit down, Bella,' said Johnny. 'Put the kettle on, Eliza, and make the lass a pot of tea.'

'I'm sorry, love. We've not had many visitors lately,' said Eliza sadly. 'I shouldn't need to be reminded to put the kettle on. I don't know where me manners have gone?' She went into the kitchen, and Bella heard her fill the kettle with water.

'The constable came back to see Mr Sopwith today,' said Bella. 'He thinks he knows who was responsible for what happened to you, but he has no proof. Did any of you hear a voice you recognised or see anybody you could describe?'

The faces looking back at her were blank. Surely, someone must have noticed something, she thought.

'Mr Lowery, when you were in the mine, did you hear the men who set the explosives that caused the rockfall?'

'Aye, I heard them. I think there was two of them.'

'Do you know who they were?'

'Mebbe. Though I couldn't say for sure.'

'If you recognised the voices, you should say so. The men should be locked up for what they did.'

'I have a good idea who was behind it,' said Jack before his father could reply.

Bella looked at him, eyes wide, hoping he would say the same name that the policeman had given Mr Sopwith.

## CHAPTER 26

'When me and Robbie tried to go into the mine, we were stopped by some fellas. Tommy Ritson and Nelson Kidd looked like they would have done anythin' to stop from us goin' in.'

'Is Nelson Kidd the man who lives in the tiny house tucked away behind the pub?' asked Lizzie.

'Aye, he is,' confirmed her father. 'What difference does it make where he lives?'

'Well, if it's him, I think I heard him outside our house the night we were smoked out.'

'Lizzie!' exclaimed Bella, 'If you heard him, that's as good as seeing him.'

'Do you think that will be enough to put him behind bars?' asked Johnny.

'Yes.' Bella smiled back at him. 'With what Jack and Lizzie have just said, I think that would be enough to convict him.'

'That's good 'cos I think it was him I heard in the mine.'

'Thank you,' said Bella. She would tell Mr Sopwith what she had discovered first thing in the morning.

The following Monday, the defeated miners queued outside the mine office, their shoulders slumped and their heads bowed. The strike had failed. After five months without any pay, they were returning to work on the same terms as the previous year. They begrudgingly agreed to their bargains and to work eight hours a day on weekdays.

Jack stood beside his father, aware of the comments directed at him from the other miners, but now that the strike was over, what did it matter that his father had gone back to work a few weeks earlier than the rest of them?

Jack was of the firm opinion that family was family and that family should stick together whatever their differences, unlike his father, he thought, who had thrown him out at the first opportunity. It still troubled him that his father had turned against him so readily.

'Can you see Bill and Frank anywhere?' asked Johnny.

'No, I cannot,' replied Jack, looking around. 'Mr Heslop isn't here either, and a few of the others.'

'They're being daft. What are they goin' to do if they don't come back to work?'

Jack shrugged his shoulders. He was surprised his father was interested in the welfare of Bill and Frank when the two families were not on speaking terms. Only the day before, he'd seen Bill go indoors to avoid contact with his father. If they weren't Bella's kin, Jack wouldn't give a damn about them after the way they had behaved, especially Bill for forbidding Bella from seeing him and stopping them from getting married.

He hoped Bella would be waiting for him after she finished work. He hadn't seen her for a few days and he missed her terribly.

Jack and Johnny paired up with Robbie and his younger brother and agreed on a bargain with Mr Sopwith in the office. Mr Sopwith rewarded the partnership by allowing them to continue to work in the exceptional vein where they'd been working before the New Year, all because Johnny had gone back to work before the end of the strike. The amount he offered them for the ore was lower than the previous year, but they had expected that. Jack was confident that they would still get a decent payout at the end of the quarter. They all shook Mr Sopwith's hand and left the building, their futures secured.

Later that day, Jack climbed the stone wall that surrounded

the grounds of Allenheads Hall and waited for Bella under the shade of an old sycamore tree. He saw Bella walking down the drive and called out to her. Her face lit up when she heard his voice, and she looked around for him. Spotting him under the tree, she ran across the grass to meet him, and they stepped behind the tree, where they couldn't be seen, and melted into each other's arms.

'It's so good to see you,' Jack whispered.

'It's been too long,' Bella looked into his eyes and cupped his face with her hands. 'I hate sneaking around like this.'

'Bella, I promise that I'll marry you on your twenty-first birthday, with or without your father's blessin'.'

'But that's not for another year!' Bella protested.

'I know, love. But if he won't give us his consent, we don't have any choice. We'll have to wait.' Sighing, Jack said, 'God, I hope he changes his mind soon. I want you so much.'

Pushing her up against the tree, he kissed her longingly until they were breathless.

'God, help us,' he said as he closed his eyes and held her close.

The following morning, Jack was standing outside the mine with his father when Robbie and his brother walked over to them.

'What's goin' on?' asked Robbie, looking at the men loitering in the yard. 'Why's nobody gone down yet?'

'Sopwith's asked us all to wait here,' said Jack. 'I think he wants to say a few words.'

The men shifted uncomfortably as they waited for Mr Sopwith to begin his speech. Jack wondered what there was left to say. They'd agreed to his terms. They'd gone back to work. What else did the man want from them?

'Thank you, gentlemen,' Mr Sopwith's voice cut through the chatter. 'Before I begin, is Nelson Kidd here?'

Nelson held up his hand and walked over to his boss.

'Ah, there you are, Mr Kidd. Constable Heaviside would like to have a word with you.' Mr Sopwith pointed to where the constable stood, and Nelson went over to him.

'Mr Kidd,' said the constable sternly, 'I'm arresting you for the attempted murder of John Lowery and his family.' Then he took a set of handcuffs from his pocket and tried to put them on Nelson's wrists, but Nelson stepped back, out of reach.

'It wasn't me!' he exclaimed, backing further away.

A couple of miners standing nearby had heard what the constable said and held Nelson's arms so that he could be cuffed.

The constable thanked the men who had helped him, and then said, 'Come on, Mr Kidd. I'm taking you to the lock-up, and you can tell me your side of the story there.' He led Nelson away from the crowd.

Mr Sopwith resumed his speech to the miners. 'The reason I wish to speak to you this morning is a matter of the utmost importance. Thank you for seeing the error of your ways and returning to work this week. However, the recent behaviour of some men in my employ has been unsatisfactory. Very unsatisfactory, indeed. In fact, I find it utterly deplorable that a small number of you miners encouraged your fellow workers to strike, resulting in abject poverty for some families in this district. The men I'm talking about stood by and watched their fellow miners suffer and did nothing to help them or their families in a very un-Christian manner. I congratulate those of you who ignored the ring leaders and thought for yourselves and came back to work willingly. Your loyalty to the company has not gone unnoticed, and it will be rewarded.'

Holding up a piece of paper, Mr Sopwith continued, 'Here is a list of one hundred names of those responsible for inciting the strike. I will pin this note on the office wall. If your name is absent from this list, then you are to begin work at the mine immediately. However, if your name appears on this list, you are dismissed from your employment with immediate effect and you will vacate your property by the end of the week. I will not tolerate trouble-makers in my mines. Do you hear me?'

The men looked at each other in disbelief and pushed forward, eager to check the list for their names.

'I asked, do you hear me?' shouted Mr Sopwith.

Replies of 'Yes, Mr Sopwith' and 'Aye' were heard from the crowd as the men followed their boss to the office.

After waiting for about ten minutes, Jack was at the front of the queue, and the list was in front of him. He ran his finger down the names, checking twice, before stepping to the side. He nodded at his father, who was waiting on the verge a few yards away.

'We're not on the list.' Jack smiled as he approached his father. 'Robbie and Davey aren't on it either. Thankfully, we've still got our jobs and a decent bargain.'

'What about Bill and Frank? Are their names on it?'

'Aye, Bill and Frank's names are on the list. They've been dismissed.'

Johnny hung his head. Jack understood his father's disappointment. If the Dixon men were no longer employed at the mine, they'd have to move out of their house at Briar Place.

Anxiously, he thought about Bella. What would happen to her if the men in her family were forced to move away to find work?

All day, as Jack shovelled rocks into tubs and drilled shot holes in the rock face, Bella was at the forefront of his mind. He couldn't wait to get out of the mine at finishing time and go to see her. He needed to know what her family intended to do.

# Chapter 27

### Allenheads, Northumberland
### May 1849

'I cannot get a job anywhere! There's none of us can,' said Bill Dixon, standing with his back against the mantle, even though there was no fire burning in the grate. 'And it's not for the want of trying! We've asked at all of the lead mines that Sopwith has nowt to do with, but they'll not take us on. We went to Durham. There's loads of work in the coal mines there, but as soon as they hear our names, they want nothin' to do with us.' Shaking his head, he said, 'This is Sopwith's doin'. He's blackened our names so we cannot get work.'

'What are we goin' to do?' asked Martha, as she folded the clean laundry on the table. 'We cannot stay here if there isn't any work. You said we had to be out of the house by the end of the week.'

'Aye, that's right. I heard Sopwith's taken on thirty men from Alston to replace us,' said Bill sourly. 'No doubt he'll give them our houses as well as our jobs.'

'Is that true?' asked Martha, looking at her husband.

'Aye, Jimmy Lee told us. His brother's a clerk in the office. The Alston lads start on Monday.'

'Hmph! After all the years of hard graft you've given them, and that's the thanks you get.'

'Me and the fellas have been talkin' and we think we should try America.'

'America?' squeaked Martha. 'You've got to be kiddin' me?'

'No, I'm deadly serious. There's plenty of work over there, and no matter how high and mighty Sopwith thinks he is, there's no way his influence will carry that far!'

'I should hope not.'

'Willie Pearson has a cousin who works in a lead mine in Illinois. That's where we'll go.'

'Oh, I don't know, Bill. Aren't we gettin' on a bit for startin' over somewhere new? Everyone we know is here in Allenheads.'

'But that's the point, Martha. They won't be in Allenheads anymore, will they? A lot of them will be goin' with us.'

'Have you said anythin' to Frank and Bella?'

'Frank's all for it. He's excited at the prospect. He thinks it's all a big adventure. And our Bella, well, she'll do what she's told.'

Martha shrugged. She knew that if Bill wanted to go to America, it wouldn't matter what the rest of them wanted. His family would have to go with him. At times, she hated her husband. He was controlling and domineering, and he didn't care about anyone but himself. And Frank was just like him. Her life would have been unbearable without her daughter. She hoped Bella would go with them willingly because she couldn't bear to be parted from her. She'd lost her youngest daughter, Lucy, and as good as lost her best friend, Eliza; she couldn't bear to lose Bella too.

'The passage costs about three pounds per head,' said Bill,

## CHAPTER 27

'and that includes the food. Then, there's the rail fare from Haydon Bridge to Liverpool, and we'll have to get a train to Illinois.'

'For the four of us, that'll be fifteen pounds at the very least! We haven't got that kind of money. We cannot afford to go.'

'Don't you have a bit saved up?' asked Bill.

'I did have a few pounds, but it was spent on food during the strike.'

'We'll have to find the money somehow, love. Look,' said Bill, stepping forward and taking Martha's hands in his, 'we haven't any choice. You said it yourself. We can't stay here without work. I'm hoping our Bella and Frank might have a little put away to help us out. And we'll sell everything we've got 'cos we cannot take it with us - the furniture, the lot.' He waved a hand at everything in the room. 'Those dresses that Sopwith's missus gave Bella must be worth a bit. Why don't you have a sort out and see what you can find?' Bill raised his eyebrows.

Martha fought back her tears and said, 'Alright. I'll go and have a look.'

Bill went to the door, put on his boots, and said sadly, 'I've finally got this garden just how I wanted it. It's taken years to get that soil right, and now someone else will get the benefit of it. I'll have to start all over again somewhere else.' He stepped outside and closed the door.

When she was alone, Martha's tears began to fall. This cottage was her home. She'd come to it as a bride, her three babies had been born there, and she'd expected to spend the rest of her days in it. It had been a wonderful place to live when they were on friendly terms with the Lowerys. She hated being estranged from Eliza; she missed their chats. They had laughed together, cried together, and had always been there for each other.

Martha slowly climbed the stairs and went into Bella's room. She took out the dresses from Bella's wardrobe and laid them on the bed, and she recalled how lovely Bella had looked in them, especially the blue one. Martha had expected that it would be her daughter's wedding dress. But Bill was right; the dresses would fetch a good price at Hexham, and if they needed the money, they would have to be sold.

She felt unsteady on her feet and sat on the chair by the bed. The gold locket that she had tucked away came to mind. That had to be worth something too. She'd kept it hidden for years in case there should ever come a time that she needed a bit of money, and it looked like that time had come. As sad as it was, she knew there was no future for her in Allenheads.

When Bella returned from work that evening, she said, 'You'll never guess what I heard on me way home. There's talk in the village that the Dickinsons and the Ritsons are leaving. They're going to America!'

Her parents didn't look surprised by her news.

'You already knew, didn't you?' she asked.

'Aye, we heard,' said her father. 'They're not the only ones either. There are five families from the village going so far, but I'm sure there'll be more.'

'But why?'

'Isn't it obvious, lass? There's no work for them here, and without work, there's no place to live and no money to live off. There's plenty of work to be had in America. The Irish are goin' in their droves 'cos they cannot make a livin' in Ireland with the potato crops failing year on year.'

## CHAPTER 27

Bella lowered her eyes. She knew that her father was in the same situation as the families who were emigrating, and it suddenly hit her that he too might be thinking about going to America.

'Me and your mother have been talkin',' said her father. 'We've agreed that we should go an' all. There's nowt left for us here.'

'But what about me? I've got me job.'

'Aye, you've got a job,' said her mother, 'but it doesn't give us a roof over our heads or feed us all.'

Bella's voice rose as she said, 'And me and Jack are getting married!'

'Oh no, you're not,' said Bill firmly. 'I've already told you that I'll not allow it. You're comin' to America with us.'

'I won't!' Bella stepped away from her parents. 'You can't make me!'

'Yes, you will, young lady.' Her father stood up and towered above her in a menacing fashion, making Bella even more determined that she would not bend to his will. But her mother's eyes met hers, pleading with her to back down, and Bella's resolve weakened.

'Please, come with us,' said Martha. 'Our Frank's keen to go. And if your father's made up his mind, I'll have to go. We wouldn't want to leave you here on your own.' With tears in her eyes, she added, 'You're me only daughter now.'

'Aw, Mother.' Bella had tears in her eyes too as she thought of her little sister, Lucy, who would always be little in their memories. She went to her mother and hugged her. Her mother clung to her and began to sob loudly.

At that moment, Bella knew that whether she stayed at Allenheads or went to America with her family, her heart would be broken, as would the heart of someone she loved. How could she say goodbye to her mother or Jack, knowing she was unlikely to see them again?

Her mother still clutched her in her arms, but the sobbing had subsided.

'Don't worry, Mother,' said Bella, her eyes brimming with tears. 'I won't leave you.'

Out of the corner of her eye, she saw her father lean back against the fireplace and heard him breathe a sigh of relief.

After the plans had been discussed, Bella went to her room and sat on her bed. She tried to summon up the strength and courage that she would need to tell Jack that she was emigrating to America with her family. After a long while, she went to the Lowerys' door and knocked quietly.

Lizzie opened the door and greeted her warmly.

'I need to see Jack. Is he in?'

'Aye, I'll get him for you.'

Jack came outside and ushered Bella around to the side of the house, where they couldn't be seen or heard. The concern on his face was evident. He was about to put his arm around her, but she stepped away from him.

'What is it? What's wrong?' he asked.

'My family's going to America, and I'm going with them.'

Bella didn't know how she had managed to get those words out, but she had, and with them, she knew that she'd inflicted the most horrific pain on Jack, hurting him deeply. It broke her heart to do that to the man she loved, but what choice did she have? Her mother would never manage the journey to America or to set up a new home without her help, and she would be so miserable with only her father and Frank for company. And that's if she saw much of them, for they would probably spend their evenings out drinking, leaving Martha at home alone.

Bella knew that this wasn't the time to be selfish. She had to deny what she wanted, which was to spend her life with Jack. She had to support her mother. She couldn't bear to think about the lonely existence her mother would suffer in a faraway country without her.

Jack stared at Bella, his mouth open as her words sank in, and then he cried, 'No! You can't go. You can't leave me.'

'I have to. Me mother's going and she needs me.'

'But Bella, I need you. We're goin' to get married. The banns have been read. Everybody knows that we're goin' to get married.' He looked around helplessly, desperately trying to think of a way to make her change her mind, to stay with him and be his wife as they'd planned. 'We could go to Gretna Green tomorrow and get married there. Your father couldn't stop us. And if you're my wife, Bella, he wouldn't be able to take you away from me.'

When Bella didn't answer him, Jack got down on his knees in front of her. 'Please, Bella, don't leave me. What would I do without you?' He put his arms around her and pressed his face against her belly.

'We can't get married, Jack. Not unless you come to America and we wait until I'm twenty-one.'

That thought hung in the air for a moment while Jack considered it. Briefly, Bella's hopes lifted. Would Jack drop everything and go to America with her? But then his eyes met hers, and she could see the desolation in them. She knew what his answer would be.

Jack stood up and took her hands in his. 'I'm so sorry, love. I cannot go. It would be no different over there. Your father wouldn't let us see each other. And with all the trouble me family's goin' through, I need to be here to look after them.'

Bella couldn't help it. Her resolve slipped away, and a tear trickled down her cheek. She felt Jack wipe it away before resting his brow against hers.

His voice broke as he said, 'I'll miss you more than you could ever imagine.'

Her arms went around his body, and they clung together, sobbing, both reluctant to let go, knowing it would be the last time that they would hold each other in their arms.

# Chapter 28

### Allenheads, Northumberland
### May 1849

The next day, Bella walked slowly up the drive to the Hall. The spring in her step had gone, and she felt as though she'd aged twenty years overnight. She didn't want to go to America with her family. She wanted to stay with Jack. Poor Jack! Yesterday, he had begged her to stay with him, and she was sure that he would have done anything in his power to marry her and stop her from leaving. But she couldn't marry him. Not now.

Bella remembered the look in her mother's eyes when she'd asked her to go with them to America. That one look had taken away any choice that she'd had. How could she deny her mother anything? The woman who had given her family everything and had asked for nothing in return, until now. Her mother needed her more than Jack did. There was no doubt in her mind about that.

When she moved away, Jack would forget all about her. He would move on and find himself another wife. Bella was sure of it because he was the kindest, funniest and most attractive man she had ever met. Who wouldn't want to marry Jack?

She stopped outside the kitchen door and dried her eyes on her sleeve before going into the Hall.

'What's the matter with you?' asked Mrs Vickers.

'Is Mrs Sopwith around?'

'She's still in bed. I don't think she'll want to be disturbed.'

'Mr Sopwith?'

'Mr Sopwith's in his study.'

After thanking the cook, Bella went to the master's study and knocked on the door.

'Come in!'

Bella entered the room where Mr Sopwith sat at his desk sketching with a pencil. She wiped her sweaty palms on her skirt and waited for his attention.

'Yes?'

'I've just come to tell you that I can't work here anymore.'

Looking up at her, he said, 'Of course, I should have expected as much. I heard the banns being read out in church. Who is it that you're marrying?'

Bella stood in front of him, her eyes wide like a startled deer, and then she rushed out of the room. She ran to the kitchen where Mrs Vickers was tending the oven and sat heavily on a chair.

'By! What's got into you today?' asked Mrs Vickers, her voice full of concern.

The master appeared in the doorway.

'Sir, is there somethin' you want?' asked the cook.

'Bella seemed upset,' replied Mr Sopwith. 'I just wondered, was it something I said?'

Bella turned to face him. 'I'm not getting married, Mr Sopwith. I'm going to America with me family.'

'Oh, I see.' Bella thought he looked sad at the news. 'It's

## CHAPTER 28

none of my business, but couldn't your marriage take place as planned, and then you could stay in Allenheads with your husband?'

'Me mother couldn't manage over there without me. Me father and Frank would be of no use to her. So, you see, I don't have any choice in the matter. I have to go with them.'

'We'll be very sorry to lose you, Bella. When will you finish?'

'I'll work the day out.'

'Come to my study before you leave. I'll write a reference for you and settle your wages.'

'Thank you, sir,' said Bella.

Mr Sopwith nodded and turned away.

Mrs Vickers went over to Bella and hugged her, covering her black dress in flour.

'You poor, darlin'. I don't know how you can leave that lad of yours. It's obvious he worships you.'

'It's me mother. It would break her heart if I stayed. She's already lost one daughter.'

'Your mother's lived her life. Now, it's time for you to live yours, lass.'

'I wish it was that simple.'

'It might not seem simple to you, but really, it is. That lad loves you. You love him. You should be together, and that's all there is to it.'

'But we cannot.' Tears brimmed in her eyes, threatening to spill over.

'Well, that's your choice, hinny. I might not agree with what you decide to do, but I wish you all the very best. I'll miss you. You've been good company for me these past few years.'

'Thank you, Mrs Vickers. I'll miss you an' all.'

Sniffing loudly, Bella grabbed the furniture polish and cloth and began her work.

When Bella returned home that afternoon, two men stood outside their door at Briar Place.

'Excuse me,' she said as she attempted to pass them to enter the house.

'I'm sorry, miss,' said the older man. 'But I can't let you in.'

'But why? I live here.'

'Not anymore, you don't. Your family have to move out now. The house is needed for the new miners that are comin'.'

Martha came to the door, her face stony and her head held high. She carried two blankets, one over each shoulder. Bella guessed that they were filled with clothes and bedding.

'Where will we stay, Mother?' she asked.

'The Pearsons have offered us their barn for a few days.'

Bella was shocked. 'We're goin' to sleep in a farmyard? But Mother-'

'Beggars can't be choosers, Bella. At least we'll have a roof over our heads. That's more than some folks have.'

Bella wished she hadn't spoken out about the barn. It was good of Mr Pearson to let them stay on his property.

'I'm sorry,' she said. 'What shall I take?'

Martha handed the blankets that she held to her daughter and went back inside to gather more of their belongings. The bailiffs stood and watched the proceedings with disinterest.

Bella noticed the curtains twitch in the Lowerys' window, and she was embarrassed that someone was watching her family being evicted from the only house that she'd ever called home.

Within a few minutes, her father and brother came out of the house, carrying what they would need and anything of

## CHAPTER 28

value left that they could sell before they set off for America. Most items had already been sold.

The older bailiff closed the door from the outside and put his hand out for the key, which Bill gave to him, with a sour expression on his face.

'You disgust me,' said Bill, 'Puttin' honest hard-workin' people out on the street. How can you sleep at night?'

'I'm just followin' orders, and I sleep fine.'

The younger bailiff moved closer when he sensed that his colleague might be in danger, ready to step between him and Bill if necessary.

'Come on, Bill,' said Martha. 'Let's go.'

Begrudgingly, Bill turned away and began to walk briskly down the road, his anger apparent in his heavy stride. The family picked up their things and followed him.

Just days later, Bella and her family thanked Mr and Mrs Pearson for their hospitality and made their way to the village, carrying only what they needed for the journey. Sixty people were leaving Allenheads that day to begin the long trip to America, and they assembled around an array of carts and traps parked in front of the village inn. The atmosphere was tense and emotional.

Bella leaned against a cart and waited. Excited children ran around the carts, weaving in and out between them. At one time, she would have smiled at their antics. A young woman cried unashamedly in her sister's arms until her new husband dragged her away and helped her onto a trap. An older man shook hands with a young man and then kissed the cheeks of the man's wife and children, and Bella guessed that he was saying farewell to his son or daughter and his grandchildren, and she idly wondered if he would ever see them again. She doubted that he would.

'Did you hear about *The Spencer?*' she heard one man ask another.

'What's *The Spencer?*' came the reply.

'A ship. I read about it in the paper. It was sailin' from America to Liverpool, but it ran aground on a Scottish island a few days ago. The passengers were all rescued. That was an unusual turn of events though. Most often, they perish at sea.'

'Don't talk to me about shipwrecks, will you? I'm worried enough about the crossing already.'

'Aye, well, you've every right to be. Do you know how many die on those crossings?'

Bella couldn't imagine a worse thing to say to someone who was about to cross the Atlantic and wondered how the man could be so thoughtless.

Although she was aware of the many emotions surrounding her, Bella felt nothing. Ever since she'd told Jack that she was leaving, she'd felt nothing. Nothing at all. It was as if all of her emotions had been used up that day, and there was nothing left for her to feel.

The travellers moved towards the conveyances for the first leg of the journey. Bella was crammed into a cart with her family and the Ritsons. She had seen a map, and she could visualise the route in her mind. They would travel to the railway station at Haydon Bridge and take a train to Newcastle, where they would change trains and head for Liverpool. There, a ship would be waiting at the docks to take them to America.

The horses and carts formed a procession as they set off through the village. Most house doors stood wide open, the villagers standing on the road outside, watching their friends and relatives leave. Most waved and wished them luck, but some just stood there as though they couldn't believe that they were witnessing a mass exodus from the village of Allenheads.

Bella's eyes searched for a last glimpse of Jack as they passed Briar Place. His sisters were lined up outside the house, waving and smiling at everybody, but Jack was not there. She noticed that her family home was still unoccupied. There had been no need for her family to sleep rough in a barn after all, and she knew that she should feel anger or bitterness at their mistreatment but she felt nothing.

A little further down the road, a movement on the hillside made Bella look up, and there he was, standing alone, looking down at her, his face expressionless.

She longed to be there with him, standing by his side, holding his hand, kissing his lips, being held in his arms, and it suddenly struck her that she would never see his smile again, never hear his laugh, never feel his touch, and she would never hear his voice telling her that he loved her. How could she live without Jack?

# Chapter 29

**Allenheads, Northumberland
May 1849**

On the makeshift bed in the corner of the front room, Jack sat with his head down, hiding his silent tears. Despite his family's best efforts to cheer him up and draw him into their conversations, he hadn't spoken to anyone since Bella had left that morning. Even the younger girls in the house were subdued because their big brother was upset.

Upset. That was the word his mother had used, but it was an understatement, thought Jack. His heart was broken, shattered into a thousand tiny pieces. Already, he missed Bella more than he could ever express in words, for what were words when his beautiful Bella was gone?

He wished he had never gone up the hill to watch her leave. That picture of her seated on the back of a cart, that expression of love and anguish and pain when their eyes met, would be ingrained in his mind and haunt him forever.

Desperately, he tried to remember her face that day when they'd gone to see the vicar and arranged their wedding. She had been glowing then, so happy, and he grew frustrated that the image wouldn't come back to him.

## CHAPTER 29

Tomorrow would be the eighteenth of May. The day that they should have become man and wife and started the rest of their lives together and the night that he would have finally bedded her. He had longed to make her his for so long and he still did. It would never happen now. A small moan escaped from his throat.

Mary, sensing Jack's despair, wandered over to him, sat on his lap, and wrapped her tiny arms around him. Instinctively, Jack hugged the small child to him for comfort, and they sat together for the longest time while the family worked and ate and played around them.

The longer he sat there, the more Jack realised that life would go on in the same fashion at Briar Place whether or not he was there. Now that the dispute was over and the men had settled back into work, there had been little trouble. The constable's questions had caused problems for a week or two because his father had been blamed for getting them involved, but since Nelson Kidd's arrest, their lives at Allenheads had returned to some kind of normality. He had felt so guilty for not being there to help them when they'd needed him, but did they need him now? Surely, his father could watch over them; his wife and children were his responsibility after all.

If he stayed at Allenheads, Jack envisaged endless days, months, and years of working at the mine, coming home for his tea, and then wandering aimlessly on summer evenings, alone. Perhaps in the winter, he'd end up at the village inn, night after night, as his father and Bill had done for most of their lives. The prospect was bleak.

He wondered if he would spend the rest of his life alone. There was no way that he could ever love another woman as much as he loved Bella, but he supposed marriage might not be out of the question or a family of his own. Almost imperceptibly, he shook his head. That wouldn't be fair on the lass he chose or on himself, for it would deprive them both of the love and happiness they deserved.

There was only one thing that would ever make him happy and that was spending the rest of his life with Bella, and there was only one way that that could happen.

Mary had fallen asleep on Jack's knee. To the surprise and delight of his family, he lifted his sister as he stood up and carried her upstairs to bed. When he came back down, Jack stood against the stair rail and faced his parents.

'I'm goin' after her. I cannot stay here without her.' His voice breaking, he said, 'Me life would be unbearable.'

His father stood up, knocking an empty mug off the table in his haste. 'You cannot go! How will we manage?'

'I can go, Father, and I'm goin' to go.'

'You selfish -'

'Johnny,' Eliza said firmly, 'sit yourself down. It's our Jack's decision to make.'

'Hmph!' Johnny sat down and looked daggers at his wife. 'You always side with him.'

Eliza rose shakily to her feet and looked at her firstborn with glassy eyes. 'I can see that you've made up your mind, Jack. You have to do what you think is right, and if that means goin' after Bella, then that's what you should do.'

Lizzie and the girls looked desolate as their older brother gathered together his few belongings, put on his jacket and cap, and walked out of the door without saying a word to them.

Johnny picked up his cap and headed towards the door.

Eliza put her hand on her husband's arm and said, 'Let him

## CHAPTER 29

go.'

He shook his arm free and walked to the door. 'I wasn't goin' after him, woman. I'm goin' out for a drink. Don't bother waitin' up for me 'cos I might be late.'

Eliza looked at her daughters and said, 'Don't just sit there. It's time to get up that wooden hill. Lizzie, make sure that they pray for our Jack tonight. We should all pray for God to help him find Bella in Liverpool because if he doesn't catch up with her before she gets on that ship, he's got little chance of findin' her in America.'

'We will, Mother. I'll come back down after I've tucked the lasses in.'

'Thank you. I'd like that.'

As Lizzie followed the girls upstairs, she glanced down at her mother. Eliza sat rigidly on her chair, and as soon as she thought she was alone, she wrapped her arms around herself, and her body began to shake. Lizzie knew how much strength it had taken for her mother to stand up to her husband and to tell Jack to leave and follow his heart. She had done what she thought was right by her son, but she was clearly devastated that she might never see Jack again.

Jack heard the rhythmic hoof beats of a horse drawing near. He moved to the edge of the road but kept up his pace. He'd walked about a mile since he'd left Allenheads, and he had fourteen more to go before he'd get to Haydon Bridge. The horse slowed to a walk and pulled up alongside him, and Jack heard a voice he knew well.

'I thought that was you,' said Robbie. 'Where are you off to in such a hurry?'

'Haydon Bridge. To the station.'

'Jump up. I can give you a ride as far as Allendale.'

Jack didn't hesitate. He jumped up onto the cart and sat beside his friend. 'Thanks,' he said as the horse resumed its trot and the cart lurched forward.

'So, you've decided to go an' all, have you?' asked Robbie, a little sulkily.

Jack was quiet. He wasn't sure how to answer that question. Ideally, he wanted to bring Bella home to Allenheads, but if she wouldn't come back, then he'd go to America with her. That's if he could find her. What if he couldn't find her? Would he come home without her?

'Who'll take your place at work?' asked Robbie.

'You'll find someone to take me place. There's always men wantin' jobs.'

'Were you goin' to leave without tellin' me? Does your father know that you're goin'?' Robbie fired questions at Jack in quick succession.

Jack looked down at his fidgeting hands and wiped his palms on his trousers. He was starting to regret taking Robbie up on his offer of a ride. He could have done without an inquisition.

'Look, I'm sorry, Robbie. I know I'm lettin' a lot of people down by leavin' like this, but I couldn't stay. I just couldn't. Not without Bella.'

'Aye, I cannot say I blame you. I don't know why you didn't just marry the lass, and then she could have stayed here with you. Why didn't you? Why did you let her go with her parents?'

'Her father wouldn't allow us to marry, and she didn't think her mother would manage without her over there.'

'Oh! Is there somethin' the matter with Mrs Dixon?'

'No, Robbie. She's gettin' on a bit, and she's set in her ways,

## CHAPTER 29

that's all.'

Jack remembered the last time that Robbie had given him a ride to Allendale. It had been on New Year's Eve, and he'd sat in the back of the cart with his arm around Bella, her head resting on his shoulder. He wished he could go back to the time before the strike, before his father had become a blackleg, and before the feud with the Dixons. It was so painful not knowing if he would ever hold Bella in his arms again. He had to believe that one day he would and that she would be his wife.

Jack couldn't bear to talk about Bella anymore, so he deflected the conversation by asking, 'How come you're goin' to Allendale this late in the day? It'll be dark before you get back.'

'I'm takin' some timber down for me uncle. I'll stay there tonight, at his place, have a drink with him and me cousins, and then I'll head back first thing in the mornin'.' To Jack's relief, Robbie continued to talk about his uncle's family and business until they reached the town.

Robbie stopped the horse at the marketplace, and Jack jumped down from the cart.

'Thanks, Robbie.' Jack shook his friend's hand firmly.

'I hope you find her,' said Robbie sincerely. 'But if you don't, you will come back, won't you? It'll not be the same without you.'

Jack nodded. He picked up his small bundle and set off at a brisk walk towards Haydon Bridge, still seven miles away. He was determined to catch the last train to Newcastle.

An hour and a half later, Jack walked into the station and headed directly for the ticket office.

'Third-class to Newcastle, please,' he said, pulling a handful of coins from his pocket.

'That'll be three shillings and ninepence, sir.'

Jack hesitated, looking at the coins in his hand. After he paid for the ticket, he would be left with a just couple of threepenny bits. How could he get to Liverpool with sixpence? He rued the fact that there hadn't been a proper payday since he'd gone back to work. The subsistence money he'd been given was just to tide him over, and that was all he had left. But he couldn't have waited until the beginning of July to collect his pay before following Bella. Who knows where she would be by then? But he would have to manage somehow because he had to find Bella before her ship left the docks.

'The train's due in a couple of minutes. Are you goin' or are you stayin', lad?'

'I'm goin'.'

Jack gave the man the fare and took the ticket. He could hear the train approaching the station, and it soon appeared in a cloud of smoke, hissing loudly as the driver brought the engine to a stop. Jack found the third-class carriage and climbed aboard. He was grateful to Robbie for giving him a lift because, without it, he would have missed the last train.

When he arrived at Newcastle-upon-Tyne, Jack stepped out of the carriage onto the busy platform. He picked up a train timetable outside the ticket office and discovered that the next train to Liverpool was the sleeper train, leaving at ten o'clock that evening. He checked the station clock and saw that he only had thirty minutes to wait, so he found a seat and watched the hustle and bustle of the station. He still had no idea how he would get onto the sleeper train to Liverpool without a ticket because he couldn't afford to buy one.

A well-dressed gentleman and his wife walked onto the

platform, followed by a man who carried their luggage. Jack watched as the man went outside several times, returning with more trunks. Eventually, the servant bade his employer farewell and left.

Jack looked more closely at the gentleman. He recognised him. It was Mr Armstrong, the man who'd built the hydraulic engine for the mine. A plan suddenly sprang to Jack's mind.

When the train was ready to be boarded, Mr Armstrong motioned to a boy and pointed out that their luggage needed to be loaded onto the train. He took his wife by the arm and led her to the first-class carriage.

Jack stood beside Mr Armstrong's pile of trunks and bags. When the boy returned with a porter, Jack said, 'Mr Armstrong is very particular about his things. He asked me to make sure that his luggage was loaded safely onto the train and that nothing was left behind. He said I was to travel with it so nobody can interfere with it on the journey.'

'Right, you are,' said the man, who began to carefully lift the bags and trunks into a carriage reserved solely for the luggage of first-class passengers. Jack climbed up and nodded to the porter when the last item was loaded.

He heard someone ask, 'Who's that you've let in there?'

Jack peeked out of the door and saw the guard standing beside the porter.

'It's alright, Jim,' said the porter. 'He's one of Mr Armstrong's men.'

As the train chugged out of the station, Jack smiled to himself. He'd managed to get a free ride to Liverpool. He sat on the floor with his back against a trunk and relaxed, knowing that he should try to sleep. Tomorrow, he had to find Bella.

# Chapter 30

**Liverpool
May 1849**

The sound of the carriage door being pulled open woke Jack.

'Oi! What are you doing in here?' asked a porter in a gruff voice.

'I work for Mr Armstrong, an important gentleman from Newcastle. He asked me to travel with his luggage to ensure its safety.' Gesturing to the trucks and bags behind him, Jack said, 'All of these are his. Please be very careful with them.' And then he climbed down from the train and stood on the platform, appearing to wait for the bags, but as soon as the porter went inside the carriage, Jack ran out of the station and onto a wide street.

Even this early in the morning, the road was crowded with horses pulling carriages and carts. Everywhere he looked, people walked, he presumed on their way to work. Hawkers stood in the street selling their goods alongside newspaper sellers and there were carts laden with food. Jack's stomach growled. He hadn't eaten the day before; he'd been too distraught at Bella's leaving to stomach anything. A woman was selling bread from a small cart on the roadside, and he

## CHAPTER 30

asked her, 'How much for a small loaf?'

'For you, love, tuppence.'

He gave her a threepenny coin, and she handed him a loaf and his change.

'Thanks,' he said, smiling at her.

He sat on a wall and ate some of the bread, wondering where Bella and her family would have gone after leaving the station.

Not wanting to linger any longer than necessary, he tucked the rest of the loaf into his jacket pocket and decided to head towards the port. Seagulls screeched overhead, and Jack wrinkled his nose at the strong smell of fish and saltwater. He found the office of a large shipping company and went inside.

'Morning!' said Jack to a young clerk seated behind a large desk. 'I'm looking for me friends. They came to Liverpool yesterday, and they're going to America. I wonder if you know when they might be sailing?'

'What's their name?'

'Dixon.'

The clerk searched a passenger list in an open ledger, looking for the name Dixon.

'There's a load of them travelling together.' said Jack. 'About sixty. The other names are Ritson, Kidd, Pearson, Taylor, Dickinson, and a few more.'

'I have a Dixon here. Family of four booked on *The Guy Mannering*. She left port first thing this morning, headed for New York.'

A family of four. Bill, Martha, Bella, and Frank. He was too late. He'd missed her.

'They've gone already?' asked Jack in despair.

'Yes, the ship sailed at first light. Is there anything else I can do for you?'

'No, thank you.'

Jack left the office and found a seat outside. He sat on the wooden bench for over an hour, idly watching a ship being loaded with supplies in preparation for its next journey across the ocean. He wondered what he should do now. Should he return home, or should he follow Bella to America and search for her there? He knew that the people from Allenheads intended to go to the lead mines in Illinois. It might take him a while, but he was confident that he'd be able to track her down.

He went back into the shipping office, and the clerk showed no surprise at seeing him again.

'Yes, sir?'

'How much would it cost for me to go to America?' asked Jack.

'Two pounds and fifteen shillings. That's for a bunk in steerage, and it includes three meals a day. There's a ship sailing on Friday. Would you like to purchase a ticket?'

Jack had only four pence to his name. He shook his head and went outside, returning to the bench that he'd just vacated. He sat forward, his elbows on his knees and his head in his hands, deep in thought. He wondered if he should go home, collect his pay and then return when he had the fare but he couldn't afford to travel home. He'd been lucky to stow away on the train to Liverpool, but he doubted that he'd get away with that trick again. He could walk home, but he reckoned that would take about a week and he didn't have enough money to buy food for the journey.

He was desperate to cross the ocean as soon as possible because the sooner he got to America, the sooner he'd find Bella. But whatever he chose to do, he needed money, and to

## CHAPTER 30

earn money, he had to find work.

Jack walked down to the Albert dock and was mesmerised by the tall ships moored to the wharves and the vast, red-brick warehouses at the water's edge. The place was full of men, sitting and standing, wherever there was space. Jack wandered around and asked anyone who looked like a boss if they had any work for him. After a while, he realised it wouldn't be as easy as he'd thought to get a job in Liverpool. The hundreds of men hanging around the docks were all waiting for work. Talking to them, Jack learned that even the experienced dock workers were lucky to get three days of work each week.

A well-dressed man approached Jack and looked him up and down. 'You're young and strong. I need a lumper. Are you interested?'

'I don't know. What does a lumper do?' asked Jack, causing the old-timers to laugh loudly.

'You'll be carrying cargo on and off ships. The pay's seven shillings a week, if you last that long. Do you want the job?'

Seven shillings a week wasn't a great wage. He quickly calculated that he'd have to work eight weeks before he could pay the passage to America, and that was without spending anything on food or board. He needed to eat, but did he need lodgings? At this time of year, it was warm enough at night, and he reckoned he could cope with living outdoors for a few months if it meant that he'd find Bella sooner.

'If he doesn't want it, I'll take it!' shouted an elderly man. 'I haven't had any work for weeks!'

'I'll take it,' said Jack. 'When do I start?'

Again, the men around him howled with laughter.

'Right now!' replied his boss. 'Follow me.' As they walked

to a ship that had just docked, he said, 'I'm Mr Walker. Your name, son?'

'Jack Lowery.'

'You must be new around here, Lowery?'

'Aye, I just got here this mornin'.'

They stopped next to the large ship, and Mr Walker motioned for a tall, lean man to come over. When he joined them, Mr Walker said, 'Walsh, this is Lowery.'

Jack nodded, and Walsh gave him a cheery smile.

'The cargo needs to be offloaded from this ship before six o'clock,' said Mr Walker. 'Follow Walsh. Copy what he does. Alright?'

'Thank you, Mr Walker. I won't let you down.'

Jack followed Walsh onto the ship and into the hold, where there were hundreds of canvas bundles and an overpowering pungent smell.

Walsh groaned as he picked up a bundle. Jack picked up a bundle too, and he was shocked by its weight. He guessed they must be around a hundredweight.

'What are these?' Jack asked Walsh as they carried them off the ship.

'Tobacco.'

He followed Walsh into a large warehouse, passing porters with sets of scales at intervals, and put down the bundle next to Walsh's.

'One down, quite a few more to go.' Walsh laughed.

The two men continued to work, going backwards and forwards carrying bundles of tobacco until lunchtime.

'We have twenty minutes,' said Walsh. 'Are you coming for a pint?'

'No, thanks. I don't drink.'

## CHAPTER 30

'A lumper that doesn't drink! I've never heard of such a thing.' Laughing, Walsh walked away.

Jack found a public water fountain and drank his fill of water before finding somewhere quiet to sit and eat some more of his bread.

When Walsh returned to the dock, the men continued with their work until the last bundle of tobacco had been removed from the ship, well before the six o'clock deadline.

Mr Walker came back to check on their progress and was astonished that they'd finished with so much time to spare.

'Good job! You've worked well together today. I want you both back here tomorrow morning at six.' Without waiting for a reply, Mr Walker turned on his heel and walked away.

'Don't suppose you've changed your mind about drinking yet, have you?' asked Walsh, chuckling.

'No, thanks. I couldn't afford to even if I had.'

'That bad?' said Walsh. 'Come on. I'm buying. It's the least I can do after your first day on the job.'

Jack was used to hard work, but he felt exhausted. Having a cold pint and some friendly company sounded appealing.

'Thanks, Walsh. I'll take you up on that.'

Walsh slapped Jack on the shoulder, 'Come on. The boozer's this way.'

# Chapter 31

**Allenheads, Northumberland
June 1849**

Four weeks had passed since Jack left Allenheads and there had been no word from him. Lizzie thought he must be aboard a ship crossing the Atlantic, on his way to America, or else he would have written to tell them his news. She wondered if he had caught up with Bella and they were travelling together or if he had yet to find her.

Eliza had hardly spoken a word since the night Jack walked out of the door. His leaving had affected her mother even more than Lizzie had realised.

Lizzie sat by her mother's bed and held her hand, knowing that she was unlikely to get out of it again. She was sleeping peacefully. She slept most of the time now. Lizzie wondered how much longer she could survive without eating. Although there was plenty of food in the house now, her mother simply refused to eat.

It was as if she had made up her mind that she'd had enough, that she was tired of living and didn't want to carry on anymore, thought Lizzie. Life had been hard for them all that year, with the hardships they'd endured during the strike,

## CHAPTER 31

falling out with the Dixons, Deborah's death, the shame of having a blackleg in the family, and then Jack leaving home. There was only so much that anyone could bear, and losing her beloved son had been the final straw for Eliza.

She had waited for a letter, day after day, but none came. After a fortnight had passed, Eliza stopped waiting for the postman. Lizzie assumed that her mother had accepted that Jack had sailed to America and left his family for good. She knew of many people who had emigrated to America, Canada, New Zealand and Australia and none of them had ever been seen again. Lizzie missed Jack too. She longed for her brother's return but did not expect it.

She yawned. As well as caring for her mother, Lizzie cooked and cleaned the house, but she enjoyed being busy and she loved her family, so the work didn't seem so hard. Still, she was grateful for Hannah's help looking after their younger sisters.

When Lizzie heard her father come home from work, she went downstairs.

'How is she?' asked Johnny as he went into the kitchen to wash the dust off his hands and face.

'Just the same,' she replied. 'How was work?'

Johnny picked up the towel and dried himself. 'Just the same.' Then he shook his head, 'No, it's not. We do the same thing every day, clearing, drilling, and blasting, but it's not the same. It hasn't been the same since the strike. It's all changed. It was the men that made it a good place to work, you know. There's no laughin' and carryin' on like there used to be. The lads are too frightened of losin' their jobs now. They hardly dare say a word 'cos they don't know who to trust.'

'That strike has a lot to answer for,' said Lizzie bitterly.

'Aye, lass, it has. Before the strike, there wasn't a day that I worked without Bill by me side. It's strange him not being there. It's like I've lost a part of meself.'

Sensing her father's melancholy, Lizzie changed the subject. 'I got some beef bones this morning and made a pan of broth. It'll be tasty with a bit of bread.'

'Your mother always said you were a godsend, and by, she was right!'

'Aw, Father. Give over.'

Lizzie served out the meal and went to fetch the girls inside for their tea.

The following day, after her father left for work, Lizzie took her mother a cup of tea. Eliza was awake, and Lizzie propped a pillow behind her back to make her comfortable.

'I'm sorry, Lizzie,' said her mother. 'I'm so sorry for everythin'.'

'Don't be silly. What have you got to be sorry for?'

'It's my fault that Jack left.'

'Jack would have gone no matter what you'd said. He was determined to find Bella.'

'If your father hadn't treated him so badly, he might have stayed. He loves you girls, but he's always resented Jack.'

'They haven't been gettin' on well since the strike, but before then, they were alright.'

'No, love. They weren't.'

Lizzie looked perplexed. She tried to recall what her father's relationship had been like with Jack before the strike.

Taking Lizzie's hand, Eliza said, 'I know I'm not much longer for this world, and there's somethin' I need to get off me chest before I go. I should have told Jack this, but I'll not get the

## CHAPTER 31

chance now.'

Eliza closed her eyes for a moment and sighed, and Lizzie wondered if she was falling asleep, but her eyes opened, and she gripped Lizzie's hand more firmly.

'Your father would never say anythin' about it, so I must.'

'What is it?' asked Lizzie.

'It's about Jack. Jack isn't your father's son.'

Lizzie's eyes widened, and she felt her mother squeeze her hand. If Jack wasn't her father's son, that meant he was her half-brother. For some reason, that didn't come as a shock to her. Jack had always been different. He was the only one in the family who had black hair; the others had red or brown. He was keener to learn than the rest of them, and he had been an exceptional scholar. Jack had opinions on everything and a confidence about him that seemed at odds with the family. Yes, what her mother said made sense.

'Lizzie, please don't think badly of me. Years ago, I loved a man, a wonderful man, but he…he died before I could tell him that I was expectin' his child.' Eliza's eyes were wet with tears, but she carried on, eager to get her secret out. 'Your father knew I was carryin' another man's child, but he stepped up and told everybody that the baby was his, and he has done ever since.'

'And Jack doesn't know?'

'No. Just your father and me, and now you. Promise me; don't tell Jack about this while your father is alive. It would destroy Johnny. He's tried his hardest to love Jack as much as the rest of you, but he couldn't. Every time he looked at Jack, he saw Jack's father.'

'Who was he? His real father.'

Eliza swallowed and paused before she whispered, 'That, I

would rather not say. All Jack needs to know is that he was a good man and that I loved him dearly. He looked so much like my dear Jack.'

'Don't you think Jack should know who his father was?'

'I've given this a lot of thought, love, and some things are better forgotten,' said Eliza before closing her eyes and drifting off to sleep.

Lizzie sat with her mother and wondered why she was not shocked, or even surprised, by her mother's confession. She wished her mother had told her who Jack's father was; she thought her brother had a right to know. But would she ever have the opportunity to tell him?

# Chapter 32

**Liverpool**
**June 1849**

Jack continued to lump cargo from ships to the docks, working alongside Walsh. Everything was going according to plan. Mr Walker had been as good as his word and paid him seven shillings at the end of each week, and he'd found a quiet place to sleep at night. The local cemetery. Very few people went there after dark, and as yet, nobody had seen him sleeping behind the snowberry bushes. All he needed to do was continue to work until he saved up enough money to pay for his passage to America.

One evening, after a tough day unloading bags of corn, Jack was ravenous by the time six o'clock came around. After parting with Walsh, he went out onto the streets near the dock to find something to eat. He spotted a street vendor selling warm pies, and they smelled delicious. His mouth watered. He strode over to the cart and bought a large meat pie, which he carried in his hand until he found a bench further along the road where he could sit and eat it.

He quickly devoured his meal and then lingered there, watching the comings and goings in the town. He was in no particular hurry. He had nothing to do until dusk when he would make his way to the cemetery for the night. In the distance, something caught his eye. A young man walked along the edge of the road, and for some reason, Jack was drawn to him. His eyes returned to the distant figure, and then the reason that this particular person had caught his attention became clear. Jack knew the man. He was Frank Dixon, Bella's brother. But Frank was supposed to leave for America a month ago. What was he doing in Liverpool? Jack's mind worked overtime. If Frank was still in the town, could Bella be there too? His heart soared at the possibility that she may be close by and that they may not be a vast ocean between them after all.

Jack stood up and walked towards the place where he'd seen Frank, and when he reached it, he looked around in all directions to see which way he'd gone. He spotted Frank walking up Hanover Street and followed him, hoping that he might lead him to Bella.

Staying a safe distance behind, so Frank wouldn't see him, Jack walked through the narrow, crowded streets, keeping Frank in sight. Frank turned off the road and disappeared into a courtyard. Jack ran the rest of the way to catch up, desperate to see where he was going. As he turned the corner, Jack saw a door close and realised that must be where Frank had gone.

He surveyed the area. Scruffy children ran around the courtyard in bare feet. Washing hung wherever there was space for it. Most of the house windows were open, and Jack could hear a baby crying, a couple rowing, and a woman giving birth. A putrid stench rose from the shared netties, which were teeming with flies. He had never seen anywhere like this in his life. Could the Dixons be living in this slum? Or had Frank decided not to travel to America with his family? Maybe he'd stayed in Liverpool and was boarding in cheap digs until he found a place of his own?

Pondering the situation, Jack stood at the street corner, watching the house for about an hour before the door opened and Frank stepped out. He walked towards Jack with his head down and jumped when Jack said, 'How do, Frank! Fancy seein' you here.'

'Jack!' Frank looked him up and down in disbelief. 'What are you doin' here?'

'I'm lookin' for Bella.'

An expression crossed Frank's face that Jack couldn't fathom.

'Is she here?' asked Jack.

'Aye, we're all stayin' here, just for a bit. Mother took bad when we got to Liverpool, and they wouldn't let her on the ship in case she was infectious. We're goin' when she gets better.'

'Would you tell Bella that I'm here?'

'Now, hold on, Jack. You know me father would go crazy if he knew you were here for our Bella. He forbid the match. I cannot get in the middle of all that. I'm sorry.'

Frank marched away, shaking his head.

Jack walked to the cemetery and lay down in his temporary shelter between the bushes and the high stone wall and wondered what he should do. But he was so tired, sleep came before he managed to finalise a plan.

The following day, Jack took a few pieces of white gravel from one of the graves, telling himself that nobody would miss a handful. He began work at six o'clock, and for the first time since he'd started at the docks, he was desperate for the twelve-hour shift to finish. The day dragged, and he kept glancing at the dockers' clock on the Victoria Tower. Eventually, the hands turned to six o'clock and, despite labouring all day, Jack set off at a run.

He returned to the Dixons' lodgings and watched the house. There were no signs of life, so he took a piece of gravel from his pocket and threw it at the upstairs window. An elderly lady looked out and said, 'What do you want?'

'I'm lookin' for Bella Dixon.'

'I don't know her.' The lady pulled down the sash window, and that was the end of their conversation.

Taking another piece of gravel, he tossed it at the ground floor window. A small boy came to the opening and stared at him.

'Hello,' said Jack. 'Do you know Bella?'

The boy shook his head.

'Thank you.'

There was a lower window to a basement room. Jack threw a piece of gravel at the glass and was surprised when Bella's shocked face looked up at him through the window. She quickly disappeared from view, and seconds later, the door opened, and Bella came flying out of the building, running down the steps towards Jack. He held open his arms, and she ran into his embrace.

'Jack!' she said. 'You came!'

'Thank God, I've found you,' he said into her hair. 'I missed you so much.'

'I love you,' she said with sincerity. 'It's so good to see you.'

When they parted, there were tears in Bella's eyes.

## CHAPTER 32

Noticing that they were being watched from most of the windows in the courtyard, Jack took her hand and said, 'Come on, let's go somewhere quieter.'

They walked out onto the street, where they were not overlooked by the courtyard windows, but some of the children peered around the corner to see where they had gone and stood and watched them.

'What are you doing here, Jack?'

'I'd have thought that was obvious. I came to find you.'

'But why?'

'After you'd gone, I knew I couldn't live without you. Whatever happens, wherever we go, we have to be together.'

'Oh, Jack!' Bella put her arms around him. 'I can't believe you're really here.' They stood holding each other in silence for a few minutes.

'How's your mother doin'?'

Puzzled, Bella asked, 'How do you know me mother's not well?'

'Frank told us.'

'Our Frank knew you were here, and he didn't tell me! That little-'

'He didn't want to get involved, Bella. He's frightened of your father.'

'Aye, and I don't blame him. Me father scares me sometimes.'

'Your mother?'

Bella looked up at him and said, 'I think she's improving, but it's taking time. Father and Frank are out at work. Do you want to come in and see her?'

'I don't know, Bella. How do you think she'll feel about seein' me? Even though we're miles away from Allenheads, I'm still the son of a blackleg.'

'Me mother has nothing against you, Jack. She never has had. It's just me father. I think she'd be glad to see someone from back home, to be honest.'

Jack nodded and followed Bella to the house, where they climbed up three stone steps and went through a wooden door with cracked glass. Inside, there were wide steps going up and narrow steps going down. They took the small staircase that went down to the basement room. Bella opened the door and invited Jack in.

The room was dark and gloomy. There was only one small window that Jack had used to get Bella's attention earlier, and there was no fire burning in the hearth. The smell of dampness permeated the room. Three make-shift beds were set up on the floor and in the far corner was a narrow bed. Jack was surprised when he saw Martha. Even in the poor light, he could see her cheeks were hollowed, her eyes were set back in dark sockets, and her lips looked blue.

'Hello, Mrs Dixon,' said Jack cheerfully.

She turned her face to look at Jack.

'Jack. Is that you?'

'Aye, it's me. How are you?'

'I've seen better days, lad. I wish your mother was here. She was always such a comfort to me.' Pulling the blanket up to show him her swollen feet and ankles, she said, 'She would have known what to do with these. Our Bella's been bathin' them in cold water and has had them strapped up.' Looking down at her feet, she said, 'You know, I think they might be goin' down a bit.'

'I'm sure Bella's takin' good care of you.'

'Aye, she's a good lass, is our Bella.' Martha looked puzzled for a second, her gaze moving from Jack to Bella. 'Aren't you

## CHAPTER 32

two gettin' married?'

Bella held her mother's hand and looked at Jack, smiling. 'We are goin' to get married, Mother.'

'That's good. I'm pleased that's sorted out.'

'I'd better be goin', Mrs Dixon. It's been good to see you.' He bent down and kissed Martha on the cheek.

'Bless you, lad.'

As Jack left the room, he heard Martha coughing. Bella followed him out and pulled the door closed behind them.

'Bella, you know it's her heart, don't you? Me gran had heart trouble, and she looked the same.'

'Aye, I thought as much. I think she's improving though, and as soon as she's well enough to travel, me father will have her on a ship. He can't wait to get to America.'

Jack tenderly brushed the hair back from Bella's face and said, 'If you go to America with them, I'm goin' with you. Promise me you won't ever leave me again.'

'I promise,' she whispered, kissing Jack on the lips. He wrapped his arms around her, pulled her closer, and returned her kiss.

'What the hell is goin' on here?'

Bella and Jack jumped apart at the sound of her father's voice in the corridor.

'I told you that you're not marryin' me daughter. Get yourself back home where you belong. Do I make myself clear?'

'I'm not goin' anywhere, Bill. Not until we've had a talk.'

Bill moved forward menacingly. 'What did you say?'

'You heard me.'

Bill lifted his fist and aimed a punch at Jack's face, but Jack moved quickly, and it missed its target, landing on the door behind him with a thud.

'Bill,' said Jack calmly, looking Bill in the eye. 'I think you'll agree it's only fair that Bella has a say in her future. I'm sure you want her to be happy, just like I want her to be happy. We both want what's best for her.'

Bill stepped back and listened.

'I let her leave Allenheads without a fuss,' said Jack, 'because I thought she didn't want me anymore, but I was wrong.' Taking Bella's hand, he said, 'She didn't leave me because she didn't want me. She left me because you made her choose between her mother and me.'

'That's not true!' countered Bill. 'She wanted to go to America.'

Bella could not meet her father's gaze.

Bill's large form seemed to shrink before them.

'I love your daughter, and I know she loves me,' said Jack. 'We want to be together. I don't care where that is, Allenheads, Liverpool, or America, just as long as we're together. If it wasn't for her mother lyin' on that bed in there, I'd steal her away from here right now.'

'And what have you got to say for yourself?' Bill asked his daughter gruffly.

'Jack's right. I never stopped wanting to marry him. I'd live anywhere with him, but…but I can't leave Mother. Not the way she is. But if you're too stubborn to give us your permission,' said Bella bravely, 'we'll just have to wait until I'm twenty-one. We'll get married next May.'

'Oh, Bella!' said Bill wretchedly. 'Why did you have to fall for him, of all people? His father's a bloody blackleg.'

'You cannot choose who you fall for - and you cannot choose your parents,' she replied.

## CHAPTER 32

Jack was surprised to see Bella standing up to her father and squeezed her hand in support.

'You were best friends with Jack's father before the strike,' she continued. 'The strike is finished now, over and done with, so why should any of that matter?'

Bill's eyes grew wider as he drew in a long breath. 'Don't get me started on that! Johnny betrayed me an' I cannot forgive him for it. Let's leave it at that.'

'Me father wasn't thinkin' about you when he went back to work,' said Jack. 'All he had on his mind was gettin' food for his starvin' children. I know what he did was wrong in your eyes, but he's paid dearly for it. We lost our Deborah. Me father nearly died when he was trapped in the mine. I got to him in the nick of time. And then someone tried to smoke the whole family to death. Isn't that enough?'

'Aye, well. What did he expect would happen? Sufferin' always comes with a strike, but I'll tell you somethin', it comes ten times worse for them that break it.'

'Can we stop talking about the strike, please?' said Bella impatiently. 'It's not helping anything. Me and Jack are back together now, and we will get married one way or another. Will you give us your permission to marry or not?'

The young couple stood before Bill with such love and hope in their eyes that, despite his previous adamance that he would never allow them to marry, he heard himself say, 'Are you sure that's what you both want?'

'Yes.' They answered in unison.

'Right, then, as long as our Bella goes to America with us and helps her mother like she promised, I suppose the two of you could get married.'

'Thank you!' Bella stepped forward and hugged her father

229

tightly.

When they parted, Jack held out his hand to Bill.

'I can't say I'm overjoyed about the union. I'd rather I was givin' her to someone else, anyone else for that matter, but I can see that she's got her mind set on you. You'd better make her happy!' With that threat, Bill took the proffered hand and shook it firmly.

# Chapter 33

**Allenheads, Northumberland
June 1849**

The day of Nelson Kidd's trial finally arrived. Lizzie's hands shook as she dressed in her Sunday clothes, brushed her hair and fastened it up with pins. When she was ready, she went downstairs where her father was waiting for her.

Johnny smiled reassuringly, and asked, 'Are you ready, love?'

Lizzie nodded. Her father took her arm and led her outside to Robbie Dodd's horse and cart. Lizzie climbed onto the cart, sat next to Robbie, and shuffled a little closer when her father sat on the end of the seat. There wasn't much room between the men, but she didn't want to sit in the back and dirty her good dress.

It was a beautiful day as they travelled to Hexham. The sun shone and there was hardly a cloud in the sky. Her father talked about the trial, explained what would happen and coached her on what to say, and she wondered how he was so knowledgeable about such things.

When they arrived, Lizzie and Johnny were ushered into the courthouse and shown to their seats. Lizzie was surprised to see Nelson Kidd standing in the dock, clean, smartly dressed, and contrite. She had only ever seen him in his work clothes before, and his usual expression was mischievous.

The magistrate sitting on the bench was Mr Atkinson. He cleared his throat before beginning the proceedings.

'Mr Kidd, you are charged with the attempted murder of Mr John Lowery, Mrs Eliza Lowery, and their five daughters. How do you plead?' he asked.

'Not guilty, Your Honour,' Nelson replied clearly.

Mr Atkinson called Mr John Lowery as the first witness. Johnny walked to the stand and faced the people in the room. He placed his hand on the bible and swore an oath to tell the truth. Then, he told the story of how he was trapped in the mine and left to die and how he would not have survived if it hadn't been for his son, who'd gone into the mine to search for him, despite being threatened by Nelson Kidd and the other pickets.

Lizzie looked down at her hands when her father mentioned his son. Ever since her mother had confided in her about Jack, she had been thinking about who his real father could be. Why had her mother told her half a story? She must have known that her curious mind wouldn't rest until it had worked out the rest. But hearing her father speaking so proudly about Jack, she knew that she could never broach the subject with him.

'Mr Lowery, did you see the men who set off the explosive that caused the rock to fall and block the tunnel?' asked the magistrate.

'No, sir. I didn't see them.'

'So, you can't be certain that Mr Kidd was the man responsible.'

'Before the explosion, I heard Nelson talkin' to another fella.

## CHAPTER 33

At least I thought it was him. Then, after the explosion, they were both laughin' and one of them was definitely Nelson.'

'How can you be so sure it was Mr Kidd?' asked Mr Atkinson.

'If you've ever heard Nelson Kidd laugh, you'll know that his laugh is unmistakable. He sounds like a donkey with a sore throat.'

Lizzie looked at the people in the room, many of whom were trying to stifle their laughs at her father's colourful description.

'It might not have been him that lit the fuse,' continued Johnny, 'but he was there in the mine when it was lit.'

Miss Elizabeth Lowery was called as the next witness. Lizzie wiped her palms on her skirt before standing up and taking her father's place. She swore on the bible that she would tell the truth and recounted the events of the night when the windows, doors and chimney of their house had been blocked, preventing her and her family from leaving their house as it was filled with smoke.

She explained in great detail what she had seen and heard and identified Nelson Kidd as one of the men who had been outside the house. She had not seen him either, but she confirmed that she was certain she recognised his voice.

Nelson Kidd was led to the stand by a constable, and Mr Atkinson questioned him about his whereabouts on the dates that those particular events had occurred.

'I was at home with me wife,' he said. 'She'll tell you the same.'

'Do you have any recollection of being in the mine at any time during the strike?'

'None at all, Your Honour. I would never set foot in a mine

durin' a strike. I'm not a blackleg.' He glanced vindictively at Johnny.

'In recent months, have you been in the vicinity of Briar Place, where Mr Lowery lives with his family?' asked the magistrate.

'I've walked past the place from time to time. That's all. I wasn't there the night when that lass said I was.' Nelson glared at Lizzie and pointed in her direction. Lizzie shrank back in her seat when she saw the hatred in his eyes. Until that moment, she hadn't thought about what might happen if Nelson was not convicted of the offences he was charged with. If he was set free and returned to Allenheads, she wouldn't dare leave the house in case she ran into him. Her sisters wouldn't be able to go out on their own either. Perhaps he'd even go back to work at the mine with her father. It wouldn't be safe for any of them. The thought of living in fear again, as they had done throughout the strike, sent a shiver down her spine. They'd lived in fear for long enough. How she wished Jack was there to keep them safe; he hadn't been frightened of Nelson Kidd.

Mrs Mary Kidd took the stand after her husband returned to the dock. As she swore the oath to tell the truth, Lizzie noticed that she had yellow bruising on the side of her face and wondered how she had come by it.

'Mrs Kidd,' said Mr Atkinson, 'please could you tell us the whereabouts of your husband on Tuesday the tenth of April, the day an explosion occurred in the mine trapping Mr Lowery, and on the evening of Thursday the twelfth of April, when he and his family were barred in their home and their chimney blocked.'

The woman hesitated and looked towards her husband.

## CHAPTER 33

'Mrs Kidd,' said the magistrate, 'You must answer the question.'

'He...he was out both times. I don't know where he was.'

Nelson's face turned red, and he glowered at his wife.

'Is that the truth, Mrs Kidd?'

'Aye, it's the truth. He asked me to say he was at home with me. When I told him I couldn't tell a lie in court, not when I'd sworn on the bible, he did this.' She pointed at the fading bruise on her face.

'Are you telling me that your husband asked you to provide him with a false alibi, and then he assaulted you when you refused?'

'Aye, I am.'

'Thank you, Mrs Kidd. You may return to your seat.'

Addressing the dock, the magistrate said, 'Mr Kidd, you will face trial at the Crown Court in Newcastle-upon-Tyne on the same charges brought against you today. You will be held in custody until the trial.'

Lizzie noticed the look of relief on Mary's face and realised that she wasn't the only person who had been worried that Nelson Kidd might be released after the trial.

'But it wasn't me that did them things!' Nelson protested.

'Mr Kidd, you had your chance to tell the court your version of events, and you will have an opportunity to do so again when you appear before the judge at Newcastle.'

'I was there, both times, I'll admit to that, but I didn't do it. I could tell you who did, though.'

'It's a little late for that, Mr Kidd.'

'It was Frank Dixon.'

Lizzie gasped and looked at her father, who looked shocked to the core. Frank was one of his partners in the mine and had lived next door since he was born. Johnny would have trusted him with his life.

'It was all Frank's idea,' continued Nelson. 'He did all of it. We just got him what he asked for. We didn't know what he was plannin' to do with the stuff.'

'But you didn't stop him, did you?'

'No, sir.'

'Can anyone corroborate your story?' asked Mr Atkinson.

'Aye, a few of the lads can. They were with us. Will Lightburn. Tommy Cain. John Thompson. They all know that it was Frank that did it, not me.'

'I see.' Mr Atkinson paused for a while as he decided how to proceed. 'In light of the new evidence, I believe the best course of action in these circumstances would be to reopen the investigation. I hope that you and your friends will co-operate with the constables this time so that the real culprit, whoever he is, can be brought to justice.'

'I will, Mr Atkinson, sir. Thank you.'

'In the meantime, you are free to go home.'

Mary Kidd was visibly shaking in her seat, and she looked to the magistrate for help.

'The constable will call on you every day until you reappear in this courtroom. If he suspects you have laid one finger on your wife, he has my authority to arrest you and hold you in custody until the investigation is complete. Do you understand?'

'Yes, Your Honour.'

Johnny took Lizzie's arm, and they walked outside together.

'Frank!' he said, shaking his head. 'Well, I never! I wouldn't have thought he'd have it in him to do those things. He's still

## CHAPTER 33

just a lad.'

'No, he's not,' said Lizzie. 'He's a grown man, and he's just like his father. A bully.'

'Has Frank been botherin' you?' asked Johnny, looking quizzically at his daughter.

'He's never bothered me, but I always kept a close eye on Hannah when he was around. I think he had a fancy for her.'

'The lad will be in America by now. There's nowt the justices can do.'

'That poor woman,' said Lizzie. 'Havin' to live with a man like Nelson.'

'There's no excuse for a man to hit his wife, ever.'

'There's no excuse for what they did to us either,' said Lizzie sadly.

Johnny looked down at his feet.

'It wasn't your fault, Father. You shouldn't blame yourself.

'Well-'

'There's no well about it,' said Lizzie adamantly. 'I believe Frank was responsible, and I'm pleased he's gone away. But the other men aren't free of blame. They could have put a stop to it. They're all as bad as each other.'

'There's no disputin' that. Come on. Let's find Robbie and get ourselves home.'

After a restless night's sleep, Lizzie got up early to light the fire and was surprised to see her father sitting in his armchair, fully dressed.

'You're up early,' she said as she knelt on the hearth mat and put a match to the newspaper and sticks that she'd set in the hearth the night before. She watched the fire take hold, and then she carefully placed small pieces of dried peat on top of the sticks to build up the fire.

Realising her father hadn't replied, she turned to him and asked, 'Are you alright?'

'Aye, lass. But there's somethin' I need to tell you.' Leaning forward, Johnny swallowed deeply and said, 'It's your mother. She died in her sleep.'

Lizzie put her arms around her father's shoulders and held him until he said, 'You'd better get the porridge on. It won't cook itself.'

Lizzie wiped her eyes and then hung a pan of oats and water on the hook at the back of the fireplace. Then, she went upstairs to help Hannah dress their sisters.

When she returned downstairs with all of the family, their tearful father told them the dreadful news. Her death didn't come as a shock to them, they had been expecting it, but still, the children were devastated by the loss of their mother.

Two days later, Eliza Lowery's body was laid to rest in the plot next to her daughter after a moving service by the vicar.

# Chapter 34

**Liverpool**
**June 1849**

On a beautiful sunny morning, Jack walked to St Peter's Church with a huge grin on his face, and when he arrived, he saw the vicar leaning against the church wall, basking in the sunlight.

'Good morning, sir,' said the vicar as Jack approached him.

'It certainly is!' said Jack.

'What can I do for you?'

'I'm Jack Lowery. Me and Bella Dixon would like to get married here.' He pulled a marriage licence from his pocket and proudly handed it to the vicar, who took the document from him and read it carefully.

'Everything appears to be in order. Your intended is underage, but her father has signed to confirm that he's given his permission for the marriage to go ahead.' The vicar looked up at Jack. 'So, all we need to do, Mr Lowery, is arrange a suitable date and time, and take a payment from you on behalf of the church.'

The clerk who had issued the licence had informed Jack that he'd have to pay fees and seemed to take pleasure in telling him that it would be more expensive because they were marrying in a parish where they hadn't been born. The church fees would eat into the money he'd saved since coming to Liverpool, which would delay his passage to America, but that was of little consequence now that Bella was becoming his wife. That's what he wanted more than anything.

'I was thinkin' as soon as possible,' said Jack.

The vicar looked up at Jack quizzically.

'We're goin' to America soon, and we want to be married before we leave.'

'I see. If the wedding must take place on a Saturday, I'm afraid the church is fully booked until October. But if you're able to take time off work, this Friday morning is available and any day next week except Tuesday.'

Could they get married this Friday? Jack was concerned that he might lose his job if he took time off during the week. The men hanging around the docks would jump at the chance of his job. He hoped Mr Walker looked upon him favourably enough to keep his job open. He'd made it clear to Jack that he was a good worker; he'd told him that he could offload ships in half the time it took some of the older men.

'Friday, this week,' said Jack. He would take the risk. He didn't want to wait a second longer than necessary to make Bella his wife; he'd waited long enough already.

'Right you are. If you'd like to come inside, I need to take a few more details from you before the service can take place.'

When he left the church, Jack went directly to the Dixons' room in the courtyard. He knocked at the basement window, and Bella opened the front door to let him in. Following her inside, he was amazed to see Martha sitting on the edge of the bed, fully dressed, supping a cup of tea.

## CHAPTER 34

'Morning, Mrs Dixon. You're lookin' well.'

'I'm feelin' much better, thank you,' she said, smiling at him. 'Have you brought us some good news?'

'I was about to ask the same,' said Bella. 'Did you see the vicar?'

'Yes,' he said, smiling broadly. 'We can get married at St Peter's on Friday morning!'

Bella's smile reflected his own. 'I wasn't expecting it to be so soon,' she said. 'That's wonderful.'

'Your father and Frank will be at work on Friday,' said Martha. 'They won't be there to be witnesses.'

'I know,' said Jack, 'but there wasn't a slot available on a Saturday until October. Anyway, the vicar said he can arrange for witnesses to be there if we need them.'

Bella took Jack's hand. 'You made the right choice,' she said. 'Father's hoping we'll be on our way to America by October, so we might not even be here then.'

'I'll come to the church,' said Martha. 'I want to see me daughter get wed.'

Bella and Jack both looked at Martha in surprise. Although she had improved lately, it seemed far-fetched to think she would be able to walk to the church in just a few days.

Seeing the disbelief on their faces, Martha said, 'I'll do it. I'll be there. Just you wait and see.'

On Friday morning, Bella waited for Jack in the courtyard lodgings. She was wearing her Sunday dress, which was decent and clean, although no longer new. Her mother had curled her hair, as she had done for Jack's birthday party, and she said it looked pretty. There was no mirror in the room for Bella to see for herself.

'It's such a shame we had to sell that blue dress you got off Mrs Sopwith,' said Martha, looking over her daughter's attire. 'It would have been perfect for today.'

Bella sat down on the edge of her mother's bed, thinking that so much had changed since she'd worked at Allenheads Hall. If anybody had told her then that she would marry Jack Lowery in Liverpool, she would never have believed it.

She had felt unsettled ever since she'd left Allenheads. It wasn't just leaving home, leaving Jack, the upheaval of the journey to Liverpool, her mother's illness, or having to live in a hovel until her mother was well again. It was more than that. Something deeper. She didn't know the exact cause, but she thought it had something to do with the rift between her father and Jack. She hoped the feeling would go away after the wedding and that her father would accept Jack as his son-in-law.

There was a knock at the door. Without looking to see who was there, Bella ran to the door, knowing it would be her future husband.

'Bella, you look beautiful,' said Jack. He leaned forward over the doorstep and gently kissed her lips. 'Are you ready?'

'Aye, I'm ready.' She smiled at him. 'Me mother's determined she's coming an' all.'

'In that case, she'd better come along,' said Jack brightly. 'I can carry her there if I need to. I'm used to lumping heavy things around all day.'

Bella laughed loudly at the thought of Jack carrying her mother to the church and nudged Jack with her elbow. 'Shush! She'll be here in a minute.'

Martha appeared in the doorway. 'Come on, then,' she said. 'What are we waitin' for?'

## CHAPTER 34

Jack took Martha's arm and helped her down the steps, and then Bella took her other arm. Between them, they managed to walk Martha to the church, stopping several times for her to catch her breath. When they arrived, she insisted that she sit at the front so she could see them clearly. They walked her up the aisle and helped her onto the front pew.

The vicar was already at the church, and he introduced the young couple to the registrar and then to his housekeeper and groundsman, who he had invited to join them in case they were required to witness the marriage.

The service was mundane. The vicar knew nothing about the couple he was marrying, and he made no effort to make the service personal to them. Bella thought he must conduct marriage ceremonies very frequently to go through the motions with so little enthusiasm. Weddings were supposed to be happy events, and she thought how pleased the vicar at Allenheads would have been to perform their marriage rites. But, as long as they were married at the end of it, did it really matter?

Eventually, the vicar finished the preamble and prayers and began the vows. Jack took a thin brass ring from his pocket and placed it on Bella's finger. The vicar then pronounced them man and wife, and Jack kissed her. When they turned around, they saw Martha crying into a handkerchief, and there were tears in the housekeeper's eyes too. The small congregation offered them their best wishes, and then the registrar asked them to sign the marriage register. When they were finished with the formalities, Bella couldn't stop smiling. She had never been happier. Jack Lowery was now her husband.

The newlyweds helped Martha back to the courtyard. They

went inside and Bella made a pot of tea while her mother sat on the edge of her bed.

'You never said where you were stayin', Jack,' said Martha. 'Is there room there for both of you?'

Jack had avoided that subject, and he shifted uncomfortably under his mother-in-law's gaze. None of the Dixons, not even Bella, knew that he'd been sleeping rough to avoid wasting his hard-earned wages on lodgings.

'You have got somewhere to stay, haven't you?' A look of horror passed over Martha's face, and she looked across the room to her daughter.

'Don't worry, Mother,' said Bella, bringing her a cup of tea. 'I'm sure Jack's got somewhere sorted for us, haven't you, Jack?'

'I've got somewhere lined up for the weekend,' said Jack. 'When I told me boss that I was gettin' married today, he said he owned a place that would be vacant until the new tenants move in on Monday and that we could stay there for free this weekend as a wedding present. Wasn't that good of him?'

'Just for the weekend? What will we do after that?' asked Bella, her voice full of concern.

'I'll work somethin' out, love.'

'Bill won't let you stay here,' said Martha. 'Agreein' to the weddin' was one thing, but I'm sorry, lad, he'll not let you live under his roof.'

Since leaving Allenheads, Jack had been living one day at a time. He didn't want to think any further than this weekend, the first weekend he would spend with his new wife. Right now, nothing was going to spoil that for him. He'd worry about next week when the time came.

'Will you be alright on your own if we go now?' Bella asked her mother. 'Frank will be back in an hour or so.'

## CHAPTER 34

'I'll be fine, love. Go on, get yourselves away!' Martha shooed them out of the room. 'I'm tired anyway. I could do with a lie-down.'

Bella made sure that her mother was comfortable in her bed before they left, and then she took Jack's hand and led him out of the basement room.

They wandered along the streets of Liverpool for about ten minutes before Jack said, 'We're here.'

The address Mr Walker had given Jack took them to a narrow street lined with terraced houses on both sides. Although the houses were small, they were well maintained. There was no peeling paint or boarded-up windows on this street. Bella noticed that fewer children were playing outside, and those she saw were clean and wore shoes on their feet. After living in the courtyard, Bella thought this quiet area of the town was like heaven.

They walked hand in hand until they found *Number 47*. Jack turned the key in the lock and pushed open the front door. Lifting his bride off her feet, they grinned at each other as he carried her across the threshold. He closed the door behind them and then lowered her to the floor.

Bella looked around the front room, which was furnished with two armchairs, a sofa and a table with two chairs. She went through to the kitchen, which was light and clean. The house was much better than the room she'd been sharing with her family. She turned to Jack and said, 'This is perfect.'

Jack moved to stand in front of Bella and gently tucked her hair behind her ear, and in a low voice, he said, 'Perhaps we should take a look upstairs, Mrs Lowery?'

On Monday morning, Bella was reluctant to leave the little

house where she and Jack had spent their first wonderful weekend together as a married couple. She rushed around the rooms, ensuring she'd cleaned everything properly. It was five-thirty already, and Jack had to be at the docks by six.

On the doorstep, Jack held Bella close and kissed her. 'Stay with your mother today. I'll come for you after work.'

Bella nodded and hugged him. She had been dreading this moment when they would have to leave the house. She was worried about where they would spend the next night and the night after that. She hoped that he'd find somewhere they could be together. She pictured herself having to move back in with her parents while her new husband slept under the bushes at the cemetery. It had taken her ages to get him to tell her where he'd been staying since he arrived in Liverpool, and she could hardly believe it. Who would choose to sleep in a graveyard? But she supposed he'd had good reason; he'd needed to save quickly, and board and lodgings would have cost him half his pay. At least, his intentions had been good.

She set off in the direction of the courtyard, and as she walked, she remembered when her family had been refused admission to the ship and they'd needed somewhere to stay. The clerk at the docks had told them about the courtyard rooms. They were the cheapest lodgings in town, he's said, and there were always rooms available. Bella had hated the place on sight. She couldn't imagine a more squalid place to live. No amount of cleaning could shift the awful stench, and there were rats in the buildings. Several times when she'd been lying on the floor trying to sleep, she'd felt them climb over her. During her time there, Bella had heard some shocking language, curse words that she'd never heard before, from the women as well as the men. The people were dirty,

## CHAPTER 34

their clothes filthy and worn, and she suspected the children were covered in lice because they scratched constantly. She couldn't wait to get away from there.

Suddenly, she felt homesick. Allenheads had been a paradise compared with the courtyards of Liverpool. Her family had not known how well off they'd been at Briar Place, in their stone houses with large gardens, plenty of fresh air, and surrounded by friends.

At the end of his shift, Jack rushed along the dock. He was in a hurry to get back to see Bella, and in his haste, he almost collided with Mr Walker.

'Jack! Just the man I wanted to see.'

'Hello, Mr Walker. What can I do for you?'

'It's about the house.'

'We left the place clean and tidy this mornin'. Bella made sure of that.'

'Yes, the house was in perfect order. It's just that the new tenants didn't show up today, so it looks like the place will be vacant until the end of the year. I just wondered if you and your wife might be interested in taking it on?'

'Bella loved the place, Mr Walker, but I think it might be a bit above our means.'

'You're earning enough to cover the rent. Of course, there is cheaper housing in the town, there's no doubt about that, but I'm guessing you wouldn't want to leave your wife alone all day with the ruffians that live in the courtyards?'

Jack knew the rent would take most of his weekly wage, and after buying food for the two of them, he'd be lucky if there was any money left to put aside for his passage to America. But Bella had loved the house, it was in a decent part of the town, and it wasn't far from the docks or for Bella to visit her mother.

'Thank you, Mr Walker. We'll take it.'

The men shook hands, and Mr Walker handed Jack the key, saying, 'Your missus will thank you for it.'

Jack nodded and went to collect Bella from the courtyard. With a brief greeting to Martha, he led Bella outside and onto the main road.

'Where are we going?' asked Bella, her voice betraying her anxiety.

Jack held her hand firmly as they walked along the narrow streets. 'You'll soon see,' he said.

Bella didn't like this game, not knowing where Jack was taking her, but she hoped that wherever it was, it was clean and free from vermin. She had already decided that she would never lower herself to sleep outside with him in the cemetery. If that's where he was taking her, she would walk away and return to her parents' place. She'd rather do that than sleep outdoors.

What would her father say if Jack had married her but couldn't provide her with a roof over her head? She didn't even want to think about that. He'd be so angry with Jack, calling him irresponsible for taking on a wife without a thought for her care. He'd be mad at her too for choosing Jack in the first place and for persuading him to let them marry. Then, she guessed that he would gloat that he'd been right about Jack all along. She wouldn't be able to bear it.

They turned a corner, and Bella recognised the street next to where they'd stayed for the weekend, and then they turned onto that exact same street. She looked at Jack, silently asking the question, and he nodded at her with a wide smile. She hugged her husband in the street, and when they parted, she took Jack's hand and led him to their door.

For the next few weeks, Bella spent her days with her mother and nights in the charming little house with Jack. She couldn't understand how they could afford the place when Jack was supposed to be saving to go to America with her and her family, but it didn't bother her too much. She was happy to be living in a clean place, with running water, a private netty, and no vermin.

Since the wedding, her mother's condition had improved, and her father was becoming increasingly impatient to continue their journey. She knew that her father had the money for all four of his family to travel overseas, but now that she was a married woman, she wondered if he might expect Jack to pay for her ticket. Bella wasn't sure that Jack had the money for his own fare, never mind hers. Had she acted rashly in marrying Jack? Perhaps she should have waited until they'd landed in America before becoming his wife and responsibility. But even as that thought crossed her mind, she recalled the wonderful nights they had spent together since their wedding day and she knew that she'd made the right choice. She would never regret marrying Jack Lowery.

# Chapter 35

**Allenheads
June 1849**

While the family were walking back from Eliza's funeral, the reality of his wife's death hit Johnny hard, and by the time they returned to Briar Place, he was inconsolable. He slumped down at the table, his head on his folded arms, his body racked with sobs.

Lizzie didn't know what to do; she'd never seen him cry before, not even when Deborah had died.

'Hannah, take the lasses out for a walk,' she said.

Wondering what her mother would have done, she took a whisky bottle from the top of the kitchen cupboard, picked up a glass, and poured her father a drink.

Johnny lifted his head and took the glass from her, swallowing the amber liquid in one gulp, and then he held out the glass for a refill. After his fourth whisky, Johnny wiped his eyes on his sleeve, sat back in his chair and stared at his empty glass. He began to talk, and Lizzie wasn't sure if he was talking to himself or to her.

'When I went back to work,' he said, 'I reckoned that would be it. That would be the end of all of the sufferin'. But, our

## CHAPTER 35

poor little Deborah! Why did that have to happen, eh? And after I'd gone back to the mine and we had food comin' into the house again. Was that God's idea of retribution because I turned against me fellow men? Eeh, I've never known a lass that was so full of fun as our Deborah was. She was such a lovely lass.' He smiled at the memories of his daughter, his eyes still brimming with tears. 'The others haven't been the same since she went. And then our Jack. Runnin' off like that with hardly a word. How could he do that to us? It broke his mother's heart.' Starting to sob again, he said, 'My Eliza. She was the only woman I ever loved. What am I goin' to do without her?'

Lizzie went to her father, intending to put her arm around his shoulder to comfort him, but he didn't see her there. He rose to his feet and said, 'I'm goin' out.'

'Where are you goin'?' she asked, surprised that he wanted to leave the house in the state he was in.

'The pub,' he said as he walked out of the door and closed it quietly behind him.

Hannah and the girls came home for their evening meal, but their father didn't appear. Lizzie was worried about him and waited up for him that night, listening for his footsteps outside the door, but all was silent. When he hadn't returned by midnight, she decided to go to bed; she needed to be up early in the morning.

The following day, Lizzie lit the fire and set the porridge to boil. By the time she'd finished preparing her father's bait, she was surprised that he wasn't up yet. Lizzie knocked on his bedroom door, 'Father, wake up. You'll be late for work.'

When there was no sound from his room, she knocked

loudly and opened the door. Her father was not there, and his bed was still made. Panicking, she realised that he hadn't come home the night before. In all the times he'd gone out drinking with Bill, he'd always found his way home.

Lizzie asked Hannah to get the girls ready for school, then walked briskly to the village inn and knocked at the door. There was no answer, so Lizzie pounded at the door with her fists. A man in his nightshirt lifted an upstairs window and shouted, 'For God's sake! I've just been in me bed for a few hours. What do you want? It better be somethin' important to interrupt me sleep.'

'Me father didn't come home last night. I wondered if he was still here?'

'Yer father? Would that be Johnny Lowery?'

'Aye!'

'He's not set foot inside this pub since he went back to work. Nothin' personal, but the other miners wouldn't have stood for it.'

Lizzie was shocked by this revelation and wondered where her father had been spending his evenings if he hadn't been at the pub as he'd said.

'Have you any idea where he might be?' asked Lizzie.

'No idea, hinny. But I hope you find him.' The landlord lowered the sash window and drew the curtains.

Lizzie didn't know what to do. Where could her father have gone? On the other side of the road, she saw a parish constable chatting with a young lad who was leading a string of ponies towards the horse level. Lizzie crossed the road to speak with him.

'Good morning. Could you could help me, please?'

The constable stopped and asked, 'What can I do for you,

## CHAPTER 35

young lady?'

'I don't know if I should be botherin' you with this, but me father didn't come home last night. He's never stayed out all night before and I'm worried about him. We buried me mother yesterday and he was upset. Very upset. He said he was goin' out for a drink last night, but he didn't. I've been to the pub and the landlord said he hadn't been there and I've got no idea where he is.'

'Calm down, miss. I'm sure he'll be alright.' The constable took out his notepad and pencil and asked, 'What's your father's name?'

'Johnny Lowery.'

'And where do you live?'

'Briar Place. Number Two.'

'Can you tell me what he looks like?'

'He's about five foot ten. His hair is dark. A bit thin on top. He has a dark beard an' all.'

'Do you remember what he wearing when he went out?'

'We'd been to the church so he was dressed smart. Trousers, jacket, waistcoat, shirt, and he had his hat on. He always wears a hat.'

'I'll ask around, see if anyone's seen him. Try not to worry, miss. Get yourself home in case he comes back, and I'll call round later.'

'Thank you.' She smiled at the constable.

Instead of going straight home, Lizzie went to Robbie's house and knocked at his door. Robbie's brother answered it, clearly surprised to see her, He invited her in and she explained to the brothers that her father was missing.

'Don't worry, Lizzie,' said Robbie. 'Me and our Davey won't go into work today. We'll go out and look for him instead.

But I'm sure he'll turn up safe and sound.'

'Have you any idea where he might be?' asked Davey.

'I wish I had,' she replied. 'If he wanted a drink bad enough, he could have walked to Spartylea or Sinderhope. And if he wanted to be alone, he might have gone onto the fells or into the woods.'

'So, he could be anywhere,' concluded Davey.

Robbie put a reassuring hand on Lizzie's shoulder. 'Try not to worry about him. You Lowerys are made of strong stuff!'

'Thanks, Robbie. I wish our Jack was here. He would have known what to do.'

The lads nodded, followed her out the door and headed towards the mine yard. She guessed they had to tell somebody that they wouldn't be going into the mine that day before they could begin their search.

Lizzie walked back to Briar Place with a sense of foreboding that she just couldn't shake off. She tried to distract herself by watching the wild birds flying to their nests and studying the tidy front gardens as she passed them, with their pretty flowers and bits of purple and amber spar, but she was too concerned about her father to pay them much attention.

When Lizzie reached for the door handle, Hannah opened it from the inside. Hannah laughed, oblivious to Lizzie's worries, and said, 'I'm takin' the bairns to school now. I'll be back soon!' The girls streamed out of the house after Hannah with smiles on their faces.

'See you later!' said Lizzie, trying to sound cheery.

When Hannah returned alone, Lizzie told her the reason that she had visited the village earlier, and when she'd finished her tale, Hannah was worried for their father too. They kept themselves busy that day with housework; they cleaned and

## CHAPTER 35

scrubbed every surface in sight.

Around noon, Robbie and Davey checked in with them, but they had no news to share. Nobody had seen Johnny. Lizzie had prepared some food for them, and after having a bite to eat, they continued their search.

Later in the afternoon, while Hannah was collecting the children from school, the constable came to the door.

'I don't want to worry you unduly,' he said, 'but nobody's seen anything of your father since he walked home from the church yesterday afternoon. Can you think of anywhere he might have gone? A favourite place he goes to? Somewhere he likes to walk? Anyone he goes to visit?'

Lizzie shook her head. 'He went to the pub a lot before the strike, but we know he's not there. He spends a bit of time lookin' after his hens, but that was the first place I checked. I cannot think of anywhere else he might be.'

'If you don't mind me askin', what did he say before he went out yesterday?'

'He was feelin' sorry for himself and he'd had a few drinks. He talked about our Deborah. His daughter. She died a couple of months ago. And about our Jack who's gone to America. At least we think he has, we've not had word from him. And about his wife. He said he didn't know how he would manage without her. Then, he said he was goin' out and lied to me about the pub.'

'I see.' The policeman shifted uncomfortably. 'Well, we'll carry on lookin' for him.'

That night, Lizzie was woken by loud banging at the door. She got up and opened the curtain slightly, the sun was starting to rise, and she guessed it must be about five o'clock in the morning. The pounding on the door continued. She dressed quickly and ran downstairs to open it. On the doorstep stood the same constable.

'Miss Lowery, it's about your father.'

'Yes,' she replied hesitantly.

'I'm afraid we've found his body.'

'He's dead?'

'Aye, miss, he's dead. I'm sorry.'

Lizzie stepped back, her hand rising subconsciously to her mouth. Her mind was working overtime.

'But how did he die?' she asked.

'May I come in?

'Yes, of course.' Lizzie moved to the table and lit the oil lamp. The flame flickered and then illuminated the room.

'Please sit down,' said the policeman, with a sympathetic smile.

Lizzie sat down, wringing her hands together.

'Are you alright, miss?'

'Aye,' she said, feeling far from it.

'It looks like your father took his own life. We found him in the reservoir. Drowned.'

Lizzie could hardly believe it, and her head shook ever so slightly. Only the night before, her father had opened up to her. Yes, he'd been feeling sorry for himself, and he had every right to be after everything that had happened. She had tried her best to comfort him but she mustn't have done enough. He'd chosen the coward's way out. He'd left her and her sisters to fend for themselves. She didn't know if she was angrier at his selfishness or more upset by his death. Either way, she was disappointed that he hadn't cared enough about his children to stay with them. They had just lost their mother and they needed him. Through the haze, she tried to figure out what

## CHAPTER 35

this news meant for her and her sisters.

'If you're sure you're alright, I'll leave you to it,' said the constable, with a weak smile. 'You'll have arrangements to make in the morning.'

After he'd left, Lizzie paced up and down the small room, thinking about what she needed to do, desperately trying to hold back her tears. She could grieve for her father and wallow in self-pity later. For now, she had to find somewhere for the girls to stay because as soon as the agent heard about her father's death, he would be at their door to give them notice to leave the cottage. They hadn't wasted any time in turning out the Dixons.

She wouldn't let the girls go to the workhouse, not if there was anything she could do to prevent it. There had to be other options. Lizzie knew she needed to act quickly, or that's exactly where they would end up.

After gathering together some writing paper, a pen and an ink bottle, Lizzie sat at the table and began writing. She wrote to every one of their relatives that she could think of and hoped she hadn't missed anyone. By the time she had finished the letters, her hand ached. She stretched out her fingers and sat back in her chair, pleased with her work. Daylight peeped through a chink in the curtains and landed on the neatly stacked pile of letters that she'd written.

Lizzie stood up, opened the curtains and then lowered the wick in the lamp, extinguishing the flame. It was time to start on breakfast, and she prepared a pan of porridge for her sisters, dreading the moment when they would come downstairs and she'd have to tell them that their father was dead, that he'd taken his own life, and that they were orphans.

# Chapter 36

**Allenheads**
**June 1849**

Three days later, Johnny Lowery's funeral took place at Allenheads. It was attended by far more people than Lizzie had expected. The news of his tragic death had come as a shock to the villagers. Many of them had known Johnny their whole lives, and they turned out in force to show their respects. Dozens of miners stood in the churchyard. Lizzie eyed them suspiciously and hoped the men who had harassed her father after returning to work felt rotten for what they'd done, for she believed they were partly responsible for her father's death. But it was the strike that she blamed the most. Without the strike, none of the awful things that had happened recently would have occurred. Her family would still be living at Briar Place with the Dixons next door, and Jack and Bella would be married with a house of their own.

As Lizzie stood by her father's grave with her sisters, holding hands, she noticed the sympathetic looks on the mourners' faces, especially those of the women. She wondered what was going through their minds—three burials in two months, a good man brought down by circumstance, five girls left to

## CHAPTER 36

fend for themselves. Thinking about their situation from an outsider's point of view, she could understand the mourners' reactions, but Lizzie couldn't allow herself to think that way. Now that she was responsible for her family, she was determined to stay strong and vowed to do everything she could to find the girls somewhere to live.

Every day since her father's death, Lizzie had feared eviction. She tried to continue with their regular routine for her sisters' sake. The younger girls continued to attend school while she and Hannah cleaned the house, washed their clothes and cooked their meals. Their food supplies were dwindling quickly, and Lizzie had no means to buy more. She was grateful that the hens were laying well for at least they would have eggs to eat.

After returning from the funeral, Lizzie wandered into the Dixons' garden. Bill had planted some crops before he'd left for America, and even though the garden had not been tended since he'd left, she could see carrots, onions and small potato plants growing between the weeds. There were also rows of cabbages covered with hairy caterpillars.

Lizzie picked a gooseberry from a bush and put it in her mouth. She bit into the fruit, but it wasn't ripe, and she spat it out. Then, she picked a few stalks of rhubarb and took them home, along with an onion, a handful of spindly carrots and a cabbage, after removing the pests. Nobody would mind, she thought, as the house was still unoccupied.

In the kitchen, Lizzie made some pastry and stewed the rhubarb with a handful of sugar for the pie filling, knowing it would be tart, but hungry mouths couldn't be picky mouths. Lizzie heard a knock at the door. She wiped her hands on a cloth, opened the door and greeted the postman, who stood on the doorstep holding a letter in his hand.

'Miss Elizabeth Lowery?' he asked.

'Yes, that's me.' Lizzie said a little prayer to herself as she took the letter from him and closed the door. She ripped open the letter, eager to read the response, whether it be good or bad. She skimmed the letter, and when she'd finished it, she held the letter to her chest and sighed.

Hannah came downstairs and asked, 'Was that the postman?'

Lizzie nodded and held up the letter.

'Who's it from?' asked Hannah as she drew closer.

'It's from Aunt Jennie, Father's sister. She has a dressmaker's shop at Alston. I went there once with Father.'

'Well, what does she say?'

'She said that as her boys have all left home now, she and Uncle Sep would like to take in Jane and Catherine.'

'Both of them?' Hannah squealed. 'That's fabulous news!'

Lizzie's beaming smile matched that of Hannah's.

'And that's not all,' said Lizzie. 'Aunt Jennie goin' to teach them how to make clothes. With a skill like that, they'll always be able to fend for themselves, come what may.'

'That's wonderful, Lizzie. Are they comin' to collect the girls or should we take them over there?'

'They're comin' over here tomorrow,' said Lizzie, thinking how great it was that the two girls could stay together; since Deborah's death, they had been inseparable.

A cart pulled up outside Briar Place the following day at around noon. Lizzie opened the door, and an elderly couple approached the house. Lizzie hardly recognised her Aunt Jennie, whom she hadn't seen for years. Underneath her plumed hat, her hair was white, her shoulders were stooped, and she wore silver spectacles with small round eyeglasses.

## CHAPTER 36

'Jane, Catherine, come and meet Aunt Jennie,' called Lizzie.

The two girls sat at the edge of the room, smartly dressed and well-behaved. They stood up together and came forward to greet their aunt.

'I can see that you're good, strong girls just by looking at you,' said Aunt Jennie, peering over the top of her spectacles at them. 'When you come to stay at my house, I'll teach you everything you need to know about making clothes. I'll expect you to get up early in the mornings and to work hard for most of the day. In return, you'll have a room to share and three meals a day. How does that sound?'

'Very good, thank you,' said Jane.

'Thank you, so much,' said Catherine, with a huge smile.

'You'll love your room,' said Aunt Jennie, smiling kindly at them. 'I've made some new curtains with lace edgings. They're very pretty. And the bed's plenty big enough for the two of you.'

The girls looked at each other and grinned, unable to believe their luck.

'We can't wait to see your shop,' said Jane. 'Lizzie said she's seen it.'

'I'm surprised you can remember, Lizzie. You can't have been more than five years old when your father brought you over to see us. I was the best dressmaker in Alston in those days,' said Aunt Jennie proudly, 'but my eyes have failed me lately.'

'The girls can do the close work for you,' said Lizzie. 'They'll soon learn.'

'I'm sure they will.' Looking at the two girls, she asked, 'Are you ready?'

'You will take good care of them, won't you?' implored

Lizzie as the girls moved to the door.

Aunt Jennie took Lizzie's hands in her wrinkled ones, looked into her eyes, and said, 'Of course, I will. You have no need to worry about these two.' Turning to Jane and Catherine, she added, 'And a town is a much better place for young women to live, rather than out here in the wilds. There are always civilised events going on. You'll love it!'

'We don't have any decent clothes to go to events,' said Catherine.

'Ah! You'll soon be making your own clothes, and when you can do that, you'll never be short of something to wear, whatever the occasion!'

'I can't thank you enough for taking them on,' said Lizzie sincerely. 'They can be a bit of a handful at times, but they'll be good workers.'

'They'll be fine with us, I promise you. I'm only sorry that we couldn't take all of you, but we don't have the space. I hope you find somewhere for the rest of you soon.'

'Thank you.' Turning to her sisters, Lizzie said, 'Be good for Aunt Jennie, and I'll come over and see you when I get the chance.'

'We will, Lizzie,' said Catherine. 'We're lookin' forward to stayin' with her.'

'I'll miss you,' said Jane, hugging her eldest sister.

Up until now, the tall figure of Uncle Sep had been standing quietly behind his wife. While the girls said their farewells, he slipped some money into Lizzie's hand with a discreet nod.

'Thank you, Uncle. That's very kind.'

He held out his hand for Lizzie to shake and mouthed, 'You're welcome.'

When it was time to leave, the excited girls giggled as they

## CHAPTER 36

climbed onto the back of the cart. Lizzie watched them go until the cart disappeared from view, wondering when she would see them again. She wiped a tear from her eye before going indoors and sitting at the table; she couldn't let the others know she was upset.

Lizzie was delighted to have secured homes for the two of them, but Hannah and Mary still needed somewhere to stay. She wasn't concerned for herself. She was confident that she could get a live-in job as a nanny or maid. She may even be considered for the position of housekeeper in a small establishment. Her face straightened. She was sure of one thing: no matter how desperate she was, she would never ask for a job at Allenheads Hall. She couldn't bring herself to work for the Sopwiths. Mr Sopwith could have ended the strike whenever he wanted, but he'd chosen not to, and because of that, Lizzie blamed him for her family's downfall and for everything that had gone wrong in her life. If it hadn't been for him, they would not have fallen out with the Dixons, Jack wouldn't have left to go after Bella, her parents and Deborah would still be alive, and she wouldn't be sending her sisters away to live with people she barely knew. Her hands trembled with the strength of her feelings, and she held them together on her lap.

When the postman returned to the door the following day, Lizzie and Hannah were waiting for him. They jumped up to answer the door, and Lizzie took the letter from his hand.

'Open it!' said Hannah excitedly.

Lizzie tore open the letter and read it to her sister.

'Dear Lizzie, I was sorry to hear about the death of your father so soon after the dreadful news concerning your mother, who was my dear sister. Your Aunty Polly and I have a small farm near the town of Corbridge. Unfortunately we were not blessed with children of our own. Therefore my wife and I would dearly love to offer a home to your youngest sister Mary. She will be treated as our own daughter. If you are willing to relinquish her into our care, we will come to Allenheads on Tuesday afternoon and take her home with us. Your loving Uncle, Robert Walton.'

'Tuesday,' said Hannah. 'That's today!'

'Go and fetch her from school,' said Lizzie. 'We need to get her ready.'

Hannah grabbed her bonnet, and as she rushed to the door, she quickly fastened the ribbons under her chin, and shouted, 'I won't be long!'

Lizzie put some water on to boil and carried the tin bath into the house, and by the time Hannah returned with Mary, there was a warm bath ready for the child.

Lizzie and Hannah bathed their little sister and dressed her in her Sunday best. They packaged up her few things, including the old rag doll. Then, they sat and waited.

It wasn't long before they heard a knock at the door, and Uncle Robert and Aunt Polly entered the house. Lizzie couldn't remember meeting them before, but she liked the couple on sight. They had no airs and graces about them and showed genuine concern for the girls. Aunt Polly had brought a food basket as a gift, and Lizzie's mouth watered when she placed the sugar, dripping, bacon, flour and apples in the larder.

Hannah made a pot of tea for their guests, and while they drank it, Lizzie and Hannah told the couple everything they could think of about their little sister. When it was time for

## CHAPTER 36

them to leave, Mary began to search the room.

'What are you looking for?' asked Hannah.

'Maisie. I can't find Maisie.'

'Who's Maisie?' asked Aunt Polly.

'My doll.'

Hannah took the rag doll from the small bundle she'd packed earlier and handed it to her sister. Mary snatched it from her and held it tightly against her chest.

Lizzie knew that Mary did this when she was anxious, so she knelt beside her little sister and said, 'Maisie is very excited today.'

Mary held the doll at arm's length, looking at her sceptically.

'Why is she excited, Lizzie?'

'Because she's going to stay at a new house, and she wants you to go with her.'

'Does she? Well, I can't let her go on her own. She might get lonely.'

'That's right,' said Lizzie. 'You can keep each other company, and Aunt Polly here will be your best friend too.'

Mary smiled up at Aunt Polly and introduced the doll to her.

Uncle Robert held out his hand and asked, 'Would you and Maisie like to ride in our trap?'

Mary jumped up and down on the spot and beamed. 'Can I, Lizzie?'

'Aye, you can go with them, but you must be a good girl. Promise me.'

'I will,' said Mary, and her uncle lifted her onto the leather seat.

Lizzie's heart was breaking at having to part with her youngest sister, but she could see that her aunt and uncle were smitten with Mary already, and she was sure they would take good care of her.

After they left, Lizzie and Hannah sat at the table and shared an apple, cut into slices, savouring the taste.

'Now that the little ones have gone and it's just us that's left,' said Hannah. 'I think we should look for work. We can't wait around for someone to rescue us.'

'Aye, I know. We could get thrown out of the house at any time. I'm surprised it hasn't happened yet.'

'I'm nearly fifteen, and you're seventeen,' said Hannah. 'We should be able to get a job.'

'Allendale will be the best place to try. We'll have to walk there, though. We can't waste money on the coach.'

Hannah pulled a face. 'I suppose not.'

'We'll go tomorrow and see what's on offer.'

'Wouldn't it be good if we could stay together?' said Hannah. 'Like Jane and Catherine.'

'Aye, it would. But we'll have to take what we can get.' Realising her reply had sounded harsh, she smiled reassuringly and added, 'It'll all work out. I know it will.'

Lizzie didn't feel as confident as she sounded. It was unlikely that they'd be taken on at the same place, but ideally, she would have liked to keep an eye on Hannah. Her sister was a bonny lass with a kindly disposition, oblivious to her effect on men. Lizzie was concerned for her sister's safety and reputation, and although she'd just said they'd have to take whatever was going, she hoped she might find a place for Hannah in a house where there were no men, perhaps as a servant for a widow and her family or as a lady's maid.

A knock on the window startled them. A well-dressed man poked his head through the open doorway and said, 'Hello! Is

## CHAPTER 36

anyone at home?'

Lizzie and Hannah stood up quickly, aware that this was the moment that they'd been dreading. Standing tall, Lizzie said, 'I'm Lizzie Lowery. And who are you?'

'Mr Bagley, Mr Beaumont's land agent. I've been informed that your father is deceased and that your brother has gone away. As you know, this house belongs to the company and as nobody here works for the company anymore, I must ask you to leave. I shall expect the house to be vacated by Friday.'

'I don't suppose you know if there's any jobs goin' at the mine, do you?' asked Hannah.

Mr Bagley looked from one girl to the other with a puzzled expression. 'Is there someone else living here who could work at the mine? Another brother that I don't know about, perhaps?'

'No, there's just us.'

'We don't take on young women at the mine. You must find somewhere else to live this week, or you'll be evicted on Friday. That's how things stand.'

He nodded before turning and closing the door.

Seeing that Hannah was close to tears, Lizzie hugged her. 'It'll be fine, Hannah. We'll find somewhere. Don't worry.'

# Chapter 37

**Allenheads**
**July 1849**

The following day, Lizzie and Hannah dressed in their best clothes and walked the seven miles along the dusty road to Allendale Town. It was market day, and the streets were busy with horses and carts and people on foot.

'Where should we start?' asked Hannah.

'Let's ask at the shops. The shopkeepers might need help or know of customers who are lookin' for someone.'

They went into every shop in town, and the answer they received was always the same. 'No, they didn't need any help and they didn't know of anybody looking for servants.'

By midday, the girls were hot, thirsty and despondent. They went into a tearoom in the marketplace and sat at a table. A middle-aged woman came over and asked them what they would like. As the sisters ordered a pot of tea, Lizzie asked, 'Do you know of any work goin' in the area?'

'Now, let me think,' she said. 'I did overhear something the other day. Now, what was it?' She thought for a moment and then said, 'Never mind, it'll come back to me. I'll get you that tea.'

## CHAPTER 37

When she returned with a fully-laden tea tray, she placed the items onto the table and stood back. 'I've remembered what it was that I heard. There's a big house on the left-hand side of the road when you come into town from the Allenheads side. The people there will likely need a new maid. One of them has just left.'

'Do you know why she left?' asked Lizzie.

'Aye, she had a belly out here,' said the woman, holding her hand at least six inches away from her abdomen, before returning to the kitchen.

Lizzie looked across at Hannah and felt anxious. But just because the girl had been in service didn't necessarily mean that a man at the house was responsible for her condition. She could have been walking out with another fella outside of work. Lizzie had to believe that because if there were a job available at that house, Hannah would have to take it.

When they left the tea shop, Lizzie thanked the woman for the tea and her help. She and her sister walked towards the edge of town and saw the large house looming over the road. They stopped at the white-painted door, and Hannah pressed the button to ring the bell. Within seconds, a stuffy-looking housekeeper opened the door.

'We wondered if you were in need of a maid or a nanny here,' said Lizzie.

The housekeeper looked them both up and down. 'We have a vacancy for a maid. Just one. Would you come inside?'

Both girls went indoors. The large hallway was filled with furniture and plants, so there was little room to stand.

'Come through to the kitchen. We don't want to disturb the family.'

The sisters sat at a kitchen table with the housekeeper on

the opposite side, facing them.

'What do you expect a maid to do here?' asked Lizzie

'Haven't you been in service before?' came the reply. 'It's the same as any maid's job - cleaning, serving at meals, some fetching and carrying, making tea and light refreshments, and such like.'

'Is it a live-in position?' asked Hannah.

'Yes. The servants' rooms are in the attic. The family employ two maids and they share a room. Breakfast is at six o'clock, lunch at noon and dinner is after the family has eaten, which is usually around seven.'

'May I ask about the family?' asked Lizzie. 'Who lives here?'

'Mr and Mrs Burn, and their three sons. Mr Burn is a solicitor in the town, as is his eldest son. The twins are at college in Newcastle during the week but they come home at weekends.'

Lizzie guessed the sons were all young men, probably in their late teens or early twenties, and she tried not to frown. She couldn't let Hannah stay in this house, especially when she knew why the previous maid had left.

Could she work here? With her red hair and lack of curves, Lizzie knew she was less likely to be noticed by the men, and in any case, she was strong enough to fend off their advances. Perhaps she should take it, but not until she'd found a decent place for Hannah.

'Thank you for your time.' Lizzie stood up. 'I'm interested in the position, but I can't start until Friday. Would that suit you?'

'I'd rather you could start straight away, but Friday will be alright. You haven't asked about the pay?'

Lizzie smiled. She'd been so concerned about finding a

## CHAPTER 37

place to live that she hadn't considered the pay.

'It's five shillings a week,' offered the housekeeper.

'Thank you. That's very fair.'

The housekeeper escorted Lizzie and Hannah through the house and out the front door. The sisters walked up the road for a while before Hannah turned to Lizzie and said, 'That was a nice house, Lizzie. Why did you say that you would work there rather than me?'

'You're a bonny lass, Hannah,' said Lizzie. 'Men are attracted to you, and there were four men living in that house.'

'What are you sayin'?'

'I don't want you goin' there and endin' up like the last maid, with a bairn in your belly.'

Hannah grasped Lizzie's meaning and said, 'But you don't know it was one of them that did it.'

'No, I don't. But when a live-in servant ends up in the family way, the odds are that's what happened.'

'But what about you? Will you be alright there?'

'It's not ideal but it'll have to do,' said Lizzie sadly. 'Unless I can find something better by Friday.'

The following day, the sisters were about to leave the house in search of work when the postman knocked at the door. He waved a letter in the air. 'This is becoming a habit!' he said, smiling. 'I've got another one for you.'

'Thank you,' said Lizzie, returning his smile. She took the letter and opened it apprehensively. Hannah stood over her, tapping her fingers on the table.

'It's from Aunt Kate at Lanehead.'

'Where's Lanehead?'

'It's a little village in Weardale.'

'Well, what does she say?' asked Hannah.

'She says she's a widow now. Her husband died last year. She's been tryin' to keep the farm goin' by herself, but she's findin' it difficult. She would like it very much if a couple of the older children could stay with her to help on the farm, and that she'd appreciate some company in the evenings.'

Hannah hugged Lizzie tightly.

'Thank God,' whispered Lizzie.

There would be no workhouse for them and no more begging for jobs. There was a home waiting for them in Weardale, where they could stay together and where Lizzie could keep a watchful eye over Hannah. It was as if her prayers had been answered.

On Friday morning, Lizzie and Hannah packed their clothes and belongings into two parcels and set off to walk the four miles to Lanehead in the neighbouring valley of Weardale. When it was time for the girls to leave home, an air of sadness surrounded them. Lizzie turned back for one last glance at Briar Place. The two cottages stood empty and silent. The Dixons and the Lowerys had all moved on.

Lizzie and Hannah walked through the village, and as they climbed the hill out of Allenheads, the sadness gradually receded and was replaced by a sense of excitement. The young women were going to live in a new place, where they would meet new people and begin a new life.

# Chapter 38

**Liverpool
September 1849**

Three months passed without incident for the newlyweds. Jack was happier than he had ever been before, living in the terraced house with Bella. He was pleased that he had managed to save a little too. He'd discovered that if he went to the market at the end of the day, he could pay a fraction of the price for food. At this rate, he reckoned that he would have enough money to pay for his passage to America by the end of the year. Everything was going well.

One evening when Jack went to collect Bella from the courtyard after he'd finished work at the docks, he opened the door and was surprised to see that everyone was at home. Bill and Frank were grinning about something. Martha looked anxiously from Jack to Bella and back again. Bella's eyes were large and they seemed to bore right through him. Jack reckoned that something must have happened that pleased the men but troubled Bella and her mother.

'Jack!' said Bill. 'Come on in. We've got some good news. Martha says she's well enough to travel!'

Looking at Martha, Jack said, 'That is good news. I'm glad

you're feelin' better.'

Bella came over and stood by Jack's side. She slipped her hand into his and gripped it tightly. Jack felt his heart pounding in his chest. He knew what was coming next.

'Father's been to the ticket office,' said Bella, looking up at him. 'He's bought tickets to go to Boston. The ship's leaving on Tuesday. He's got one for me an' all.'

Jack clenched and unclenched a fist behind his back. Bella was his wife. Her father shouldn't be paying for her fare. He should be the one to provide for his wife. The anger he felt was rapidly replaced with despair. He didn't have the money to pay for his own fare, never mind hers. There was no way that he could travel with them next week.

Jack felt everyone watching him, waiting for his reaction to the news. It felt like the walls were collapsing in on him and in his panic, he heard himself say, 'Are you sure you want to go to America, Bella? We could go back to Allenheads if you want.'

'What do you mean by asking her that?' said Bill, glaring at Jack. 'She left Allenheads to come with us. She's made it clear that she wants to stay with her mother, and she promised to help her mother in America when I agreed to your wedding.'

'But things are different now, aren't they? We're married, so she doesn't have to go if she doesn't want to,' countered Jack, looking down into Bella's sweet face, hoping that she would agree to return home with him. He could easily afford the rail tickets to travel back to Northumberland. He'd even buy first-class tickets if only she would say yes.

'I want to stay with me mother, Jack. That's what we agreed. She cannot travel all that way without me, and I want to see her settled over there. But I want to be with you too.' Tears

## CHAPTER 38

formed in her eyes. 'You will come with us, won't you?'

Jack's shoulders drooped, and he looked down at the dirty mat on the floor. He couldn't let Bella go to America without him. He couldn't be parted from her again. But how could he get the money he needed before Tuesday so that they could travel together?

He had some pay owing to him, but there would be little to spare after paying the rent. Certainly not enough to buy a ticket. He couldn't ask Bill to loan him the extra money; he was too proud to do that. So what could he do?

'Jack?' pleaded Bella. 'You have to come with us.'

If he hadn't taken on the house, if he hadn't married Bella, if he'd still been sleeping at the cemetery, he would have had enough money saved up by now to pay for his passage, and they could have travelled across the ocean together.

And then another thought crossed his mind. If he didn't have the rent to pay, he might just have enough. What if he took his wages but didn't pay the rent? Then, he could leave with Bella and her family on Tuesday. He wouldn't have to hand Bella over to her father until he could join them at a later date. He didn't want to be separated from his wife for a single night; he wanted to be with her always.

'Aye, alright,' said Jack. 'The ticket office will be closed now, but I'll go in me dinner break tomorrow and sort it out.'

Bella's smile confirmed that he'd said what she longed to hear. She opened her arms and wrapped them around him, hugging him tightly. He could feel her body sobbing with relief.

Martha smiled weakly at Jack and looked away. He guessed that she knew about his money situation from Bella, and he thought that she must be wondering how he could afford to pay for his ticket. She could never know what he was about to do. He couldn't tell Bella. He could hardly admit it to himself. What he planned to do was tantamount to stealing, something he had never done in his life, nor would he have considered doing it. But these were exceptional circumstances, he told himself, and he could justify his actions by believing that he had to be on that ship with Bella, no matter what. Letting her leave him again was not an option.

'We're goin' on *The Cambria*,' said Frank, breaking through Jack's thoughts. 'She's one of the Cunard steamers.'

Jack nodded. 'Thanks, Frank.'

'Come on, we should be going,' said Bella, taking Jack's hand. 'We'll be off now, Mother. I'll see you in the morning.'

The Dixons said their farewells, and Jack and Bella left the courtyard. When they walked along the street, she asked, 'How can you afford a ticket, Jack? I know you don't have the money.'

'Don't you worry yourself about that. I'll see to it.' Changing the subject, he asked, 'What are we havin' for tea tonight?'

Jack hated keeping anything from Bella. They had confided in each other ever since they were children, and they had never kept secrets from each other, until now.

Jack carried the last barrel off the ship, took it to the warehouse, and added it to the pile he'd already removed. He wiped the sweat off his brow with his shirt sleeve and looked for Mr Walker. He found him in the weighing area, talking to a man in a suit - someone from the customs house, Jack presumed. When the official left, Jack approached his boss.

'Mr Walker, I'm leavin' for America tomorrow with my wife and her folks. I wondered if I could have the pay that I'm due?'

## CHAPTER 38

'Of course, Jack,' Mr Walker pulled out some coins from his pocket, counted them out on the table, and passed them to Jack. 'I knew that was your plan all along,' he said, 'but I didn't expect you to be leaving so soon. We'll miss you here. I wish I had a dozen men that worked as hard as you.'

Jack smiled awkwardly.

'I wish you and Mrs Lowery all the best for your new life in the New World!'

'Thank you, Mr Walker. That's very kind of you. I'll bring the rent and the house key over in the mornin'.'

Jack turned away, and his face fell. As he walked to the ticket office, he was riddled with guilt for what he planned to do.

The following morning, after their belongings had been packed and Bella had cleaned the house, Jack said, 'I have to take the key and the rent over to Mr Walker. Why don't you go to your parents' place and make sure they have everythin' that they need and help them down to the docks. I'll meet you there.'

'If you're sure that's alright. It's a long way for me Mother to walk down to the docks and I think she would appreciate the help.'

Jack was relieved that Bella had agreed so readily. Taking her hand and pulling her towards him, he said, 'Come here, Mrs Lowery,' and he kissed her gently on the lips.

'I'll see you down there,' said Bella, grinning. 'I can't believe that we're really going!' She turned back and waved at him as she crossed the street.

Jack stood in the doorway in silence, his conscience pricked by what he was about to do. Mr Walker had been so good to him, giving him a job, paying him a regular wage, gifting them his house for their wedding night, and taking them on as tenants. The man didn't deserve this.

But Jack had already bought his ticket, and there was no money left to pay the rent, so he had to see it through. As he wrote a note of explanation to his landlord, he vowed to send the rent money that he owed Mr Walker as soon as he could afford to, with a little extra to cover the interest. Looking around the house for the last time, he picked up his bag and stepped outside, closing the door behind him. Then he turned the key in the lock and dropped the key and the letter through the letterbox.

# Chapter 39

**SS Cambria
October 1849**

Jack and Bella stood on the deck of the Cambria and watched a commotion unfold at the docks. Several police officers appeared just after the ship had departed, and they were motioning towards the vessel as though they wanted it to return to its moorings. The couple could hear them shouting at the port officials, who shook their heads. Jack thought he'd heard the words 'Northumberland' and 'Dixon' but he wasn't sure.

'I wonder what the policemen want?' said Bella.

'They're probably lookin' for someone who's on board this ship. A criminal making his escape to America. That wouldn't be a bad plan, would it?'

He hoped it wasn't him that they'd come to arrest; by now, Mr Walker would have had time to tell the police that he'd left without paying the rent.

'I suppose it's not. It's quite a good idea, actually,' said Bella, playing along with Jack.

'The ship won't turn back,' said Jack confidently. 'Not once it's set off. They'll not catch him, whoever he is.'

'I hope it wasn't a nasty crime.' Bella frowned. 'We don't want to be stuck on board a ship for weeks with a violent criminal.'

The couple stayed on the deck gazing at the shoreline until the spires and the smoke of Liverpool disappeared into the distance. Jack leaned against the rail and sighed, wishing he'd had more time to save up before the crossing. He was taking his wife to a new land with hardly a penny to his name. Since he'd agreed to travel with them, Bill and Martha had offered to pay for his rail fare from Boston to Illinois, for which he was grateful, but it meant that he would be indebted to Bill until the debt was paid.

At Allenheads, Jack had faced danger every day working underground at the mine but never before had he felt the excitement and anticipation that coursed through his veins. He and Bella were leaving England to start a new life in a new country, and he couldn't wait to set up home with her. Of one thing he was certain, this trip with Bella would be an adventure. Turning to his wife, he surprised her by kissing her passionately.

'What was that for?' asked Bella when Jack's lips parted from hers.

Looking into her eyes, he replied, 'That was a promise of the beautiful life that lies ahead of us in America.'

Bella smiled and snuggled into his side, hoping that Jack's words were true and that they would have a beautiful life there. She'd had her doubts about going to America and wasn't sure if she would be happy there. If it hadn't been for her mother, she would have gladly returned to Allenheads when Jack had suggested it the other night. Bella had been happy at Allenheads, especially when she and Jack were courting before the strike. Her life had been perfect then. There was absolutely nothing that she would have changed about it. If the miners hadn't gone out on strike, she and Jack would have married at St Peter's church and been living in one of the new houses at Allenheads by now. The notion of emigrating would never have entered their heads. But here they were, on board a steamship, beginning a long voyage across the ocean.

'Come on,' she said, taking Jack's hand. 'It'll be dark soon. We should find our beds.'

'Bunks,' Jack corrected her.

'Why does everything have a different name on board a ship? I'll never get used to that.'

They climbed down a wooden ladder to the lower deck and entered a large room filled with long rows of straw mattresses. Bill was in the far corner. As they walked between the beds to reach him, they saw large groups of children huddled together with their parents, and Jack noticed that many of the passengers spoke with Irish accents, like a lot of the men at the docks.

When they reached Bella's parents, Martha was asleep, lying on a mattress in her day clothes.

'Where are the sheets and blankets?' asked Bella. 'I'll go and fetch them.'

'There isn't any,' replied Frank. 'We were supposed to bring our own. There's just the mattresses.'

Bella rolled her eyes, wondering why she hadn't been informed that they should take their own bedding.

Bill took off his jacket and placed it over his sleeping wife.

'This one's yours,' he said to Bella, pointing at the mattress next to Martha's. 'And Frank's on the other side of me.'

Bella turned up her nose at the arrangements, realising that for the duration of the voyage, she and Jack would be sleeping fully clothed next to her parents; they would have no privacy whatsoever. She hadn't considered that.

'Goodnight,' she said to her father and brother with a fake smile.

'Goodnight, love,' replied Bill, smiling weakly. 'It's just for a couple of weeks.'

Bella climbed onto the mattress next to her mother. Jack lay beside her, his front to her back, and he put his arm around her, pulling her against him protectively.

'Your father's right,' he whispered in her ear. 'We'll be in America before we know it. It's just a few weeks. No time at all.'

Time on the ship dragged for them all. Even after the time spent cooking meals on the deck and cleaning up afterwards, they had countless hours to fill. The men played cards and dice for fun, not money, as nobody in steerage had coin to spare. The women knitted, crocheted, sewed, sang and prayed. Children played games and read books to one another.

Frank's stomach had been badly affected by the lurching movement of the ship riding over the foamy waves, but it soon settled. The others were grateful that they did not suffer from seasickness.

Jack and Bella wandered slowly around the deck, passing children playing hopscotch and shuffleboard and adults idling away their day, reading old newspapers and books, or simply looking out to sea.

Martha did not visit the deck. She preferred to stay below, to keep an eye on their bunks and belongings, so she said.

## CHAPTER 39

Bella took her mother's meals down to her. The food was not appetising. They had porridge for breakfast every morning, and the other two meals were meat stew that was full of fat, with stale bread or potatoes.

As the first week on the steamer came to an end, Martha had completely lost her appetite and turned up her nose at her rations. Bill and Frank were grateful for the extra food, but they were all concerned about Martha's health. Nobody commented, but they were aware that the blue colour had returned to her lips. Bella spent more time below deck with her mother, leaving Jack to socialise with the other passengers.

Around three weeks into the crossing, Martha attempted to rise from her bed one morning but stopped suddenly, her hands grasping her chest. The pain had been there for over a week now, but it had never been as bad as this. She hadn't mentioned it to her family because she didn't want them to worry, and there was nothing they could do about it anyway.

She fell back down onto the mattress and tried to call for her husband, but only a groan escaped her mouth. It wasn't Bill's face that appeared above her but Bella's.

'Mother! What's wrong?'

Martha's hands still clutched at her chest, and she gasped for breath. She tried to sit up, but the exertion covered her body in sweat, and she lowered herself back onto the mattress.

'Stay there! I'll get the doctor. Don't move.'

Bella left her mother and ran up to the deck shouting for a doctor. As well as Jack and her family, the ship's captain heard her cries and came to her aid. They all helped to search for a doctor, but by the time they returned to her mother's bunk, it was too late. Martha was dead.

Bella looked down at her mother's body in disbelief. She hadn't been away long, it couldn't have been five minutes. Instead of going to get help, she wished that she'd stayed by her mother's side and comforted her while she'd taken her final breaths. Instead, Martha had died alone in a strange place. Bella's eyes filled with tears, threatening to overflow. Jack's hand gripped hers, and with his support, she explained to the doctor what had happened.

'It appears she had a weak heart,' said the doctor. 'Has she had spells like this before?'

'She was ill for a few months before we left, but she'd improved enough to make the journey. She must have felt well enough, or she would never have set off.'

'I'm sorry, my dear, but a sick heart does not get better.'

'I'm sorry for your loss,' said the captain. 'I'll need your mother's details so we can record her death, and then the burial will take place this afternoon. I'll send some men down to wrap her body and carry it up to the deck.'

'But how can we bury her?' asked Bella. 'Are we close to Boston already?'

'She will be buried at sea.' The captain touched her shoulder in sympathy, and he and the doctor left the grieving family.

Frank looked down at his mother's body in horror, his stomach churning, and he turned away and walked quickly up to the deck for some fresh air.

Bill took his wife's hand, tears in his eyes, unable to believe that she was gone. Looking at Jack, he said in a low voice, 'You're to blame for this, lad. What a bloody pathetic first-foot you turned out to be. I knew you'd bring us nothin' but bad luck, and I was right.'

'But Father,' pleaded Bella. 'Mother was ill. This had nothin' to do with Jack.'

'She was fit and healthy until this year. Of course, it's his fault!'

Bill stood up to his full height and towered over Jack, and he punched Jack in the face. Jack fell to the floor, holding his hand to his nose, and then wiped away the blood that trickled from his nostril.

'Father!' exclaimed Bella, bending down to help Jack to his feet. 'That was a rotten thing to do.'

Jack walked away, anger seething through his veins. He couldn't hit Bill back because the man had just lost his wife and had reason to be upset. If it had been Bella lying dead on the bed, he would want to hit someone too! He went to the deck and leaned against the rail, thinking that when Bill cooled off, he would realise that he'd acted irrationally and apologise to him when their paths crossed.

A few moments later, Bella was at Jack's side. 'I'm sorry, Jack. Me father's upset, but he shouldn't have hit you or said what he did. It's not your fault. None of it.' She wrapped her arms around her husband's waist. 'Are you alright?'

'I'll have a shiner in the morning, but aye, I'm alright.' He turned to Bella and hugged her.

That afternoon, a small crowd gathered around the captain as he performed the funeral rites for Martha Dixon. The service was short and straightforward, and within ten minutes, the sailors dropped her body from the deck into the dark ocean below.

Jack held Bella's hand tightly throughout the proceedings, and afterwards, he found a quiet area on the deck where they could be alone. Bella clung to him and wept silent tears of grief.

Sniffling, she lifted her head from his chest and said, 'What will happen now?'

'What do you mean?' he asked.

'I agreed to go to America for me mother's sake, so I don't have to now. We could go back to Allenheads, couldn't we? We could go back to our old jobs. You know, your family would be over the moon to see you again.'

'Oh, Bella. That sounds wonderful.' He kissed her brow. 'But when we get to Boston, we won't have the money to return to England.'

He felt Bella slump in his arms, and her tears resumed. He held her tightly against his body, and she cried into his shoulder.

Jack wondered if Bella was intent on returning to England or if she'd only suggested it because she didn't want to go to Illinois with her father and brother. Of course, Jack wanted Bella to be happy and he would make sure that she was, but after the effort that it had taken to get this far, he didn't want to work in Boston for a year just to earn their return fares to England and leave America without seeing the country. He wanted excitement and adventure. For the first time in his life, he felt as though he and Bella were free from restraints; they could go anywhere and do anything.

When Bella recovered from the shock of losing her mother, he wondered if she would be open to new ideas. Before they reached Boston, he would broach the subject with her and they could explore where their future might lie.

# Epilogue

**Weardale
January 1855**

Snowflakes floated to the ground as Lizzie walked along the road, leaving a trail of footprints in the newly fallen snow. She lifted her shawl over her head and stopped to admire the steep slopes of Weardale, veiled in white. She loved Weardale, with its rugged heather-covered hills and rough pastures, and she was thankful that she'd found a home there. Her eyes returned to the farmstead where she had lived for the last five years, with her aunt who had treated her and Hannah kindly.

Lizzie enjoyed living on the farm, milking cows, herding sheep, lambing, hay-making, and rebuilding dry stone walls. The tasks were demanding, but she never complained. She recalled her mother saying, 'The devil finds work for idle hands,' when anyone had been sitting around doing nothing at Briar Place. Well, Lizzie could honestly say that since coming to Weardale, she'd not had a minute to spare, never mind get into trouble.

She was content with her life, although she still missed her family at times. Her parents were long gone. Jack, she presumed, was settled in America but it troubled her that he'd never written. She had visited her two sisters at the shop in Alston several times. They were seamstresses now and enjoyed living in the town. She had seen little Mary in Allenheads on one occasion when her uncle had delivered supplies to the Hall for Mr Beaumont's coming of age celebrations. Her uncle had written to arrange the meeting, and for that Lizzie was grateful. And her beautiful sister, Hannah, had recently married a young lead miner, George Watson, and they lived a few miles up the road at Killhope. She still saw Hannah regularly. Everything had turned out well for the girls and she commended herself for that. They could so easily have ended up in the workhouse.

Walking towards her on the narrow road was a young man. He stopped by her side and said, 'Miss Lowery?'

Lizzie raised her eyebrows, surprised that the handsome stranger knew her name. 'Yes, I'm Miss Lowery.'

'I've got a letter for you.' He pulled an envelope out of his pocket and handed it to her, smiling kindly.

The address on the front was *2 Briar Place, Allenheads, Hexham.*

'The postmaster at Allenheads is a friend of mine,' explained the man. 'He knew you'd moved over to this side of the hill and lived somewhere near me folks. I told him we were practically neighbours, so he asked me if I'd bring the letter over for you.'

Lizzie stared at the letter in her hand. Slowly, she turned it over and saw that it was from her brother, Jack. She had thought it was his writing but after all this time, she hardly dared to believe it. Her eyes filled with tears.

'Are you alright, miss?' asked the man, fishing around in his pocket for a handkerchief, which he found and offered to Lizzie.

She took it gratefully and wiped her eyes.

'Aye. I'm alright, thank you. This has just come as a bit of a shock, that's all.'

'Who's it from?' he asked.

'Me brother. He left after the strike. We think he went to America, but we never knew for sure because we never heard from him.' She held up the letter and said, 'Until now.'

'That was a bad do, that strike. I'm a miner an' all. I've been workin' over at Rookhope for a while, but I'm startin' at Sedling next week. By the way,' he said, holding out his hand, 'I'm Benjamin Featherstone, but me friends call me Ben.'

She smiled as she shook his hand and said, 'Well, as you know, I'm Lizzie Lowery. I'm very pleased to meet you, Ben.'

'I live up at Pry House,' he said, pointing to a small house on the hillside, just a couple of fields across from her aunt's farm. 'Would you mind if I walked with you?'

'Not at all. It would be nice to have some company.'

They set off to walk, side by side.

'You know a lot about my business,' said Lizzie, 'so tell me a bit about you and your family.'

They chatted like old friends as they strolled up the hill to her aunt's front door.

'Can I see you again, Lizzie? It's alright if I call you Lizzie, isn't it?'

'Aye, you can call me Lizzie, and aye, you can call on me if you want. I'd like that.'

'I'll pop over on Sunday afternoon.' He smiled broadly at her. 'See you then.'

Lizzie watched as he made his way across the fields to his house. When he was out of sight, she went indoors and climbed the stairs to her bedroom in the attic of the old house. Sitting on the edge of her bed, she looked at the letter and wondered why it had taken Jack so long to write home. Had he found Bella? Where was he living? Was he well? Although a little anxious about what the letter would reveal, curiosity got the better of her, and she tore it open to read Jack's words.

2nd December 1854

To My Dearest Family

I hope you are all in good health, as am I, and that time has healed the wound that my sudden departure must have inflicted. It was not my intention to cause you any hurt.

Mother and Father, I hope you can forgive me for abandoning you and the girls, a deed that preys heavily on my mind. I hope you understand my reason for leaving. I could not stay at Allenheads without my Bella.

We were married in Liverpool and took a ship to America. I don't know if you have heard from other means, but Mrs Dixon didn't survive the journey. She had been suffering with her heart which delayed the crossing but she seemed much improved. Her condition worsened on board the ship and she died from it. She was buried at sea.

We didn't go to the lead mines at Illinois with Bill and Frank as we planned to do. With Martha gone and after the troubles at home, we decided to make a fresh start for ourselves. We parted company with them in Boston and headed to California to the gold region. The journey across the country was long and hard, so much so that it is difficult to explain just how long and hard it was. Many folks didn't make it and we buried them on the trail. God rest their souls.

We settled at a little place called Georgetown. It is surrounded by hills covered with forests. I built us a timber house. I liked working on my own account with no boss to answer to. There was a decent amount of gold in the area and we wanted for nothing. We would have been happy there except for the fighting between the army and the natives. I feared for our safety at times.

Last year, we journeyed to Australia. I have been more fortunate in New South Wales with gold mining than I was in America, in part due to hard graft, in part due to my experience at mining, and in part due to luck. Probably more down to luck if the truth be told. Anyway, I am pleased to tell you that I am now a man of means. I would encourage any miner back home to leave the lead mines and come to Australia to see for himself the rich pickings to be had here.

I have saved the best news for last. We have two sons who are both healthy. We called the eldest John after you Father and the youngest is named William after Bella's Father. I hope they will grow up to be as close as you and Bill once were.

Your Loving Son
Jack Lowery

While reading her brother's words, Lizzie was bombarded by emotions. Of course, she was delighted that Jack had found Bella and that they were married. To her mind, they had always been meant for each other. She knew where he was now, and the relief she felt at knowing he was safe and well was overwhelming, but Australia was such a long way from England, even further than America.

Jack and Bella had two boys, which meant she was an aunt, and she smiled to herself sadly, wondering if she would ever meet her nephews. She knew that Jack would be a wonderful father to his children because he'd been a fantastic older brother to his sisters. And she admired his mining success. By leaving Allenheads, Jack had done better for himself than he could ever have done at home.

It was clear from the letter that Jack thought his family would still be living at Briar Place, that nothing would have changed since he'd left, yet everything had. He had no way of knowing that his parents had died or that his sisters were living under separate roofs miles apart. She envied her brother's oblivion.

Lizzie put the letter in a drawer, unable to reply right away; she needed time to digest his news. She went downstairs and saw Ben chatting with her aunt.

'Oh!' Lizzie stepped back in surprise. 'I didn't expect to see you again so soon.'

'There you are,' he said. 'I wondered if you'd like to go for a walk now? It's stopped snowing and the sun has come out.'

Lizzie smiled broadly at him and said, 'I'd love to.'

# Author's Historical Note

The miner's strike at Allenheads, Northumberland, in 1849 was devastating for the people who lived in the East Allen valley. Strikes were not uncommon in the lead mines of the North Pennines, but this one was different. The strikers were branded as trouble-makers and black-listed by local mining companies. As they could not find work in northern England, they were forced to look further afield, and many decided to move their families to America. Around one hundred people left the small village of Allenheads and the surrounding area. This historical setting was ideal for my novel *Briar Place*.

Some characters in this novel are based on real people. However, their actions and words are entirely fictional unless indicated below.

Thomas Sopwith of Allenheads Hall was an important historical figure. He meticulously kept a diary of his life and work. He was a geologist and worked as Chief Agent for the Beaumont lead mines for twenty-six years. In the early days, the miners resisted the changes and improvements that he implemented, but by the end of his service, he was well-liked by the miners. He described the lead miners of the North Pennines as shrewd, intelligent, kindly and well-informed.

Sopwith was a member of the Royal Society of Arts and spent about a quarter of his time in London on business. He had some interesting friends from the world of science and engineering, including Michael Faraday, considered one of the greatest scientific discoverers of all time; Isambard Kingdom Brunel, one of the 19th-century engineering giants; George Stephenson, father of the railways; Robert Stephenson, designer of the steam locomotive; Charles Babbage, father of the computer, and William Armstrong, the inventor of modern artillery and renowned for his work with hydroelectricity. William Armstrong, later Lord Armstrong of Cragside and Bamburgh Castle, tested his company's armaments on the moors above Allenheads.

The Thomas Sopwith featured in this novel was the grandfather of Sir Thomas Sopwith, the aviator who designed the Sopwith Camel, one of the best-known fighter aircraft of World War I.

The genealogical information regarding Sopwith's family, his wives and children's names, births, baptisms and deaths is factual in *Briar Place*. His second wife had an aversion to London and a love for the countryside, which is one of the reasons Sopwith took the job as Chief Mining Agent at Allenheads. Allenheads Hall was built for him and his family in 1847.

The mine at Allenheads, along with many other lead mines in Allendale and Weardale, was owned by Thomas Wentworth Beaumont, who in 1831 was considered the richest commoner in England. Mr Beaumont's son, Wentworth Blackett Beaumont, visited Allenheads Hall in the summer of 1848 and was introduced to the lead industry by Sopwith. During his visit, Mrs Sopwith and her children stayed at Newhouse, the lead mine agent's house in Weardale. In *Briar Place*, his visit takes place a few months later than it actually happened to fit with the story. In 1906, Wentworth Blackett Beaumont was raised

## AUTHOR'S HISTORICAL NOTE

to the peerage as Baron Allendale, of Allendale and Hexham in the County of Northumberland.

Thomas Sopwith introduced the watcher men at Allenheads mine to improve the miners' time-keeping. He was frustrated that they would not commit to working an eight-hour day, a change he believed necessary to improve profitability.

The altercation between the miners and Sopwith outside Allenheads Hall resulted from the miners' desire to resolve the dispute. They turned out in force to show Sopwith that they all wanted the watcher men dismissed. Sopwith must have felt threatened by their sheer numbers outside his family home when he reacted rashly, calling them a 'mobbish body' and 'Irish ruffians'.

The progress of the dispute and strike is recorded factually in the novel. The lead miners met regularly and had men, including Mr Heslop, to represent them at talks. Mr Atkinson, a local magistrate, was involved in the discussions, and for a short time, the watcher men left the mine. The miners sent Mr Shield to Bretton Hall, Yorkshire to speak with Mr Beaumont on their behalf, and shortly afterwards, the time-keepers returned to the mine, accompanied by a constable carrying a pistol!

The miners requested a meeting with several impartial, well-respected men to discuss their grievances. Sopwith agreed to this but then went back on his word, which infuriated the miners. Sopwith investigated the matter himself, interviewed the men, and promptly dismissed their case.

This led to the strike that began on 1 January 1849, and as with all strikes, there would have been considerable hardships for the miners without an income.

Blacklegs were regarded as traitors and were badly treated.

A miners' meeting took place at Swinhope Chapel, and the actual words that the chairman spoke to incite hatred and violence against blacklegs appear in *Briar Place*. Readers would be forgiven for thinking that they had been exaggerated for effect in the story, but they were not. The speech clearly disturbed the locals because it was recorded at that time and appeared in several later publications.

As a magistrate, Thomas Sopwith presided over a horrific case at Wolsingham in Weardale where a man was smoked out of his house by two miners. A similar event was incorporated into *Briar Place* to demonstrate how cruel the miners' punishments could be.

Several letters from the miners were published in newspapers to inform the public about the miners' mistreatment by Thomas Sopwith. Sopwith replied to one of them. He also complained about the miners' time-keeping publicly at the opening of the new school and complimented the children. Whether his extended stay in London during the strike, which made a settlement impossible, was intentional or unavoidable is unknown.

Sopwith stood up to the miners and eventually won the battle. After the strike ended, many of his miners were refused work and evicted from their tied cottages.

Fifty-eight people from the area left Liverpool on 22 May 1849 on a ship called the *Guy Mannering*, and they arrived in New York on 28 June. The passage from Liverpool to New York cost between three and four pounds per head in the middle of the nineteenth century. It is unclear how the miners, who would have been destitute after the strike, paid the fares to take their families to Wisconsin and Illinois. Interestingly, one miner settled in Wisconsin for four years before travelling to California, and within a year, he sailed to Victoria, Australia. I discovered his story after I had written Jack Lowery's letter at the end of *Briar Place,* detailing his life and adventures after leaving Allenheads.

Allendale's traditional New Year celebrations are popular in the region. They have taken place from at least the mid-nineteenth century, but it is unknown if they occurred before that time. They may have more ancient roots in the Middle Ages or even from pagan times, but however old the custom, the tar barrel procession is an extraordinary spectacle to behold.

## About the Author

Margaret Manchester lives in County Durham, England, with her husband and sons. She was born in Weardale and spent her childhood there. Margaret's research into her family history discovered that many of her ancestors had lived and worked in the area for centuries, either as lead miners, smelters or farmers. While she studied local history and archaeology, Margaret worked as a guide at Killhope Lead Mining Museum. She was awarded a Master's degree in Archaeology from the University of Durham, and then taught archaeology, local history and genealogy. As well as writing, Margaret is currently the managing director of an award-winning business and a charity trustee at the Weardale Museum. She enjoys spending time in her garden and with her dogs.

**You can connect with me on:**
- https://www.margaretmanchester.com
- https://twitter.com/m_r_manchester
- https://www.facebook.com/margaretmanchesterauthor

# Also by Margaret Manchester

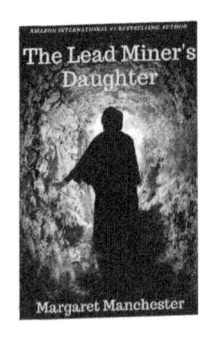

**The Lead Miner's Daughter**
Amazon #1 International Bestseller

Northern England, 1872. Mary Watson, a lead miner's daughter, leaves her childhood home to work at Springbank Farm. She soon meets a handsome neighbour, Joe Milburn, and becomes infatuated with him, but is he the right man for her?

Mary's story is woven into a background of rural life and crime in the remote valley of Weardale. Not one but two murders shock the small community.

Find yourself in the farmhouse kitchen with the Peart family, walking on the wide-open fells, seeking shelter underground and solving crimes with PC Emerson as this intriguing story unfolds.

Will the culprits be brought to justice? And will Mary find true love?

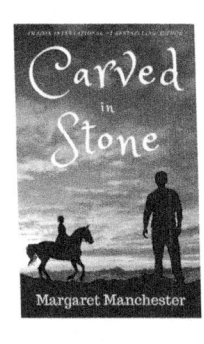

**Carved in Stone**
Amazon #1 UK Bestseller

Northern England, 1881. Sent away during her brother's trial, Phyllis Forster returns home after a seven-year absence to find the Weardale people have turned against the Forster family and she desperately wants to win back their respect. Can trust and harmony be restored in this rural community?

At twenty-eight years of age, she has almost given up hope of love and marriage, and throws herself into the management of the family estate, until two very different men come into her life.

Ben, troubled by the past and full of anger and distrust, is a shepherd who shuns the company of others until his new boss arrives at Burnside Hall.

Timothy, the new vicar, is preoccupied with the ancient past, but he takes a keen interest in Phyllis.

Will she settle for just a husband? Or will she defy convention and follow her heart?

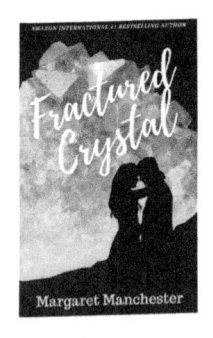

**Fractured Crystal**

Northern England, 1895. Josie Milburn meets Elliott Dawson, a man who shares her interest in collecting crystals. Defying an age-old superstition, Elliott takes Josie into a lead mine, an action that sets off a sequence of dramatic events, beginning with a miner's death the same day.

Elliott and Josie face a series of trials involving tragic loss and the unveiling of family secrets, which change their lives and fortunes in ways that they could never have imagined.

Will these traumatic circumstances bind them together or break them apart?

Printed in Great Britain
by Amazon